PILLARS OF
THE MOON

B J FRENCH

Available at amazon.com
www.pillarsofthemoon-belmopan.com
www.facebook.com/brianfrenchauthor

Cover design by Melissa Roshini
Book design by Xuanyun Malcho

ISBN: 1481960024
ISBN-13: 978-1481960021

ACKNOWLEDGMENTS

To my wife Susana, and the many Susans in my life who have given me encouragement, love, and the faith to continue on. And to the Creator, who has shown me that we truly are, all in this together.

DISCLAIMER

'Pillars of the Moon' is a work of fiction. Names, characters, places and incidents are either products of the author's imagination and/or are used fictitiously. Any resemblance to actual events or locals, or persons, living or dead, is purely coincidental.

CONTENTS

Introduction

Pillars of the Moon, is a delightful tale of North American Native intrigue. Set in recent times, this adventure spans the north western portion of modern day America, from British Columbia, the Olympic Peninsula and across to the dusty plains and mesa of the four corners area of Colorado and New Mexico.

The story begins with a hap-hazard photographer, named Brian Alexander, who inadvertently gets dragged into the cat and mouse game of hide and seek involving an ancient artifact of priceless value. Drawn into the search further by the relentless desire to be rid of head-aches and visions, a result of an accidental blow to the head, he is also intrigued by the mesmeric beauty and beguiling nature of a native woman central to his plight.

Watch for part 2   **Belmopan**

PRECURSORS

Cascade Locks, Oregon, 1936

At the far end of the restaurant bar, several suit-clad men kept making eyes at the teenage girls sitting at the table behind. The girls were vibrant but timorous as they sipped on their drinks through long straws while making account of the young men that passed outside the window of their sitting booth. Occasionally, the eldest and most mature would glance back to the men at the bar and give a blushed giggle. Several feet away, two young men, not far beyond their years, sat in the next booth, hurriedly eating burgers and fries as if pressed for time. A loud slurping noise emanated above the din of the cantina, as the one, a Native American, emptied his tall metal milkshake flask of the last remaining drop. The room went quiet as eyes turned to the young man who gallantly carried on with a mouthful of fries, not noticing the oddity he had created by his presence in the restaurant. Young and in his twenties, he had not yet tempered from the bigotry

1

and insults that surrounded him while out and about in the general public. His slightly older and equally unaffected companion was intent on finishing his lunch but held guarded concern for the girls sitting behind and the seeming harmless advances of the men at the counter.

Driving the old car down from Vancouver, the day previous had been uneventful for the two young men, but a pleasant drive. It had been slow going through the port town of Seattle, and rather rough continuing on the hard packed dirt roads to Olympia, ultimately to find a room for the night. Overall, the trip had been satisfactory, but was eventually marred by the difficulties of finding accommodations with a native. The older companion, Portuguese by birth, had near perfect Queen's English, and the wit to compliment. The pair finally came to rest when papers from the budding Archaeological Society of Vancouver, were produced and then permitted to stay in the rooms of an elderly spinster of Olympic notoriety.

With an early start to the next day's travels, they pulled away from the Inn's open gardens only to be followed, once again, by a car that had periodically been with them throughout the journey. The private cargo they had been retained to deliver was of a delicate nature and incognito. No one but a small group of academics knew of its nature and destination. For the moment at-hand, the coincidence of the familiar car would play the part and ignorance the game.

After finishing their meal and paying the bill at the register, Vincent could not help but feel the eyes that followed him and his assistant Daniel, out the door. This was more than a passing slight at his nationality and that of his companion; something signaled caution.

Pulling away from the parking lot, to Vincent's relief, no one left the diner and it did not appear that they were being followed. After several moments and then hours of driving, the comfort and freedom of the drive came back.

Both had been intent on stopping and visiting an obscure archaeological site at the Oregon, Idaho border on the Snake River. Excitement built as they pulled into a foliage-covered lane and parked their car. Pulling a small, leather bag from under the front seat, Vincent handed the object to his companion and nodded for him to tuck it down his jacket for safekeeping. Together, they disappeared up a narrow, slick crevasse.

Quietly, without notice, a black Hudson slowly made its way up the lonely lane to rest beside the old Ford. Two suited men slid from the doors closest to the Ford; the driver slowly opened his and retreated to the rear of the car. Visually scouting the area, he opened the trunk to retrieve a metal bar and handed it to one of the men. Opening the door to the Ford, the other proceeded to rifle through the belongings in the leather suitcases in the rear seat. Finding nothing, they retreated to the trunk and pried its lid. Convinced that the prize was not to be found, the eldest and most elegant of the three waved for the others to continue up the crevasse to pursue the missing pair.

Somewhere, near the middle of the trail leading back to the parking area, Vincent and Daniel met the two coming up the trail.

Recognizing them as the same as at the restaurant, Vincent whispered, "Whatever happens, you must get to Shiprock."

With that, he shoved a small piece of paper along with some money into Daniel's top pocket and gave an encouraging tap on his shoulder. Passing the two, all four had eye contact. Falling in-line behind Vincent, the enforcers followed close, there was no mistaking their intent, but what to do in these surroundings? Uneasy, the young native turned back to Vincent for encouragement and direction. There was none to give, so Vincent continued expressionless down the narrow crevasse toward the entranceway behind his young friend.

As he and Daniel broke into the clearing from the narrow slick, dirt covered path, Vincent could see the other of the trio leaning against the Hudson and the condition of his own car, "Run!"

Daniel bolted up the bank to the side of the clearing and out of sight. Vincent turned and forced himself against the two behind him. Being pushed aside and flattened to the ground, he was punched and held down tight in the slippery mud. The other assailant jumped wildly into the bush in the same direction as the young native, disappearing into the denseness. Dragging Vincent to his feet, the soiled aggressor pushed him toward the elder. With the occasional nudge, Vincent staggered toward the man now standing upright before the rear of the car. Vincent did not recognize him and did nothing to encourage conversation.

"Where is it?" the man demanded.

"I'm not sure what you are talking about."

The man struck out at Vincent with the iron rod, striking him in the temple. Vincent crumpled to the ground unconscious.

Half a mile away, the young man bolted through the brush like a young stag, his pursuer falling behind with every slippery step through the forest. Gunshots echoed through the resounding countryside as a last attempt to catch his fleeing prey failed. After an hour of fruitless pursuit, the follower retreated to the parking lot and the others who now sat in their car. Vincent still lay on the ground, motionless.

"Did you get it?

"No," came the reply of his subordinate in a thick European accent. He bent and rolled Vincent over, exposing his pale face and a trickle of blood from the gash in his temple. Reaching for his neck, he pried to find a pulse, "I think he's dead."

"Are you sure?"

Pushing the body aside, he gave a slow nod.

The elder slapped the side of the car and demanded, "Get in."

Several miles away, a flatbed truck pulled to the side of the road. A shocked and exhausted young man, dressed in denim, climbed in the front seat.

"Where to?" the driver inquired.

"Shiprock," he sheepishly replied.

"You've got a long way to go," he returned pulling out onto the road again.

Within moments, the driver glanced in the rearview mirror just in time to catch the black Hudson pulling out to overtake his truck just entering a curve in the road.

"What in the hell is this guy trying to do?" the driver spat, veering to the right to make room on the narrow shoulder of the road.

The Hudson sped by barely able to negotiate the oncoming curve. Daniel slid down in his seat as his heart sank in his chest. The sedan slowly disappeared out of sight around the curb. He breathed a sigh of relief.

5

1936 -Snake River Archaeological Site, Oregon and Idaho border

The young couple, hand-in-hand, walked up the worn tracks left by the vehicles that frequented the site. The tall grass brushed against her legs as they straddled the worn path. Unaware of the previous day's events, they entered the parking lot in jocularity, only to be sobered by the sight of Vincent's prone body. Lying by the black Ford, doors still wide open, he was pale and cold to the touch, but there was a pulse. Within several hours, State police were at the scene, an army medic from Hood River worked feverishly to revive and warm the hyper-thermic Vincent. Six hours later, he was at a hospital in Portland where a message was sent on a relatively new invention called the telephone, to Vancouver, Canada.

Vincent daLima was always in awe when in the presence of Herman Neustadt, but today, recovering in the hospital, it was an overwhelmingly mood of gratitude. Being on the payroll of the fledgling archaeological department at the University of British Columbia, was not that rewarding, but at a moment like this, the placement was somewhat worth its while.

Herman Neustadt had recently come west to avoid the seeming indifference to the Third Reich's interference with artifacts being imported from various art houses and museums throughout Western Europe. Meeting with an old friend and compatriot Max, from neighboring Austria, they had chosen to archive most of their collections temporarily until the political climate became more favorable. Neustadt had chosen to repatriate some to their former homes or places of discovery, Pillars of the Moon was one such piece.

There were those who knew of the little jade bowl's story and its origins in Central America, near the archaeological site of Lamanai, in northern Belize, and wanted to possess it. The tale of a jilted Mayan prince's gift to his betrothed bride had kept interest in this seeming trivial gift until the tribe of the bride to be was massacred in retribution. The infamy of this insignificant, jade bowl spread.

The family of Neustadt had been sympathetic to the plight of the loggers of Mahogany and the chicle harvesters of Guatemala in the mid 1800's, and were rewarded for their secretive endeavors of aid to these exploited individuals. Little gifts and appreciations began to flow from the bowels of the thick jungles in the area, and before too long, a sizable collection of trinkets and collectibles amassed. Trips to and fro from Europe had endowed the Neustadt family with much wealth and respect. Not wishing to be involved directly with the insurrection or governance of the birthing British Honduras, they chose to keep a low profile and aid in the stabilization of trade and commerce throughout the uncertain times.

As Vincent recovered in the hospital, Herman, in appreciation, had offered Vincent a place with his small team of archaeologists. Daniel, Vincent's understudy, had disappeared in attempts to get the small artifact to Shiprock, New Mexico and a trusted courier who would in turn take the bowl the last leg of the journey to British Honduras. All were waiting patiently for the young Daniel who had yet to be heard from.

New York City, two weeks later.

Footsteps echoed through a narrow alley between the two dock-houses. A single shot rang out simultaneously as steel pipes dropped from the rear of a work truck shadowing the distinctive sound. One man crumpled to the ground around the corner as another glanced to see several workers scurry to pick up the scattered pipes. A dark-clothed, masked man crept quietly along an exposed area of the main building and slid into a small service doorway leading to the large storage area within. A middle-aged man dressed in a black wool overcoat, fedora perched low on his brow, stepped over a stray pipe and approached the guard at the front of the warehouse. He offered the guard a cigarette from his silver cache and struck a match to signify the occupation. The flare of the coal at the end of his cigarette highlighted in his dark eyes the contempt he held for this soldier- the glowing embers, the hate for the Third Reich.

A mass of large, wooden crates stacked high lay within. Each had its own serial number; all were bound for Rotterdam, a short distance from their true destination, further up the Rheine. A small group of German Museum Directors and art dealers had the onerous responsibility of implementing the task of cataloguing notable works-of-art throughout greater prewar Europe, and elsewhere. Most were in close association with collectors of all nationalities who held the bulk of the works. Some of the operatives held regard for the purpose of the exercise, while others coolly did not. One such man stood fixed in front with the guard to the entrance of the storage building, stoically watching from the corner of his eye, his accomplice flitting from crate to crate in the darkness, trying to match the serial numbers that lay stenciled on the side of each crate. Within moments, the task was done, made easy with German-bound crates exposed with a small swastika burned deep into the wood planks encasing the contents. With a sly grin on his face, the gentlemen took a deep drag on his cigarette while fidgeting with the knife-blade he held in reserve deep within his pocket.

"Let's go for a short walk," he suggested in his thick German accent knowing full well he would have to kill this young guard if he did not agree.

Looking from side to side along the face of the building, the young man stomped on the remains of his cigarette and ushered, "Sure."

ONE

Now, Vancouver, BC

The Neustadt Exhibit at the Museum of Anthropology, on the University Campus, was offering an interesting evening. I had been waiting for months for its arrival since the announcement first hit the Alumni mailing list. The jade bowl artifact, strangely named, 'The Pillars of the Moon", was one of those obscure pieces of physical history that seemed to miss the notoriety of the more gregarious Haida Totems of the area, and yet held an irrepressible obsession for collectors in acquiring its possession, the few who knew of it. Intrigue, mystery and even death surrounded this little, jade object, almost too small and innocuous for its reputation.

Heading down the upper reaches of 16th Ave., ominous, gray and black clouds hung amid the bellies of the resolute mountains guarding the inlet which is English Bay; strands of their white mist reached down like fingers, writhing and dissipating as if in despair, grasping at the high-rise buildings of the North Shore. Encumbered pedestrians, beneath their multi-colored umbrellas, dodged and darted beneath the tears that rained down from above making the trip even lengthier for an impatient and already anxious driver. Ghost-like ships, anchored in the bay, behemoths waiting to be unloaded, rested from the abysmal assaults of the winter's inclement weather and battle-bound seas.

Upon entering the museum parking lot, the skies began to clear relieving the area of the day's persistent drizzle and a chance glimpse at the sun. The oddity of several security guards that had stationed themselves at either end of the lot, gave the event an heir of uncertainty. Black limousines and a variety of up-scale, late-model vehicles lined either side of the lot closest to the stairway to the museum. Further toward the gallery, Tsimshiam wall-to-ceiling carvings at the entranceway to the museum's foyer were now bordered with gray, suit-clad security guards. They glanced from time to time at the repose patrons puffing lightly on their cigarettes, just outside the full-length glass doors. The paradox of the scene did not impede the true nature and design of the museum's unique architecture, which was a marvel in itself, nestled among a line of cedar trees atop the cliffs overlooking the Spanish Shores area of the bay.

Approaching the glassed foyer, umbrella in hand, I pondered at the proceedings indoors. Elegant benefactors paraded and chatted along the central corridor among the Haida totem overseers towering high in their quiet dismay; the preliminaries had not started yet. Taking a slow breath, I turned and headed out from under the protection of the entrance portico. A bank of mist dampened my face as I proceeded along the flagstone walkway to the rear of the building. The distant North Shore was barely visible above the low fog that had drifted in off the strait. The occasional boat-with-sail drifted in and out of the fog as they scurried back to the safety of moorings in False Creek.

My cell phone chimed in my jacket pocket just as I was assaulted with a, "Whomp!"

A massive weight came crashing into me. At half stride with unsure, wet footing, I was off balance, cell phone in midair and onto the ground. Shocked and on my back facing up in the mud, I lay motionless, half on the path, half in the wet grass. Unsure of what had happened, I lay still while my head, resting on a flagstone, slowly cleared. Looking up, in a dreamlike state, I watched, as raindrops danced and floating in midair as they fell cool on my face. The silhouette of a man's head came to block the rain, then, darkened my view.

"Are you all right?" echoed in my ears.

"Yeah," trying to catch my breath. With air rushing deep into my lungs, I leaned up on one elbow and continued to gather my thoughts. Looking for my phone, a pair of dark hands clutched my arm as if to reassure me. Unaware of my muddy condition and the puddles of soggy grass that lay beneath, I hesitated to get to my feet.

"I gotta go!" he blurted.

Panting, he picked up a small, wooden crate that lay in the grass and threw me my cell. After a long gaze as if to assure me, he reached with his forearm to help me to my feet. I declined and continued to rest on my elbow. Quickly, the fellow looked about scouting for something, got to his feet, and scurried off as if endangered. I caught him briefly looking back before the young man cleared the cedar hedge by the embankment. A shock of his black hair danced on his shoulders as he vanished into the trees beyond.

Half bent, I took several more breaths to gather my composure. Reaching to feel the back of my head where it had made contact with the stone, I gently rubbed the tenderness. My leather coat was covered in mud and I could feel the cold wet that had leaked up my back as I had lain on the ground. Sluggishly, I picked up my bent umbrella, cleared the mud off my phone and made my way to the rear of the building. In the courtyard, I came to rest on a low wet bench, collected my composure and took another deep breath of cool air. With my head almost clear, I wondered, 'what in the hell just happened?' As if in reply, a Raven atop one of the frontal-totems of a long-house, chattered and carried on relentlessly. Trying for several moments to extend my crooked umbrella, I lay it aside in defeat. Attempting to brush the mud from my coat, I looked out to the bay and wondered how long the wait to the exhibit proceedings would be.

Drifting off for a moment, I came to with a start as a security guard yelled "Hey! Wake up!" Giving me a nudge he asked, "Did you see anybody running by?"

Clearing my head of the vision of an elderly native man with his gray hair tied back in a ponytail, I gave a "huh"

"Hey! Are you alright?" He looked toward my mud covered back and crooked, hapless umbrella now in hand.

Sitting motionless, trying to put the last few minutes into perspective, I imagined to myself, 'I got hit by a young man, not an old man'. Confused, I looked up at the guard and continued to answer his question,

"Well, No!" The following words turned to marbles in my mouth.

Satisfied I was all right and knew nothing; he shrugged me off and headed in the direction of the service doors at the back of the building. Baffled, I yelled at him just before he disappeared through the door, "What about the exhibit?"

"Cancelled!"

"Great!" I lamented to my crooked umbrella.

The Raven atop the totem gave a few more curt cackles and flew off toward the shoreline. After walking around the side of the building to make my way back to the car, curiosity got the better of me as I neared the front entrance again and decided to take a peek. Crouching low and inconspicuously propped in the corner beside the carved panels of the entrance doors, I peered through the glass to see what had transpired. The police and the guard, with whom I had just talked, were conversing back and forth. They eventually turned and I saw the guard point to the back of the building and then to the front. As I leaned my bruised body against the glass, he looked my way and thought he pointed me out to the police.

Not wishing to be involved in the incident, I cleared the stairs to the parking lot. Passing the cedar trees, I glanced between them to see the two officers turn down the small flagstone path to the side of the museum. Behind the wheel of my 'Black Beauty', I drove from the parking lot feeling much relieved to leave them behind. My head began to clear as I continued up Marine Drive and the eventual exit from the University. A persistent ringing in my ears and a slight headache hung behind my eyes.

As I drove along slowly, my mind replayed the scenes of the previous minutes back and forth trying to understand what had just happened. Wiping the drops of water from my brow, I began to recall, step by step the last half-hour.

Passing several pedestrians walking on the road beside the parked cars, I couldn't help but notice the familiarity of the two of them. A young man and his mother walking near the middle of the road; nothing out of the ordinary, apart from the fact they shouldn't have been walking there till I caught their full identity in the rear view mirror.

'It was him, the guy who ran into me!'

A second glance revealed that the old woman was not a woman but the old man I remembered as I sat on the bench recuperating. Slowing down, I pulled over and looked in my mirror again.

"Gone."

Stopping right in the middle of the drive, I reefed my head around to see where they might have disappeared. Opening the door and standing in the middle of the road, I looked about me, scanning the parked cars and the grassy boulevard on either side.

Puzzled and exasperated, "I need a drink."

By the time I got to the coffee bar at 64th and Granville Street, rush hour was a steady grind. The ache in my head had subsided and the sun, or what little was left, peeked through the residual, rain clouds and painted the buildings with its golden hue. The streetlights, faintly aglow, greeted the reckless hustle of the Vancouver nightlife. The Georgia Straight, a local paper, lay motionless beside me on the counter, its bold headlines beckoning me to open its sprawling pages. Rose, my sister would be at her home soon and I could confide in her as to what had just happened..

Sitting alone and sipping my coffee, blankly leafing through the paper, I began to wonder of the circumstances surrounding the exhibit and the young man who had run into me. Was there a connection with the closure of the exhibit and the running man, the elderly native man in my vision after the collision? The connection was obvious.

Pensive, intrigued with the circumstance, my eyes wandered to an advertisement highlighting the accolades of holidaying in Mexico. My mind drifted to an earlier time in that fair and steamy country.

We, my brother-in-law Steve and I, had had the opportunity to travel throughout Central America and explore some of the ruins. It was there, while taking photographs of the antiquities that I became fascinated with the Central American Indian Culture and its continent wide interwoven history that lead north to Alaska. Of most interest, at the time was the chance to explore the cenotes; those large surface holes, sometimes obscured by lush jungle, that could be several hundred feet across and as much as a hundred feet deep, and rumor had it, full of gold artifacts. Accompanied by several of the not-so-ethical local amateur archaeologists, we began our adventures examining these freshwater sinkholes of the Yucatan, only to find that the local Police were as hard to appease as the hungry, Mayan gods of old. In naiveté, a suggestion by some of the locals was embraced and we continued extracting artifacts while unbeknown to us, others, in due time, were smuggling them to the lucrative North American and European markets. Steve and I, being the adventuresome, act before you think type of guys, jumped at the opportunity for a week of fun diving until the local authorities got wind of the operation. Luckily, we were helped by a local archaeologist named Dr. Magnus, who had little to lose and much to gain, and our reputations and visas were left intact. This regrettable experience opened our eyes to the attitude and climate of exploration in the jungle areas of Central America and also, intrinsically, to the greater reality of the interconnection between the lost cultures of the Indians of Central America, and possibly to the whole of the Americas. With the jungle's hidden wealth of both culture and treasure to explore, my interest and desires were kept smoldering to this day.

A bike handlebar hitting the glass brought me out of my thoughts and back to the flurry of the little coffee bar. I eased myself from the stool and continued to the little house on 60th street, a quaint, two-story with lead-crossed windows on either side of the central, cut stone arched doorway. Ivy crept along a five-foot stone retaining wall bordering the sidewalk, giving the front yard an old English personality and afforded relative privacy from the neighbors, and vise-versa.

"Hello. Rose!" I sheepishly yelled, as I poked my head through the crack in the front door then strode through the foyer.

Crossing through the living room to the dining room, I slid a pizza on the table. Looking around, I noticed the new porcelain figurines she had collected on the sideboard and went over to take a look.

"Well, what brings you here this time of the day?" she laughed as she strode into the dining room, her hair wrapped in a towel.

"Ah, Pizza! How did you know, I've been craving a slice?"

She smiled while she grabbed a couple of plates from the cupboard, knowing that full well that it was my stomach and no concern for hers that had led me to buy it.

"Where is everyone?" I asked.

"Out." she sparked. She gave me a side-glance and smiled at me, "They're always out, especially when I need them and always here when I don't. They never let me know where they are; not that I really want to know as long as they are safe. They come home eat, then shower, get dressed, ask for money and leave. The next night, it is the same thing. I may, and I mean may, catch a glimpse of one sitting in front of the T.V. when I get home from work." She smiled at me. "Does that answer your question better?"

"Yep!" I blurted. "Can I use your washroom to get cleaned up?"

"Sure," she replied as I walked by. "What happened to you?" noticing my wet, mud soaked back.

"I'll explain in a few minutes," as I crossed the kitchen to the washroom.

As we sat down later and opened the pizza box, we talked candidly about the kids and ended with me trying to explain the incidents of the last several hours.

"How is your friend, Chief Hidden Wolf?"

She finished her mouthful and wiped the corner of her mouth with a tissue. "I guess he's fine. I haven't seen him for almost six months. He's supposed to be in the States traveling, talking about the upcoming changes in governmental land legislation.

"Oh! So he's not here?"

"No. Why do you ask?"

"Well, I saw someone today. That is, I think I saw someone today who reminded me of Hidden Wolf." I stopped and took another bite. Chewing slowly I continued, "Short, long gray hair tied in a ponytail."

Describing over half the older, native male population in the north-west, she gave me a questionable look.

"Yeah, I know. But his eyes were different. They were very bright, almost on fire."

"You are confusing me Bri. Did he have any scars?"

"I don't think so."

"Without more to go on I really can't be much help to you, Bri."

She gave me that strange look again then took another bite of her pizza.

"Look," she said gathering her plate and heading into the kitchen. "I have to catch the 9.30 ferry to Victoria to meet Steve, and I have a little over an hour to get there. The kids will be home before 11:00, so would you mind keeping an eye on things while you are here." Without waiting for a reply, she yelled, "Thanks" and disappeared into the back hall.

"Can I do some Laundry?"

Not twenty miles south at the Tsawwassen Ferry Terminal, a lone figure sauntered up the catwalk to the waiting arms of a young, native woman. She had procured their tickets to Swartz Bay. In the shadows of the ships superstructure, he handed her the small, wooden crate he had kept well hidden until then. She grabbed it and held it to her breast. Looking up to the constellations that had so influenced her ancestors, she gave a sigh of relief, "We have it."

After several hours and watching a special on the

TV about the Anasazi Indians of New Mexico, I went into Rose's study to see if I could locate several articles I had read about them in the recent past. The program I had watched had somewhat alarmed me with the inference that these farmers and potters, in their desperation, had resorted to cannibalism as a means of survival. This accusation, although not unheard of in some circumstances, seemed a little far-fetched in this instance and appeared to have been founded on supposition. There had been few facts presented. Human bones of various ages and of both genders were found at the bottom of surface, water wells and middens dotted throughout their inhabited area. There had been little else. Although not impossible, cannibalism was always a possibility, but not likely. The Colorado River and its tributaries and rivulets were in constant flux, but the Anasazi could always migrate within their local area to forage for their means of survival. There were always aggressive tribes to consider, so perhaps things were not as simple as were lead to believe. From what I understood and read of the ancestors of the Pueblo Indians, there was nothing in their customs or artwork that could point to the likelihood: the thought and its implications intrigued me.

By the time one-thirty rolled around, I had skimmed several books, watched the news, and had consumed the contents of a half dozen bottles of beer, peace offerings from the kids partying downstairs, the remains of which had collected on the table. Anxious to get my clothes, I stood at the top of the stairs and yelled for everyone to leave; it was pointless. Closing the door to the basement to confine the noise, I crept into the spare room and lay down on top of the covers.

With my head sandwiched between two pillows, my sister's pink slippers dangling off the end of my toes, I dozed off. Sleep was bliss.

TWO

The sun, reflecting through the heart-shaped prism sent its shafts of light scattering throughout the bedroom. With every whisper of wind, a small, ceramic chime gently tinkled a rhyme that seemed to harmonize with the ringing in my head. The dryness of my mouth and thickness of my tongue alluded to last evening's slow and purposeful slide into the wee hours of the morning. The contents of the six dead soldiers of the night before still remained in my bladder and were crying for release. I covered my head with a pillow in an attempt to relieve the discomfort.

Rolling over to ease the stiffness of immobilization, I noticed a small picture upon the dresser of my girlfriend Marese as we sat on the stonework fencing above the falls at Niagara. Adjusting the pillows to sit upright, I pondered our relationship and the events of the previous day, and how to explain the absurdity of it all and whether she'd believe me.

The old, Winslow clock sounded in the living-room notifying me of the late morning hour. Listening intently for any sounds of stirrings from the basement below, I made a wholehearted attempt to raise myself.

Considering a shower, I eased myself from the bed, planted my feet firmly inside the wash basket containing my clean clothes and stumbled headlong into the bathroom. Slipping on the tiled floor, I grabbed the toilet bowl to break my fall, my hand slipping inside and splashing its contents over my face. Pondering the tragic start to the day, I considered it had to get better.

Within the hour, I was sitting cross-legged in a white plastic lawn chair, sunglasses in place shielding my strained eyes, cell phone in hand, sipping fresh, brewed coffee.

Taking a deep breath, forgetting the pain and the light traffic about me, I tried to download the latest news on my phone but the battery warning started to flash. I grabbed the local paper from an adjoining table and started my perusal of the news. After briefly skimming the pages with whimsical contempt, my eye caught what I had subconsciously been looking for - a small article announcing the break in. The heading read, 'Neustadt Exhibit in Jeopardy!' Articles on loan from the Neustadt Foundation were tampered with and 'thought to be damaged' at the Museum of Anthropology, on the University grounds late Friday afternoon. Charges are pending and the investigation continues. The Neustadt Exhibit has been closed until further notice.

'Charges pending.' That meant they hadn't got anybody, and the continuing investigation meant not a clue. The young, native man must have been a thief and took something from the exhibit. 'Although', I thought to myself putting the paper down on my lap, 'I did not sense him to be so.' I remembered he had not seemed fearful or panic stricken, although he'd been in a hurry; his gaze was clear and bright.

Realizing the implications of my being on and around the premises at the same time, and that the guard had noticed me, I thought it prudent to find out more of what had happened. It would not be easy task to get information from the paper, reams of red tape to endure with no assurance of any consequence. It would have been nice to know someone there, but of course that wasn't the case.

Back in Kitsilano, excited with the prospects of the investigation, I bounced up the first few front steps and slowed in pain as I passed through the etched glass front doors. Passing the collection of my black and white photos lining the staircase walls, I limped up the old oak staircase, one steps at a time to the landing and the door to my flat. Once inside, I plugged my phone in and sunk into the couch. Reaching for the telephone directory, I keyed the number into the phone and waited patiently for a response.

"Good morning. Thank you for phoning the Frazer Sun. Help us to direct your call by listening to the following six options; if you have a touchtone phone, push 'one'."

Hanging up the receiver, I pondered my 'personal options' and decided to call my sister's house. After several rings, and a quick conversation with Vanessa, I learned that my sister had left the island with Steve on a sailing foray.

Frustrated, I put the receiver down and sat back to look out the dormer window across to English Bay and

Stanley Park. The mist along the shoreline was lifting to revealing the slow march of pedestrians along the sea wall. Tucking my hands behind my head, I tried to ease the dull ache in my head.

Playful birds chattering in the tree boughs outside the window lightened my mood and fueled my desire to carry on with the probe surrounding the robbery. An inquiry at the police station was perhaps the only viable option available at the moment.

Gathering a few of my belongings, I climbed into my 'beauty' and started off towards downtown across the Burrard Street Bridge. The traffic got heavier toward the core as bicyclists, shoppers and adventurers headed north.

Arriving in China Town, the streets were a bustle with every type of person and race this earth had labored to bring forth. Vegetable produce in boxes stacked up to the awnings, decorated the storefronts. Colorful vegetables and fruits of all shapes and sizes lined trays that obscured a clear passage for the numerous passers-by. Clothes and multi-colored flip-flops as bright as any painter's pallet were stacked high and wide in disarray. A combination of unique smells emanated from behind open stalls; the fresh fragrance of mango, the stink of calamari and shrimp, all added to the ambiance that is such a part of this gregarious area of downtown. Broad smiles from brown and olive faces brought it all to life. So matchless and wonderfully singular, this little area, once a logging town only a century ago, has been as much apart of the heritage to this part of the country as old Gassy Jack's Whisky Bar.

Once through the hustle and bustle of shoppers, I turned left on Main and walked down past the corner of Orange Street to the Police Station. Stopping atop the steps and looked back toward Number Five Orange and took a seat for a few moments. As I looked down from the steps of the station to a young woman of native decent panhandling close by, I wondered about her circumstances and the tragedy that had brought her here.

Taking a deep breath and a short glance toward the docks and the inlet, I stood reflecting for several more moments, then pushed my way through the revolving, glass doors of the station.

Impressed by the sudden roominess and grandeur of the main hall, I took a moment to appreciate its architecture. The high ceilings, almost fourteen feet, and marble floors that magnified and echoed every step and utterance, almost exceeded the noble purpose of the building.

"Hello, can I help you?" enquired a young officer, seemingly out of nowhere.

"Well, yes. My name is Brian Alexander. I'm not so sure who I need to talk to, but I'm inquiring about the break in at the museum yesterday."

"Hang on a minute and I will check to see who the officer handling the case is."

Turning from me, she glanced at a roster and skirted several desks to a terminal. After several moments on the computer, and conversations with two other officers, she came back. "Yes, that is Constable Johnston. He will be a few moments, so if you don't mind having a seat over there, he will be with you shortly."

With a smile, and a nod of my head, I strode over to sit at a bench in an area just off the sunny main foyer. Apart from the few people waiting on the benches near the front desk, the place seemed quiet for a Saturday, but then again how would I know? In boredom, I glanced at the magazines on the table trying to bide my time. Scanning the colorful magazine covers for an interesting article to read, my mind began to wander to the previous day and the old man in my vision behind the Museum.

Just as I slowly started to drift off in thought, I was startled by a loud "Hello! Mr. Alexander?"

Uncomfortable at the sudden intrusion, I looked rather unsteadily at the fellow standing before me. Trying to gather my thoughts, I sat straight, and motionless, gazing up at him, the face of the old native man from the museum still impressed on my mind.

"Yes! I would like to enquire as to the incident at the museum yesterday?"

He looked down at me the way only some people in authority can do, "Yes, well there is not a whole lot we can tell you right now as the incident is still under investigation. What, may I ask, is your connection with the case?" he asked curtly.

A little shocked by his candor, I replied "Well, I'm not really connected apart from personal interest. I am studying at the University and just wanted to know more about the article to which the theft attempt had been made."

He looked down at me with a cool, glazed countenance that implied, 'do I have time for this?' and said, "The case is still under investigation, and we cannot tell you anything at this time."

I was about to mention the encounter with the young man who had flattened me, but something seemed to grab me by the throat, and the words "Sorry to have troubled you." came stuttering out instead.

Getting up from the couch, I reached out to shake his hand, "Thank you for your time. I'll keep my eyes on the paper."

Refusing my hand, he nodded and walked away. Turning back to me he half yelled, "You may want to try the Royal Museum. There's a woman there in the Anthropology Department who is also looking for information; perhaps the two of you can compare notes." A caustic grin slashed across his face; he disappeared down the hall from view.

With a bewildered acknowledgement, I returned to him an impotent, "Yeah, thanks! What's her name?"

Without noticing, a tall, thin, fair-haired man fell in behind me and followed me out the door.

Once out in the morning air, the frustration eased and the activity of Main Street brought me back to the freshness of the morning. I was nervous talking to the officer; the thoughts of the previous day still vivid in my mind. Sitting down on the warm, front steps for a few moments to recoup, I looked down at the cement before my feet and watched the shadows of people drifting by; unobtrusive, one shadow remained stationary; the woman who had been panhandling had left. Taking a deep breath of cool air, I stood and started off in the direction of the docks through Gas Town.

The Steam Clock whistled as I turned the corner to head up the street to Hastings. The scenery drastically changed in those few blocks to the shadowy lives of the street people sleeping on park benches, harmless to all but our conscience. For some, giving up is easier. As I passed by a fallen man, empty bottle clutched in his hand, the fact of this was hard for me to ignore. I continued to my car.

Driving west to Georgia Street and on, I turned into the park and the colorful scenery. Passing the remnant zoo and rounding the corner to view the yacht club, I was struck by the disproportion of the scene. To my right, the boats with their masts pointed resolutely to the boastful buildings and skyscrapers of downtown; to my left the trees and abundant, green foliage, lush with the seasons rain heartening me to look beyond to the graceful slopes and mountains above West Vancouver. Standing noble in the foreground, the stalwart totems peered down from their height to the few subjects milling below at their feet. They spoke of a great people of long ago. Strong and proud, they stand foreboding, meritorious, encouraging us to remember the past with its raw reality; as if to announce the coming of an era. The bold, carved portraitures of birds and animals peered out toward to skyline of Vancouver, waiting to proclaim the return to a way of life harmonious to the surroundings they guard.

Sitting on the bench across from the totems, I gazed at the workmanship of the carvings. The intricacy and design of the characters was unique and conveyed their individual dispositions well. The sounds of children laughing as they played in the open field behind me along with the warm sun on my face lulled me to slumber. Drifting off into scenes from a fable of the legendary, young Makah boy Kuwatsi, who had helped, through his mischievous exploits, to save the Makah Nation from starvation, I fell asleep. A loud, progressive ringing in my ears distracted me to a presence beside me. Slowly opening my eyes, I turned my head to come face to face with the recognizable old, native man sitting right beside me. His eyes were very still, and sparkled with an intensity that appeared to look through me. His brow, straight and strong, emphasized his eyes, curving down to broad, chiseled cheekbones. His bold, square chin accented by his broad and full mouth, cut across his features. A complexion of burnt-umber glimmered in the sunlight; lined and well weathered, it alluded to his years of life. A shock of white hair starting low on his forehead and tied back flat to his temples, gave a halo of fine, illuminate hair that suggested reverence. Startled, but not shocked, I made no moves and looked patiently at him. Without fear or anxiety, we sat and gazed at each other until, without a word being spoken, he gave me a smile. Putting his hand on mine, he pointed toward two pillars of light bathing the totems that sat before us. We effortlessly drifted in that direction and to the light beyond. Something compelled me to look down to the ground where I caught a glimpse of the two of us side by side on the bench. Amazed at the height we had achieved, I became self-aware and instantly heard a loud zap and found myself back on the bench, alone; the old man was no longer there. Scared, I looked around to see if anyone had noticed anything; it appeared not. The children continued playing behind me as if nothing had happened; a young man lying on his side perched on one elbow, continued to read his novel, unmoved. My world was shaken to its core by the experience and no one had noticed. Aware of the aching in my head and slight dizziness, I slowly got to my feet and wandered back to the car beneath the tall,

Cedar trees that overshadowing the roadway by the shore.

"I've gotta see somebody!"

Easing myself back into my car, I sat for a while mindlessly staring into the space above the hood and beyond the grill. Thoughts of madness gave way to the rationale of a concussion from the fall the day before. My stomach slowly settled from its peculiarity, and growled at the turmoil. Swallowing hard and glancing in the side-mirror, I edged out into the light pedestrian traffic on the road. I continued my journey around the park to third beach.

The tide was out and the flurry of activity from the Kingfishers and gulls was a good distraction. The occasional crab poked its head from beneath a protective rock, only to retreat again from the advancing, feathered, hoards of gulls. Kelp swayed back and forth in the pulsing motion of the surf, licking at the barnacle-covered rocks. The rich, strong smell, along with the abundant life of the tidal zone, caught the attention of a number of sun worshippers as they passed the time on the elevated walkway.

A few hours passed, and the strange, hollow feeling in my head had now left me. I felt renewed from the short time I had remained resting, and felt relief from the strange encounter with the Indian sage. The sun was heading down along the western ridge of the mountains before me, while the small boats, returning from their forays up the coast, ushered me home. Catching a last glimpse of the sun's rays above the hills, I followed the sea wall to the path leading up to the lot where my car was parked. Looking back across the bay to the right of the Planetarium, I could see the line of houses that protected mine from the noise and bustle of the traffic across the Burrard Bridge. The lights of the Maritime Museum, that illuminated the large wooden craft within, lit the grassy slope, and the few people who had collected for an evening picnic. The clock, on the old brewery overshadowing the bridge, reflected the rush hour time and flashed the seconds as if testing the pulse of the traffic below.

The cars within the park had slowed while people meandered their way to the busy streets beyond its boundaries. The beds of colorful flowers on either side of the parkway, gave way to the lights of the shops and hotels along Beach Drive. As the sun set, the brilliance and exuberance of the day faded into a chiaroscurist rendition of the Vancouver skyline, splashed with a multiplicity of neon color.

THREE

Welcoming me home were the walls of my small sitting area faintly pulsing red. The telephone message indicator, with its methodical flash, illuminated the small photo-filled alcove: another picture of Maryse and I, arm in arm outside the butterfly exhibit at Niagara, sat lonely by the phone. My cell sat neglected on its charging perch. The darkness of the rest of the apartment was awash with the reflected pinkish hue of the electronic panorama of the distant apartment buildings outside the patio door. The view was nostalgic; a reminder of Christmas, only all year round with hundreds of thousands of people crammed into a nine-kilometer square section of the city, sharing the same eggnog and hydro bill. A quick flick of the light switch brought to prominence a small collection of artist's proofs, acquired during my school days; alongside, a small and sorry looking photography exhibit of my own. The wall opposite displayed a more recent collage of pictures and awards from ten years of work and play. Some of the photographs displayed a visual account of the work I had done for the Film Board; others, a collection of reflective moments, captured in time, colorful, to be visually savored. The small alcove that housed the phone and couch, displayed a variety of talented fledgling artists, some well known, and some not. My favorite, a poster size proof of one artist's interpretation of the colorful 'A Mid-Summer Night's Dream', dominated the scene. A small, bronze trophy, representative of the singular recognition gleaned from years of splicing film and reprints, sat brave amid a forest of gnarled, stunted, clay figurines atop the rough, cedar bookcase.

Wading through the physical debris of a lifetime to the kitchen beyond, I turned the kettle on for a cup of refreshment. Picking up a pair of dirty socks along the way, I threw them through the open bedroom doorway and retreated to the recliner to settle in and listen to the messages. Knowing one of them would be from Maryse still in Victoria, I put my feet up on the coffee table and with anticipation pushed the button. Listening to a short message from Justin declaring that Mom had phoned and would leave a message, Marese's sweet voice tickled my ears. My heart gave a slight tug as she announced she was out for the evening and would not have a chance to talk till tomorrow. Reaching back clasping my hands behind my head, I sat for a few moments staring out the window, wondering how I should spend the rest of the evening.

Out over the strait, beyond the low mountains of the outer harbor, the sun had set; its residue, a scarlet, vermilion ribbon, stretched out above the horizon as far as the eye could see. Feeling exhausted from the day, it appeared as if both the sun and I were going down for the count. The shrill whistle of the kettle, prompted me to my feet and over to pour the water. Leaning against the counter, I watched as the twirling spoon blended the crystalline powder, an almost frightening cacophony of unpronounceable ingredients, into a savory, steaming brown liquid. Opening the patio door, I wandered on to the open deck. With a deep breath of fresh air, I tried to exhale the languor that was building within me from the day's events. Hands gripping the rail, I gazed out to the bay and the numerous small craft dotting the water in front of First Beach - their dark shadows cutting through the reflection of the city shimmering on the water; foghorns announced their efforts to moorings in False Creek. These seeming toy boats sluggishly plodded along - green and red night-lights dotted the pools of darkness on the backdrop of the shore, dancing timeless like gilded fireflies on a warm summer's night. After minutes of timeless thoughts and watching their lackadaisical journey; the sound of the methodical, gentle rush of waves on the pebbly shore called to my tired soul and nudged me to retreat. Slumping into the old, leather recliner my father had left me, with encompassing relief, I sipped on my warm drink.

With my feet up, my mind returned to review the possibilities, apart from the concussion, to which I could attribute the headaches and strange episodes I'd been having. Together, they had brought me to the point of some concern. I considered the bump on my head from the collision at the museum, but was that all. Had someone slipped me something in my food or drink as a joke; perhaps medical help would be the answer. Taking another sip from my cup, I reconsidered the ramifications of an undiagnosed concussion, and the possibility of spending the rest of the evening in emergency. But, at the moment I had no headache, or dizziness.

A recollection of the constable's sardonic face at the station, and the mention of the women in Victoria popped into my mind; perhaps a visit to the Royal Museum, in Victoria was an idea. Maryse and I, had been spending more time apart of late, and a few days together would do us the world of good. Finding the name of the woman, on the other hand, which he hadn't divulged, would be difficult. Reassuring myself the trip would be the way to go, I pondered the mystery of the elderly native and his strange familiarity to me. Reflecting on my psychology classes, and how we had occasionally touched on out-of-body experiences, I considered the stigmatism the episode might bring to me of 'somewhere–out-there' with my friends. My drinking buddies wouldn't have a clue about an 'episode' apart from the usual out-of-body all-night binges they would put themselves through on occasion. Maryse would definitely not understand.

Taking another sip, I focused on the old man and his intense gaze. Who was he? He seemed so familiar as if out of a TV program or a picture I had seen. Thinking back to the articles I had read in the not-so-distant past, I could think of none that would bring his image to mind. The possibilities were endless but there was one TV program that could be culprit - a research piece that I had worked on a few years back, an archaeological dig in the Queen Charlotte Islands. I began leafing through the backlog of periodicals on the bookshelf that I had acquired over the years. Amazed at the collection and why I had kept the majority of them, I began the lengthy task of searching.

Sitting cross-legged for several hours on the floor, I leafed through each issue. Article after article came and went with no familiar face. Eventually, a story surfaced triggering the vague remembrance of this man, ' The Ancestry of West Coast Whalers' and the story of Kuwatsi, the boy Makah. Settling back, I perused the glossy pictures, reading the pictures sub-headings first; I was positive the mystery to the old Sage was here, somewhere hidden.

The article supported the fact the Haida had been a relatively peaceful people, living in harmony with their surroundings in the Queen Charlotte Islands. Trading throughout the region and to the north, they sustained a bountiful life style, both materialistically and spiritually, through whaling, fishing and farming. The totems dotted throughout the islands told of their rich and fruitful heritage. Although the tribes of the Haida were abundant here, their fishing territory was shared to the south with other nations, the Kwakiutl and the Nootka on Vancouver Island, and the Makah on the lower island and Peninsula. The Makah were concentrated more in the south, on the Olympic Peninsula, with relatives up the southwestern coast of the island and in the Puget Sound area. Although, very similar in life style, the four nations were very powerful with a strong sense of civil order and lineage. Not beyond the habit of taking slaves for menial labor, it has been established that these four nations harbored little ill feeling towards each other and traded continually. Even though the Haida were further north along the coast and in the Queen Charlotte Islands, they often met on hunting and fishing forays and shared in the technology and bounty of the sea.

A complimentary article with the familiar name, 'Neustadt' came across the pages. Having read articles on this anthropological philanthropist, I knew full well the circumstances under which the once great German scholar and collector had acquired the artifacts that were being displayed in most of the exhibits throughout America.

More articles highlighted the epidemics of smallpox and other diseases that were brought ashore by visiting European fur traders; these decimated Indian populations. The west coast First Nations inhabitants, in a relatively short period of time, were near extinction. The systematic wave of would-be archaeologists and collectors flooding the area later brought continued erosion and a painful near end to these once great cultures. History has yet to determine whether these white traders and academia be saints or sinners.

After the catastrophe of disease had taken its toll, most of the villages fell into decay; the encroaching forest swallowed up most of the conspicuous signs of their habitation. A paradox arose for these learned men, in one way they felt it was their obligation to preserve as much of the disappearing culture as they could before it completely vanished; the other, a conundrum, was to remove the heart of these people who relied so heavily on the spiritual nature represent in the totems and great carvings of their ancestors. A meritorious gesture by scholars, if their purposes had been genuinely noble there would have been a greater attempt to preserve, and even revive, the spirit of the remaining people.

In reflection on what I had been able to learn and read of these great people, it is the natural way of life for change, death, and rebirth. 'Why should we (aboriginals), living within the circle of earth bound life and environment, taking freely of its' natural bounty, and eventually, giving back to the earth of ourselves, worry about the things the earth has so freely given us to survive on time and time again? The spiritual entity of man, living beyond this earth, is only connected through the umbilical of the soul and body, to the earth for a short time.'

There remains to this day within the spirit of some native peoples, this truth that our modern culture, in all its glory, has yet to embrace the beauty and simplicity of earth-bound life.

In one of the old black and white photos of an archaeological dig, there was a young native fellow who bore a remarkable resemblance to my gray-haired mystery man. He was a displaced Makah carver, fisherman, helping with the dig at Ninstints.

Getting another cup of hot chocolate, I slumped back into my comfortable chair with the article on my lap, and closed my eyes. Relaxed, I drifted slowly through the scenes of the articles I had just read; slipping into a light sleep, I heard a gentle hum and felt myself soaring in the afternoon sky, above the earth, like a bird. The ground far below me was parched and dry, with deep crevasses pouring into valleys of shallow rivers. A thin, green belt of grass between the canyons gave the bleached, red landscape a focused, sharp leader on which to navigate through the severity of the earth's convolute crust. Sandstone wedges thrust high into the air, as if to cut the horizon east from west, drove me further into the ancient, volcanic remnants of this geological marvel. The sun cast elongated shadows like fingers, eastward, as monumental rock formations towered boldly above the plains and mesa. Swooping down into a narrow canyon with red rock walls closing in on both sides, a creek's white banks gave way to sculptured stone, swirled with maroon, and ivory bands. The ferns clustered in dark wet corners beneath the trickle of water, along with swatches of dark green moss, cascaded down the rocks. In the clearing beyond, a small pueblo with corn growing sparsely by the waters' edge, seemed peaceful except for a small band of women and children being corralled by a half dozen men. The bodies of two other men lay motionless and bloody in the courtyard, waiting in silence to be cared for. Soaring high into the heavens again, I found myself fearless, and bold, my wings beating furiously the cushion of air.

Next, I was sitting in human form a short distance from an open fire; the heat of the flames warmed my face. The native people staring back at me were tired, their faces etched deep with lines of burden and hunger. A dozen men and women, wrapped in dusty, woven blankets, sat on the hard ground, chanting, singing, and intermittently watching me, obviously expecting a response. Their dark eyes, reflecting the dancing flames, seemed to peer deep into my soul, as if to impress me with all they'd seen and endured. I looked over my shoulder to a fire-lit clearing, not a mile away across a ravine, with a similar fire and men dancing about it. A feeling of apprehension gripped me as I turned back to the solace of the group before me. Chants and talismans set the stage for what was about to occur. Cinders, in a great upward rush from the fire, drew me along with them to meet the stars that shone bright and clear. Horizon to horizon, they radiated a never-ending canopy of sparkling light. A gentle breeze blew in my face as I focused on the stars tugging at me harder, drawing me closer. I heard a woman's voice wailing in the background as I soared, once again, to hover above the little pueblo below the mesa plateau, not a mile away. A naked young woman, painted blue, lay tied down to a wooden bench, spread eagle on her back, her chest open and bleeding from a gash below her left breast. She lay lifeless; her eyes open to the very stars that had welcomed me aloft. A dark man in a knee-length shawl, holding up a ceramic bowl, paraded the fire-lit clearing before the half dozen men. An enormous shadow stalked about the arena as his feathered headdress bobbed back and forth from the motion of his step. With the bowl lifted high in one hand, and a staff with a carved head of an animal in the other, he jumped, and wailed away, as if in a state of ecstasy. Beyond the clearing, in the shadows cast by the fire, the helpless faces of others peered through the wooden bars of their captive cell. Until this moment, I had not been aware of emotion, but a feeling began to stir deep within me. Once again I was back before the elders at the fire in the compound above the valley. Their drawn faces seemed lifeless apart from the sparkle of the fire within their eyes. Slowly looking about to each of their individual faces, I was aware of a kinship with them. The eldest man in the group came to me, and we knelt together facing each other. While he searched my eyes, he put his hands out before me. As he opened his palms, he exposed numerous small, white chips of stones and sand, similar to tiny opals, and gently poured them from one hand to the other. The light from the moon illuminated the stones to such a degree that they appeared to send faint shafts of reflective light up into the night sky. The light, held within his palms, brightened to such a degree of intensity that the light transformed his whole being. A gentle hum, as if the universe were alive and vibrating, brought me to a state of confidence and belonging. I looked back into his eyes, and for a moment we became one spirit, drawn up, once again, to the sky, hovering above the little village below. The scene below was gruesome, as the other men, also painted blue, carved the young woman's body as if to skin her. Feeling a sickness within me, I was drawn within the circle, face to face with the abhorrent priest, now adorned with a black skin and the head of a jaguar upon his head. With the feeling of sickness intensifying, and the clamorous impulse to jump at him very strong, the intense buzzing in my ears kept me from immediate action and sent me reeling back into the heavens once again. A last glimpse back caught the priest no longer in the black robe, but dancing in the fire light with the skin of the girl draped over him like a shroud. The remains were being carved, and the bones thrown down into a hole.

I woke with a start and in a cold sweat. The chocolate I had so enjoyed and ingested just an hour before, smeared the front of my chest and magazine as vomit. Grasping the arms of my recliner as hard as I could, I tried to grasp all that had transpired in the last few moments. Dizzy and rife with fear, I gave a guttural scream that loosened my throat up into a sob.

I sat in shock, dazed, staring beyond the collage of pictures on the wall, not able to recognize any of them. The smell of the vomit was filling my head, and I could bear it no longer. The mug, lying empty in my lap, crashed to the floor, along with the magazine, as I attempted to get to my feet. The hot chocolate that remained in a pool beneath me began to leak onto the floor. A stinging sensation, as my pants separated from the chair, cautioned me to my burnt thighs. I stood, teetering for a moment as I got my balance; I staggered from in front of the chair. A glimpse of my reflection in one of the large glass covered picture frames frightened me, as I was not at all familiar with the man looking back.

Once in the bathroom, I crawled, fully clothed, into the shower and turned the faucet. The warm water rushing over my scalp sent rushes up my spine as I tried to stand erect under the pulsing water. My crotch began to sting as the warm water flowing down my pants came in contact with the tender flesh between my legs. Easing the clothes from my body, I watched as the water washed the fatty remains of chocolate covered french-fries down the drain of the tub. My head throbbed as the scene of the young painted girl entered my thoughts again. The possibility that I was very sick, and that this was all from the knock on my head, became paramount. Shutting the shower off, I left the clothes in a wet heap on the tub floor and wrapped a towel about myself. I made my way through the living room to my bedroom opposite the alcove. Ducking slightly to avoid the slanting ceilings, I took a relaxant from the bottle lying in the drawer. Looking at the pill Maryse and I had so often kidded about in my palm; I stopped and pondered the effects that this could have should I have a concussion. I replaced the pill in the bottle and returned them to the drawer. Lying back against the pillows at the headboard, with my temples still throbbing, I pulled the comforter up over me and slowly drifted to sleep. The couple next door, bounding up the stairs in a fit of laughter, woke me at twenty to twelve. Thirsty, I somehow made it to the kitchen and poured myself a glass of cold water from the fridge. Looking through the open drapes to the high rises beyond; I stood motionless, trying to figure out why this was happening and what it meant. Taking a sip of cold water, I leaned my forehead against the cold glass and rolled it back and forth to ease the burning temperature within. The thought of hospitalization entered my mind again, but at this time of night, especially on a Saturday, the collection of societal oddities that would be waiting in queue, would be more than I could bear. Wandering over to the soiled recliner, I threw a tea towel on the seat to absorb any residual wetness and turned off the lights. The couch, within the alcove looked solemn, illuminated from the faint lights from across the bay. The darkness encompassed me as I sat, TV remote in hand, contemplating the many strange things and changes that had happened these last two days. The ringing in my ears and the metallic feel in my head had eased. I dare not close my eyes for fear of relapse. I guessed the TV program of cannibalism from the previous night had affected me more than I imagined.

FOUR

It was still dark and quiet as I slowly rose from the couch. My neck, stiff and sore from lying with my head propped on the armrest for several hours, felt cold to the touch, exposed to the open alcove window. In the background, I could hear the siren of an emergency vehicle blaring from across the bay. Easing my feet from the couch to the floor, my toe came in contact with the edge of a magazine that had been on my lap. The faint smell of vomit lingered in the room. Skirting the soiled armchair, I crossed to the kitchen and grabbed a small bottle of water from the case that lay beside the patio door. Sliding the glass door open, I spewed the rancid remains of my mouth over the balcony. The lights that sparkled on the ski slopes of Grouse Mountain, marked the contour of the eastern mountain range, remaining suspended in the lingering darkness. It was a clear morning with only a light cloud cover beginning to sweep its' way up the strait from the open water toward the outer-reaches of the northern shore. The way to Tsawwassen was covered with mist; time to leave.

As I drove toward the dark entrance of the Massey Tunnel, the sky was now beginning to lighten, the clouds to clear; the stars peeked through with their timeless scrutiny, eternal witness's to primal assaults of humanity, including the scene at the pueblo the previous night, all those years ago. Down into the cement bowels of the delta I sped mindlessly; the orange sidelights flashed by me to form an unbroken fluorescent ribbon trailing in the rear view mirror. The damp-ness along the seams and cracks of the concrete slabs that made up the walls of the tunnel reminded me of the tombs and crypts I had visited in my adventure-driven adolescence. Would this be my tomb, consciously aware of many tons of water lying directly above? My foot pushed a little further to the floor.

Scenes of the previous night's dream continued to haunt me; the faces of the Indians sitting around the fire had left a lasting impression on me. The girl, of course, I was trying to forget. The thought of being with Maryse and spending a few evenings with her, excited me, and I began to feel more relaxed with every passing mile.

Cars already lined either side of the narrow causeway to the ferry. Sport fisherman and clam diggers were already making their mark in the early morning hours as they bobbed up and down in the misty reaches of the sandy, ebb tide. With the receding tide exposing the sand and pebble beach, diggers of the feathered kind pranced carelessly about harvesting the bounty that lay in the exposed shallow pools. Rocks, garnished with algae and barnacles, shadowed the seaweed-lined tidal pools from all but the loftiest of scavengers.

As I pulled into the parking lot, the sun was just clearing the mountain tops to the east, casting its yellow morning light across the shoreline of White Rock. A light mist hung white, translucent, suspended between charcoal-gray rain clouds blowing in from the north and the shimmering sea of yellow-ochre beneath. Down from the Frazer Valley, the cool air flowed like the clear waters it delivered to the open sea, parting the mist that lightly billowed in from the opposite direction, the sea. I sensed it would be a calm crossing.

There were already several dozen cars waiting at the terminal for boarding the ferry as I routed the ticket booth. Sitting quietly for a few minutes and finishing my coffee, I watched as the deck hands busied themselves with last-minute preparations. To kill the few idle moment's left, and relieve the agitation of the burn from the previous evening, I eased myself from the car and gingerly walked across the parking lot to the vending machines. The walk seemed to take forever as I carefully, and slowly, strolled bow-legged to where the machines and several people were standing smoking cigarettes. A couple of elaborately made up young women in short skirts and an equally made up young man, in leathers and earrings, gave me the eyeball as I walked by. The young man had a familiarity about him. Not wishing to ignore them completely, I gave them all a nod and kept on walking till I came to a spot, along the boardwalk beyond, that I felt was comfortable enough to rest.

The weather had not been overly cold to this point, but the late arrival of spring had definitely deepened this to a crisp morning. With a long vapored sigh, I watched and listened to the seagulls perched atop the dock piles, welcoming me with their garish arias of unabridged scat. Beyond, patches of clear, blue sky amid the clouds, drifted carelessly northward to the mountains beyond. The wet mist rolling in from the strait limited the view to the south and Point Roberts, and deposited a film of dew over my face and clothes. It felt refreshing and helped to shake the remaining weariness of an uncomfortable and fitful night from my head. As I leaned on the top rail, with a view to the blue sky intermittently reflected in the water, I couldn't help but think of the girl in my dream, and how she had been killed. It struck me as odd that this type of behavior –human sacrifice- with its roots so far back in time, has continued in varying ways to this day.

Hidden from our unsuspecting eyes, man's dark side surfaces most often in times of war and domination as if addictive behavior. What is it in man that continues to sweep him away helplessly? Do these uncontrollable undercurrents tug at our subconscious, primeval roots so hard as to leave some powerless to their influence? Perhaps it is natures' attempt to test the life force that so eludes our understanding, that it ultimately forces us to impose the seeming paradox of life. The continual reference to the afterlife and underworld, have been a part of man's ancient belief since he has been able to communicate his deepest anxieties and fears. What has caused this 'appeasement of the gods', human sacrifice, to become the malignancy that has blighted mankind into this distorted apparition of his true value and purpose? Regardless of the reason for the abhorrent behavior, the young woman's painted blue complexion, and beautiful soft face staring straight up to the stars, will be etched in my memory for a long time.

The ferry's horn sounding for boarding echoed back from the mist and close mountains. The pedestrian ramp, to the second story of the ferry, came alive with cyclists and backpackers flowing from the waiting area inside the terminal. Along with the handful of people by the kiosk, I strolled back to my waiting car. The silence broke into a rumble of starting engines and shouting, as motors and motorists ignited to life. The many vehicles, full of Sunday travelers on their way to a variety of outings and islands, began their slow procession into the bowels of the ferry. Even on a not so perfect day like today, tourists from all over the province and elsewhere, pour into the many flower gardens and shops around Victoria, and visit her many tea rooms for the experience of the proverbial 'afternoon tea'.

The channel water, even though rolling, was relatively calm which guaranteed a steady, and constant, stream of people in line for breakfast. On the more rough days, breakfast lines were shorter, with the lavatory lines longer. The more seasoned ferry traveler always knew where his most urgent natural directives were best served by gauging the pitch and yawl of the boat. Either way it is always a delightful occasion for me. Relaxing with a light meal in the cafeteria this morning would be especially pleasing as all I had eaten during the last twenty-four hours was a muffin with coffee, and a large fries, which I hadn't digested. Watching and waited patiently, napping occasionally, the line eventually shortened to just a few and I casually walked to the follow the last individual.

"Hey! That's my stuff," came the cry of an elderly man running over to the table as I pushed the refuse aside. Realizing there was an article in the Globe about the Newstadt Exhibit; I slid my tray over the paper and sat in the chair closest to the window. With a stern look, he whisked the remaining stack of papers away.

"Sorry. Were you sitting here?" I asked looking up at him. He gave me a curt look, tucked the papers under his arm and walked away.

"He isn't now," could be heard from the opposite corner.

Across several tables by the distant corner, the odd fellow from the vending machines at the terminal sat glaring at me, taking sips from a cup. I gave a nod once again, but said nothing. With my back to the wall, I made myself comfortable placing everything on my tray in order and started into my breakfast. Occasionally, between spoonsful, I read the article and glimpsed the gulls perched upon the life boat hoist, patiently watching me eat.

With the warmth of the sun beating hard through the glass, I relaxed with my feet up on a chair in front of me; my head propped against the wall, my temple against the glass.

Queen of Nanaimo Ferry

When I looked up again, we were already half way through the Channel Islands. Adjusting myself in the chair, I leaned my head sideways just in time to catch a glimpse of a familiar, dark face. Startled at what I saw, thinking it was the young native fellow from the museum, my chair fell forward with my face and forehead bumping into the glass. The cafeteria was silent as I grabbed my bag, got to my feet, and raced to the door. As I went to clear the bulkhead, the odd fellow from the vending machines, with the leathers, put his arm out to stop me and stood, blocking my way, facing me.

"Slow down. You'll get hurt," he said cockily.

Looking at him straight in the eye, "Yeah, thanks! What in the hell do you care?" I grabbed his shoulder and gave it a shove to make my way by.

Out in the fresh air, the cool wind off the bow cleared the anger that had filled me from the short confrontation, enough for me to have a second thought of the familiar face.

As fast as my impaired gait could carry me, I followed off in the direction he had headed. After several turns around the deck, through various levels, I did not manage to find him. Feeling a little discouraged at not finding him and knowing that he had initially been a part of all the oddities that had occurred over the last days, I continued to hobble around the deck trying to enjoy the scenery.

With the sound of the foghorn, the ferry maneuvered the last turn before docking at the Swartz Bay terminal. Milling down the almost vertical stairways to the lower decks, the several hundred passengers made their way down to the car decks and waited patiently till the docking was complete. Taking a quick glance around at the adjacent cars, in the off chance of that familiar face popping up, I resigned myself to the fact that I had been mistaken about his identity. With engines revving in reverse, the ferry slipped and nudged its way to an almost perfect docking. A dull thud announced the telescopic steel ramp from the dock had landed on the ferry deck. Waiting while the pedestrians and cyclists made their way off, I watched and took advantage of the motorcyclists waiting their turn by taking candid camera shots of the many makes and the unique characters who rode them. To the surprise of the deck hands, one motorcyclist in black leathers, on a colorful machine, did not wait for approval but accelerated sideways, up the steel ramp, in a puff of exhaust and disappeared from sight. The rest waited patiently for their turn and moved off slowly.

Avoiding the foot traffic, I drove cautiously out of the terminal, following the other cars as they headed south. Radio blaring and the sunroof open, I mindlessly passed hikers and cyclists dotting the paved curb-lane along the highway. Some remained with thumbs extended, backpacks piled high beside them, trying to grab my attention although two lanes over. The scenery off to the side was near 'suburban' with many houses and small farms lining the main highway. Large billboards now blocked the once scenic view through the reserve.

It felt good coming back to the island, nostalgic in a way. Maryse came mostly to Vancouver to visit me, I in return now visiting the island perhaps once a year. I had lived for several years in Victoria and the surrounding area, and had purchased land with my family, at the end of the Sooke Peninsula. The lagoon on the north side of the land was great for crab fishing, but a continuous fog bank sitting over the property from dawn to dusk made it impossible for anything to dry out. We had a lot of fun for years, fishing, gathering mussels, and hiking through the pristine woods while Rose and Steve raised the kids. We eventually sold it to move back to Vancouver and be closer to the rest of the family. Still to this day, if you look from Sooke, over the inlet past the spit, you can see a cloud of fog hanging, lifeless, over several acres of cleared land. That would be the property.

Passing the turnoff to Sydney, I made a left turn to one of the back roads to Cordova Bay. The road curved continuously and was difficult to navigate, but to see some of the old-growth forest and the open water of the channel made the detour worthwhile. Mount Baker's, snow-capped peak towered high above the shimmering, blue strait that flowing beneath a ribbon of white cloud, a humbling experience. Sannichton and Brentwood Bay, unique little boroughs just to the west, brought back the memories of the years I had spent living on the island. The humming of the car motor, the stereo, the smell of the tan leather interior, along with the beautiful scenery, were all a small part of the dream I had in returning to the island.

Enjoying the drive, but with the seat vacant beside me, I had a sense of longing - perhaps physical, perhaps emotional - that kept nagging at me; it could also have been the burn starting to heal. The sun, streaming in shafts from the forest canopy to the east, highlighted the road as if to orchestrate a winding, theatrical stage. The ocean peeking through the lichen-laden boughs as if I was in a distant dreamland, and, apart from my aches and pains, made me feel like myself once again. It reminded me of the many trips the two of us had taken throughout the island. Life, at the moment, could not have been better.

Looking in my rear view mirror, I noticed a distant motorcycle, bouncing up and down with the contours of the road. It following me around the snake-bend corners with great ease. To my surprise, he accelerated right by me without the least concern for oncoming traffic. Impressed by the power of the machine, I watched as he disappeared with not so much as a trace or care around the potholes and bends in the road. Continuing on for a short distance, oblivious to the cares of the preceding days, I enjoyed the relaxation. Within several minutes though, a sparkle of light flashed from ahead, warning me of an oncoming car. Whizzing along at ease with my surroundings, I continued without taking second notice. Coming into an extremely bright area, and then back into the dark shade of the cedars, I was thrown into near blindness. Before my eyes could adjust, I strained to see a motorcycle driving directly for me.

"Shiiiiiit!"

Pulling the wheel hard to the right and slamming on the brakes, my cell phone flew across the dash and splintered into several pieces; the car slide into the ravine and straight into a stump. Red cedar chunks flew high into the air as the car came to an abrupt stop nose up with the rear bumper low in the ditch.

"Wow!" escaped from my lips.

Motionless and gathering my thoughts, I gripped the wheel. Wondering how the motorcyclist could have been so blatantly stupid, I turned to look out the rear window. Pissed to see the motorcycle stopped twenty yards behind me, upright and motionless, I banged hard on the steering wheel. Gradually opening the door and easing my way from the seat, I stood with one hand on the roof of the car, the other on my hip.

"You bastard!" was all that rolled off my tongue.

The driver lifted his visor and stared at me with a grin on his face. He slowly pulled his helmet off as if to acknowledge the stand off. I caught a glint of light reflect from below his right ear, and suddenly I realized who he was, the punk who had tried to stop me on the ferry. As I walked back toward him, he laughed and slid his helmet back on. Cranking the throttle in a sudden burst, he popped the clutch and sped off in a trail of leaves. All that remained was his black skid mark on the pavement and the blue streak of words that I yelled after him.

Angry, and wondering what to do, I walked back to the car. Kicking a chunk of cedar that had landed on the road, I circled to the front of the car where the nose was covered in dirt and cedar chips. Down on my hands and knees, I dug around the front to expose any damage. To my surprise, very little was evident except for a bent airfoil and a gash in the rubberized skin over the bumper.

"Good," I sighed looking about to see where I might use a phone.

Heading back in the direction I had come, I saw that the sun had hid itself in the upper boughs of the tall cedars, casting cool shadows across the road. In the sun scorched areas, white steam ascended from the blacktop as wisps of vapor, perhaps an omen that I should do the same. A deep breath laden with the smell of the damp earth and new foliage lining the road helped to take my mind from the incident and relieved me of the tension. Heading back in the direction I had come, I was touched by the serenity of the surroundings. I walked for several minutes and came across a laneway lined with tall cedar hedges. As I proceeded up the lane, the most heavenly aroma I had smelled for some time drifted by my nose. The wonderful scent of flowers filled my head. Peering through the hedges, I looked upon a wild garden with an assortment of flowers and bushes scattered almost haphazardly about its perimeter. A bed of blaze roses stood out brilliantly from the distant front corner in the direction from whence I'd come. Beside them a wheel barrel, hoe and digging spade lay dormant and unattended, but attested to recent use. It was easy to see that the occupants cared for and loved the beauty that surrounded them and had brought their own personalities to the garden. As I continued along the drive, the layer of gravel crunched beneath my feet and alerted a small dog somewhere on the premises to my approach. Kicking an exposed root from the ground, I stumbled up the front steps to a flagstone landing and an old oak door with a small lead glass sidelight to the right. Admiring the large lion-head doorknocker, I lifted the brass ring and let it drop hard against the solid door. The little dog yapped viciously inside as someone came to open the door.

"Good morning," I smiled, stooping slightly to accommodate the height of the tiny elderly woman in front of me. "My name is Brian Alexander and I was wondering if I might use your phone?"

"Well, good morning." she smiled back. "I'm June and we imagined someone would be coming our way. Are you alright?"

A look of bewilderment must have come to my face for she quickly continued.

"We were out in the garden when we heard the tires of your car squeal and then the motor cycle drive off.... Please... Please come in, how rude of me." She waved me in with her hand while the little dog scampered off, long hair flying, to alert the household. "My husband will be with you directly."

The woman shuffled off in her slippers and gardening apron and retreated out of sight down the dark hallway. Within seconds, the little dog came scurrying around the corner, nails clicking on the hardwood floor, to drop a beanie baby at my feet.

"Lasa Apso's have a good sense of character," came the soft deep voice of a man from the corner of the foyer by the hall entrance.

I looked up from the dog to see an elderly, gray-haired man of slight stature. His deep blue eyes and soft-spoken nature gave me the impression he was a learned man. His graceful movement, as he reached out his hand to shake mine, gave me a sense of confidence in him.

"Hello, my name is Vincent daLima." A smile came across his face. "We were expecting a visitor and are glad to see you are alright."

"Brian Alexander." I replied with a nod. His name seemed familiar to me.

Vincent looked down at the dog between us. "They were bred as guard dogs for the palaces high in the Tibetan mountains," he stated as he bent over to pick the little dog up in his arms. "This is Lilly. She is very generous, sharing everything she has with those she likes, even her beanie babies. They are said to have an uncanny sense of hearing and even, supposedly, a sixth sense. She is sometimes at the right place at the right time, but more accurately at the wrong place at the wrong time." She wriggled in his arms and her tongue darted out to lick his nose as he looked down at her. With a sweeping motion, he lowered her to the floor to release her from his arms. "Now on your way." he ordered and she scurried around the corner and out of sight.

"I am glad to see you're not hurt. We were quite concerned when we heard the commotion outside the garden. We were not sure whether we should phone the police or not, till we heard the expression of anger and the motorcycle drive off."

"I am fine," I sighed," but I am afraid I will need some help with my car."

"Is it badly damaged?"

"No. But it will have to be pulled out of the ditch.

"Good. BMW's are well made cars, aren't they? It is an older one isn't it?"

I half smiled as he turned away, not surprised that he had bothered to look at my car. My eyes followed him to a doorway. His gesture was warm as if we'd known each other for some time and he welcomed me into his sitting room. "My wife will get you a drink, and I will give you some privacy to make some calls. The telephone is at the desk. Do you need a telephone directory?"

"No thank you,"

He smiled and left the room, door ajar. With the clicking of her nails again, Lilly made her way along the hall to stand guard just beyond the crack of the door. With one eye peeping in from beneath a hairy brow, beanie baby in mouth, she watched me. Without moving a muscle, apart from the nostrils flaring slightly as she breathed, she sat motionless like a statuette.

Within moments, I had described the circumstances of my demise to Maryse, and given the directions to my local and hung up the phone. I sat back in the chair and wondered whether or not she had truly understood the directions, but concluded it was no use to worry. A few moments later, the light shuffle of slippers on the hardwood floor came closer to the study door.

"Lilly, out of the way." To my surprise, June side-stepping the dog, entered with a tray full of china. With a smile from ear to ear she gently put the tray on the desk in front of me. I had to smile. The teapot was decorated with pink roses and brocade of gold outlining the contours of the spout. The teacups matched, with tiny finger holes that could accommodate no man's finger. A variety of biscuits adorned a plate in the center of the tray, with embroidered napkins on either side. I could see that this was to be a real 'morning tea'.

"We very rarely get visitors any more," she sighed, as she began to prepare the cups and saucers. "Since Vincent gave up his tenure at the University, we don't see many folks this way. He is such a brilliant man. It is a shame they don't use him more, although he does talk down at the museum on occasion."

"What may I ask is Vincent's area of study?"

"Well, his doctorate was in native studies, and I know he has helped with the museum's handling of artifacts being given back to the bands and tribal elders." She looked at me with a side-glance. "I think that's why they don't come any more."

A bell of recognition went off in my head as I began to look around the room. 'I think I remember this guy.' The certificates and photos on the walls all pointed to a learned and well-traveled man. The photos were mostly in black and white, while a few, more recent, appeared in color. Getting up from the chair, I did a slow walk from picture to picture, and was amazed at the scope of Vincent's scholarly career. A few pictures, showing Vincent with tribal elders in front of totems and long houses, indicated the depth of relationship this man must have acquired through his dealings.

"That was taken in the Queen Charlottes," came a voice from the hall.

Startled, I turned to Vincent as he entered the room. "Very impressive."

"Only if it amounts to something," he replied, as he sallied to the high back leather chair behind the desk.

"What do you mean?"

He smiled back at me and then returned a more direct address. "A life-time of work can mean nothing if it is not done with the intent to build and not destroy."

I said nothing and turned to continue to browse along the bookshelves. "Do you mind," looking back to him for a second, not to be presumptuous and pry into his privacy?

"Not at all, they are only pictures and impressions."

"That is a powerful statement from a man who, if my memory serves me well, has probably done more for the rebuilding of the West Coast Tribes than any other white man, perhaps in all of America."

"You flatter me, but I assure you, most of it is fantasy, and the rest is wishful thinking, by all parties."

"Excuse me!" I interrupted, a little taken back by his candor.

"Sit down Mr. Alexander, and have your tea. We have each other at a disadvantage, as I know who you are as well, through your work that was published years back. And I think also, a film documentary."

"You mean someone actually remembers my work, let alone having once upon a time read and seen it!" I smiled.

"No. I didn't say I remembered it. I remember your name."

I felt the smile drop from my face. He smiled from ear to ear as he saw he had me.

"June, pour Mr. Alexander his tea."

"Sugar?" June asked with a gentle smile.

I nodded and relaxed against the shelves across from Vincent's' desk. "You worked with Dr. Neustadt in the latter stages of his career, didn't you?"

Vincent pointed to one of the black and whites tucked amongst the books in his bookshelf. The photograph was very old with its edges frayed and the finish of the frame tarnished. In the photo, a very young Vincent standing proud, outdoors, in an over grown clearing surrounded by the stunted remnants of cedar trees. In front of him stood a tall, carved cedar interior post belonging to a long house; an elderly man, presumably Neustadt, stood by Vincent's side, leaning forward into the hood of a camera.

"Ninstints?" I questioned without taking my eyes off of the photo.

"Yes," replied Vincent with a sound of pleasure to his voice. "You have a good eye." His chair squeaked a little as he turned back to his desk to take a sip of tea. "The totems at that point were in much better condition than they were when finally transported in 1956 for preservation. Most were too far gone for transport."

I slowly skirted the room looking at the many artifacts and pictures lining the shelves to the chair and slumped into it with a 'wosh' as the air escaped from the cushion.

"You have done some wonderful work over the years, but I heard a hint of animosity in your voice when you mentioned 'our history'."

Vincent's face lit up slightly. He didn't say a word, but I knew he was searching me, and for words with which to express his feelings.

"Perhaps, Mr. Alexander," he said teasingly, "you may come back to visit us sometime to spend a few days, and we will discuss some of what I have on my mind."

I sipped my tea and smiled gently to acknowledge the invitation. He smiled back, with a glint in his eye, letting me know that the reply had been given.

Looking down at my watch, twenty minutes had passed since the phone call and I still had to do some digging to get my car free.

"Well Vincent, June, I must thank you for your hospitality and I'm on my way. I still have some work to do to free my car."

Getting to my feet slowly and smiling at them both, I stood while Lilly ran over from where she was seated at June's feet, her tail wagging, and sat down and whimpered.

Both Vincent and June laughed, "She's trying to make you feel at home. But she is not saying goodbye, she wants your left-over cookie."

June gave me the nod for permission, and Lilly scooted off out of sight, biscuit in mouth, down the hall.

I reached over the desk to shake Vincent's hand as he slowly got to his feet, "Thank you." I smiled.

"You're welcome Brian, and come back again."

I turned and walked from the study, June following close behind.

"Thank you for the tea June." We stopped by the front door. "It was very thoughtful of you, and much needed."

"You are welcome. And do drop in again and let us know how you are getting on." She smiled again as she closed the large door behind me.

Starting down the drive, the cool damp air and the strong smell of roses drifted by my nose again. I took a deep breath of the wonderful scent and felt as if I'd met two very special people. Continuing up the drive back out to the main road, I followed the gravel shoulder back to the car.

FIVE

I couldn't help but feel that Vincent and June were a couple that I would visit again. The tea and cookies were reminiscent of visiting my grandparents' farm as a young boy and left me with a good feeling. The conversation over the hour had been stimulating, enlightening and somewhat surprising.

Vincent had helped to lay the legal foundation for the return of artifacts to the First Nations, by being liaison between the government and representatives of the First Nations dotted throughout the southern B.C. area. A very difficult feat that at times must have been like rolling a five hundred pound stone backwards up a mountain. A thankless task to undertake in some respects, and at the best of times a precarious position to be in. There had been a number of demonstrations and threats of violence directed at the officialdom, but nothing had created any lasting hardship and therefore no legal action had been taken. A few years later a legal precedent was set by the courts, allowing First Nations to appeal and overturn custody and guardianship of their displaced relics by non-aboriginals that began a flood of claims. From all over North America and the world, repatriation of thousands of artifacts began. Throughout the west coast, this laid down the basis for the arduous task of documentation, which in turn led to my involvement with the Film Board. The short film featured a shrine built by the Nuu-chah-nulth whaling community on the northwest coast of the island, which was held in high regard and was scrutinized by both sides of the engagement. Vincent's name had been familiar to me, but only after our conversational jesting did I truly come to recognize who he was.

The car looked forlorn with its tail dragging on the ground. With borrowed spade in hand, I began to dig the dirt from around the airfoil to clear the way for a pull out of the ditch. Within ten minutes, there was Jufel's (Maryes' brother) black 'four by four' bobbing up and down in the distance swerving with the contours of the road. A smile came to his face as he pulled up beside me and saw the condition of my car.

"Well done!" he chuckled, rolling down the window, gloating at my predicament.

Maryse climbed down from the truck with a "Huneeee!!!"

The top of her head was barely visible as she walked from beside the hood of the truck; her small stature a understated testament to the determination of character bubbling within.

"Are you OK?" she asked, gently slipping her arm around my waist. Looking up to my face with my bruised cheek and dented forehead, she slapped my arm playfully. "What did you do?"

Limping over to the car to open the trunk for a

rope, "That's not all of it hun."

"You're limping." she screamed.

Jufel didn't say a word; certain things are better left unsaid. He pulled the truck ahead and then backed up to within several meters of the bumper.

Crawling beneath the rear, I pulled the rope through the frame securing it with a bowline knot. Within moments, the car was out of the ditch and we were heading down the road in tandem to Royal Oak Drive. Maryse sat quietly beside me tapping her nails on her skirt waiting for me to begin. It was difficult to know where to start and what to say. A lot of it made no sense and it was hard enough for me to comprehend it let alone try to explain it to someone.

We spent the next half hour driving along the coast road slowly, making the occasional detour that allowed me the time to find the words to describe my circumstance. After starting the conversation a few times, I decided it was best from the beginning, and tell all. The incidents of Friday night at the University Museum, the young man, the old native man in my vision along with my dream of the blue girl, all rolled off my tongue continuously to finally end with the motorcycle running me off the road just a short hour ago.

"It sounds awfully strange to me," she mumbled not taking her eyes off the little plaza at the corner of Cook and Hillside. Turning left, we headed for downtown. "I think you'd better go see someone. These visions, or dreams you're having, sound pretty strange."

"Yeah," I sighed in agreement. "The one last night was pretty bad, more like a nightmare."

Drifting off for a few moments in reflection there was silence in the car. The leather squeaking on the seat, as Maryse shifted, signaled her uneasiness. "I can't help feeling that there is a purpose to all of it though," I continued. "Everywhere I go, I am reminded of the incident at the museum; running into people like Vincent, because of an accident; seeing the guy from the museum on the ferry and then hitting my head against the glass."

"Sounds like someone's trying to kill you."

The car went silent as we both looked at each other.

"Nah!" was my first response.

"What is going on Brian?" Maryse asked apprehensively.

"Don't be silly hun, it's all coincidence," I said with a smile trying to convince myself.

"Maybe someone's putting drugs in your coffee."

The comment was not reassuring, and the thought of someone drugging me had crossed my mind the night before. But who on earth would care or be frightened enough of me to do something like that. We were silent in the car for the rest of the trip to her parents' house.

Turning on to Leonard Ave. from Cook, I could see the empty tennis courts and bowling-green where Maryse and I had spent much of our time getting to know one another. The parks colorful flower gardens and open walkways where lovers could walk meandered through the maze of water pools and canals that were host to a variety of waterfowl. The peacocks with their shrill cry, a call to romance, echoed throughout the southern tip of Victoria. Further behind are the hills of Beaconsfield Park, where we would sit on warm evenings and watch the dusk descend over the Strait. Port Angeles, which blossomed with its lights as darkness fell, sparkled in the distance.

The mood was rather quiet as I let Maryse out of the car. Her mom and dad were in the front yard digging in the vegetables. They were different, by western standards, and were the first people on the block to do something as revolutionary as putting a vegetable garden in the front yard getting direct sunlight from the south. Giving them a wave, I turned the car and drove off heading toward the waterfront to skirt Beaconsfield Park

Maryes' parents were wonderful people with a lot of patience. I know for a fact that they did not understand the way we do things in this country, but then again, neither do I. They had emigrated from France just after the war, where they had lived culturally sheltered lives high in the French Alps. They came on the invitation from a Canadian soldier they had befriended while he remained on an extended tour of duty near their village. He had longed to return home to the west coast and when they too arrived for a visit, liked what they saw and with his sponsorship decided to make Canada their home.

Continuing around the park along Southgate to Government Street, I passed the Royal British Columbia Museum, and knew immediately I would have to make a stop. The mystery woman from the Victoria Museum, the detective had mentioned, had been in the back of my mind since the police station visit yesterday. I had a notion that if any of this were to make sense, she could be a part of it.

Looking down at my watch, the time was almost eleven. "Well, what the heck. Now is as good a time as any."

Pulling the car around the corner to pass in front of the Parliament Buildings, I made the next left and parked a little further down past and across the street from the Vehicle License Building. Dodging visitors as they milled back and forth on the lawns of the Parliament Buildings, I walked kitty-corner across to the majestic Empress Hotel. Its ivy-covered facade stood steadfast dominating the harbor front, facing westward to the Pacific Ocean. The masts of the sailing fleet stood erect in the harbor as if to salute all who milled about in the lower walkways of the harbor front. The ferry dock remained vacant while expectant travelers crowded the paved walkway leading to the dock, and waited patiently as the distant ferry, soon to arrive, lumbered across the strait. The sun had brought the city alive, even this early on a Sunday morning.

Across the small courtyard and on to the doors of the museum, I entered not knowing what to expect of my venture or how to go about getting the information I needed. A woman who I had never met worked here and hopefully with her help the two of us might be able to find some answers to my dilemma. I had no idea what her name was, what she looked like, how old she was, or, as a matter of fact, whether she actually worked here at all. Walking past the security guard, I came to the engraved black marble directory and scanned the columns of the names hoping for one to jump out at me. It didn't. Riding the escalator up to the Native Artifacts section of the museum, I walked about hoping to recognize someone or something that might give me a clue. A young native woman working behind a counter at a computer terminal gave me a glance from time to time, but kept working as if not to disturb.

The third time I looked in her direction, she got up with a smile and came over to me from the terminal.

"Can I help you?"

Taken back by her directness and slightly stunned by her appearance in a sharply cut navy uniform, I stood motionless. Not sure how to reply, with either question or answer, I stood gazing into her eyes searching for the solution to my quandary. Was this her?

"Well yes." I stuttered. "I am visiting from the mainland and I am looking for a woman who is working with the museum."

"We have a directory in the foyer that would be able to help you."

"Yes, I know. The problem is, I don't know her name."

"Well, what does she look like?" she asked with a smile.

"I don't know that either, Shaw-Ana," I stammered, noticing her name on the tag by her lapel.

She looked up at me with a half-smile. "So you do not know what she looks like."

"Nope!" I returned with a shrug.

Her forehead wrinkled, eyebrows narrowing as she frowned and stared at me perplexed.

"I realize this sounds highly irregular, but the other day when I was visiting at the Museum of UBC, there was an attempted robbery, and I got hit in the head by a man running from the museum." Reaching my hand up in sympathy to my cheek, I smiled a light grin for reassurance, "I'm alright now though, thank you. I was hoping to determine what was trying to be taken and even locate this person.

Her brow straightened and her look of concern

turned into one of dismay.

"You were there?" she asked directly.

"Well yes, but not quite. I was around the back and, well, I got run over."

"By what?" A smile broke out on her face.

"Well, not by what, by whom," I replied.

Her look sobered up, and a bit of color came to her cheeks. Asking point blank, my eyes fixed on hers. "Did you make any inquiries at the Vancouver Police Station yesterday?"

"Who are you?" she queried without answering my question? Her eyes glared, piercing deep brown, almost black, beneath the now straight line of pencil-fine brows. She did not flinch a muscle. This woman is good, I thought to myself, realizing she knew something.

"Who are you?" she asked a little louder and reached for the phone at her side.

"Brian!" I replied quickly. "Brian Alexander, and I am not here to cause any trouble." I backed off a little. "I have been doing research with west coast whaling communities and was at the museum at the time of the break in."

After a few seconds of thought, with me standing before her like an idiot with a half grin on my face, she softened her response.

"Well Mister Alexander!" putting her phone back in its holster and looking straight back at me with disconcerting coolness, "I cannot really tell you anything, but the media have already started with the inquiries, and it is only a matter of time before they publish all there is to know. The break-in came to us as a bit of a surprise, but not entirely unexpected. News does travel fast within the community, as you well might imagine, but because of the security surrounding the exhibit, the incident was to be kept quiet. The only information I am at liberty to say is that a very valuable piece was taken."

With a look of surprise on my face, "How valuable?"

"Very." She directed me over to the desk where she had been working and to an extra chair by its side. She cleared the screen and shut several drawers she had been working from. I could not help but notice her sculptured beauty and fine shoulder length black hair. She was thin with fine facial features and skin texture and color that the women of her race have been so praised for. She could not have been any more than mid-twenties, but her demeanor and confidence gave the impression of a woman twice her age.

"Please, if you don't mind I would like you to fill out an inquiry report and if there is any more we can tell you at a later date, we would be more than happy to do so. OK!"

She continued to clean around her station as I filled out in brief some nonsense about the exhibit.

"Did you happen to get a good look at the guy who hit you?" she asked, not taking her eyes from her work.

I thought to myself I had not mentioned it had been a man that hit me.

"Yes." I said slowly, "Yes, I did."

"Did you give a description to the police?"

Without answering I sat and looked at her wondering how to answer. A small bead of sweat began to rise on her brow just below her hairline. She was very cool, but I knew she was nervous and it was beginning to show.

"No, I didn't." I replied, leaning back in my chair

watching her for a moment and continued, "At the time I was very confused as to what actually happened and did not see any purpose in getting involved with the police. All I got was a bruised cheek and a sore back," Pointing to my yellowish cheekbone again.

The tension melted from her face as she shifted in her chair to a more relaxed position, "Mr. Alexander, the reason I cannot tell you more is because no-one knows. The piece is called 'Pillars of the Moon' and has only been out in circulation several times before and only for a limited number of days at a time." She shifted again in her chair to get more comfortable and crossed her legs.

"But what is it?" my voice rose slightly at the inquiry.

She tapped her finger on the arm of the chair and gave my question some thought, "I believe it is a bowl. A small engraved jade bowl."

I sat back and thought for a moment, "Jade! It cannot be of west coast origin then."

"The engravings suggest Central America."

"Of what era, Aztec - Olmec - Toltec?"

"No one knows. The inscriptions are all similar but the piece has never been out long enough in circulation to study thoroughly.

"Oh, that's interesting, any photographs?"

She smiled back at me tapping her fingernail repeatedly on the arm of the chair. "There is nothing more I can tell you."

Considering the implications for several moments, I thought about what she had said. "Are you sure?"

"Yes, Mr. Alexander."

"Call me Brian." I suggested, resting my chin on my up-raised closed fist.

"I'm sorry Mr. Alexander," she said with a smile. "I really should be getting back to work - if you'll excuse me."

She gave me a side look and knew if I pursued the issue any longer, it could mean the loss of a valuable contact.

"Thank you ever so much, Shawna. I hope we have a chance to talk again."

She nodded, "You're welcome. Come again, any time."

Returning the gesture, I walked away without turning back. Passing several glass displays, I turned to the left and ducked behind a large exhibit of a wax fur trader and his sled. From between his arms, I watched as she worked away at her terminal. After several moments, she looked up to see if anyone was watching and reached for the phone. After a few moments of what seemed heated conversation and frustration, she put the phone down and continued her work.

Slipping down the escalator unnoticed, I passed the security guard again and glanced at the museum hours stenciled on the glass by the front doors. Out into the fresh air once again, I slowly walked back to the car rethinking all that she said and wondering whether she had been entirely honest with me, probably not. Why should she be?

Rounding the block in my black beauty, I headed back out past the Empress and up Government Street to Johnson and over the bridge to Esquimalt.

Opening the door to Jufel's apartment was always a bit of an experience. One never knew what could be lurking in the confines of his small one-bedroom flat. A pull out couch tucked against one wall of the living room was usually down and cluttered with clothes and magazines; but today, it was up, and relatively clean. Most of the usual refuse had made its way to the coffee table, which sat in the middle of the room cluttered with magazines, movie videos and leftovers from the previous night, or nights. The decor was simple with the obvious splash of bachelorhood. Pizza boxes and beer bottles graced all the available horizontal surfaces, and some that were not. Throughout the living and kitchen area, stacks of empty beer cases and other leftovers, pizza crusts included, seemed to creep their way about like ground foliage on a tropical isle. The many colorful posters that lined the walls gave the living area a nightclub co-ordination that could only be appreciated by those who created it. It was obvious Jufel was enjoying himself and was in the constant mode of entertaining his friends.

Placing my small suit case and shoulder-bag of camera equipment on the floor by the front door, I waded through the debris to the opposite side of the room to open the vertical blind exposing the sliding door. Giving the door a tug, I felt cool air rush passed me, entering to relief the staleness from the night before. The smell of old smoke that impregnated the very fabric of the furniture lingered momentarily while the freshness from the outside made its way throughout the room; the culprit, a tray half full of cigarette butts, was centerpiece on the small square mahjong table. The oblong, ivory tablets of the Chinese game were neatly stacked across the deck as though left in anticipation for the next game to begin. A fallen stack of discarded coins remained at one edge, abandoned for the moment, but hopefully like the phoenix, to rise again from the ashes of defeat.

Outside, visible through the glass of the sliding

door, a small group of boys played a game of catch on Tillicum Common. Behind them several joggers in their near-fluorescent regalia, bobbed up and down as they circled their way around the gorge. My mind wandered to the many times I had run the entirety of that same walkway with much enthusiasm, but of late the opportunity and determination just were not there.

'What a mess!' I sighed turning back to the clutter of the room.

I stacked a few of the papers that were left scattered across the couch to make room to sit down. Pulling a throw blanket about me, and lying down, I let my head sink into a velvet pillow with unconcern. I gazed at the stucco ceiling for a few moments and tried to empty my mind. The conversation at the museum was intriguing. Shawna's demeanor and her body language had alluded to her knowing much more than she let on. Then again, she knew me not from Adam. Why should she divulge any more than she did, or anything at all. I was a complete stranger, but not for long.

The sound of the birds chirping in the trees just beyond the balcony rail began to ease the heaviness I felt. From the direction of the sliding door the gentle draft of fresh air, laden with the scent of new foliage, drifted by and within a moment my eyes closed of their own accord. My mind wandered at the events of the morning and I soon found myself drifting into a light sleep.

It had been delightful seeing Maryse this morning, even more-so if the circumstances had of been different and we could have spent some time down by the water, perhaps picking mussels or looking for the interesting garb that washed up to the shore along the strait. Of

late we had taken delight in the simpler things that
living by the coast had to offer, often going clam
digging, hiking and treasure hunting. We had known
each other for several years before we had dated, and
when the realization that we both felt the same way
about each other, and the opportunity arose to do
something about it, we jumped.

As I slipped deeper into sleep I was aroused by the
sensuality we had experienced during our first intimate
relations together.   Sensing that my body was
responding to the stimulation, I came to the realization,
with a start, that I was not alone. Feeling a weight on
my legs, I opened my eyes and I looked down beneath
the blanket that covered me; Maryse' piercing brown
eyes peered up at me; a mischievous little giggle, she
sounded so often to get her own way, escaped her
moist half open lips. Stealing up my chest, she nestled
her face against my shoulder and slipped her hand up
underneath my shirt.

"What do you think you're doing?" I half laughed
giving her a squeeze as she snuggled further up on top
of me, her face tucked beside my neck. "You could
have given me a heart attack waking me up like that!"

"Oh don't be silly, I am tired too." she sighed.

I knew I was defeated with not so much as a word
on the subject and within a few moments the pain of
the burn was forgotten and all the rest seemed to be
functioning, as it should.

We slept the afternoon away in each other's arms
warm on the couch till there was a loud bang on the
patio door. Two boys screaming at the top of their
lungs, just beyond the balcony, startled us out of our
slumber. Pulling my shirt close about me, I strolled out
onto the balcony and tossed a ball over the rail to the

thankful boys below. As I turned to come back inside, out of the corner of my eye a familiar shadow caught my attention. There, tucked beneath the trees just beyond the walkway in the parking lot, a familiar motorcycle was sitting. Taking a second glance and squinting to see the size of the bike and whether a familiar body came along with it, I turned and re-entered the apartment. Pulling the curtain almost shut, I stood back in the shadow and watched. Sure enough, after several moments, the familiar black leather bike suit, with something detestable inside, strolled across the grass in the direction of the bike. My first instinct was to jump the rail and chase after him.

"Do you feel lucky today, punk!" flashed across my lips in remembrance of my favorite movie line? But looking down at my skinny legs and bare feet, I decided 'he wouldn't have a chance' and aroused Maryse from her sleep.

"Come on Maryse, we gotta go!"

My watch showed it was a few minutes past four and I wanted to revisit the museum and Shawna before closing.

"Come on honey, let's go!" I gave her a nudge and pulled the blanket from her and made my way to the washroom.

Maryse remained sitting on the couch, hands clasped between her closed knees, still half asleep. As I crept over to the patio door to peek outside again, I gave her an upward waving motion with my hands to encourage her to action.

"What on earth are you doing Brian?" she drawled getting up from the couch and proceeded to stand beside me. In broad daylight she yawned, arms up-stretched oblivious to the assault on our privacy from outside. Pulling her to one side, she struggled and pulled away.

"What is wrong with you?" she yelped.

"Maryse! Stay away from the door. There's someone out there."

"So!"

"No. There is someone out there watching us." I motioned her over to sneak a peek through the corner just in time to see the motorcycle pull out of the parking lot.

"Yeah, right? You're going to have to do better than that," she mocked, wading through the debris to the bathroom. "My brothers a pig. Look at this place." Those were her last words as she disappeared behind the closing door.

"Darn!" looking over my shoulder to the camera bag by the door. "I have a zoom lens in my case. I could have got a good shot of the guy." Strutting over I bent down and unzipped the bag and prepared the lens and camera for the next encounter with this guy that I was sure would happen.

"Come on Maryse, let's go!" I yelled again donning the rest of my clothes and jacket. Flinging the camera bag over my shoulder, ready to go, I stood perched by the door with my hand on the knob. I could not believe my ears. The shower was running.

SIX

The trip back to downtown Victoria didn't take long. Wharf Street, although busy with traffic, was running relatively smooth. The obvious delays of pedestrians, as they sauntered across the paved crosswalks to view the upper harbor, was the only near irritation on this Sunday evening. Thick, ominous, rain clouds overshadowed Victoria, and gave the impression of the time being much later in the day than it actually was.

Barely able to look above the car windowsills, Maryse busied herself with looking about at the variety of people that walked the streets and stopped by the shop windows to peer in. She hated to ride in my car, let alone drive it, because of the low leather seats. Whenever she did, she would use a booster cushion to enable her to see over the dash and was always a very defensive driver. Needless to say it did not happen very often.

As we slowed down and rounded the corner by the Visitors Center, the harbor-front came to view. Almost full of boats, their masts gently swaying with the gentle motion of the waves, the docks were alive with activity as sailors and onlookers prepared for nightfall. Captains from all over the area had been cautious enough to navigate the rocky shores in the rough seas and elude the onerous weather to moor in this protected little harbor. The Empress Hotel, loomed pretentious on the left, its lights accenting its Victorian dignity. The Parliament Buildings ahead and to the right, were almost void of visitors now and looked gray beneath the ceiling of rain clouds. Busters and musicians danced and played to the few remaining pedestrians walking the lower harbor walkway to finish up the daylight hours. Raindrops had already started to fall leaving dots of spit on the windscreen. Turning right, to pass the front of the Parliament Buildings, we proceeded up Menzies, to a parking spot.

"Do you mind waiting here for a few moments while I go into the museum," putting my hand on Maryse' knee?

She looked back and grinned sarcastically, "Not on your life." She pulled her lip to one side, "The last time you asked me that, I was in the car for over an hour."

Climbing out of the car, I reached back behind the seat to retrieve my crumpled umbrella. Trying vainly to straighten the spokes to instill some semblance of normality, I came to terms with its condition and left it down to carry it alongside. We slowly crossed the street and over the lawn to the museum. The courtyard was now empty and very few people remained in the foyer of the museum. Riding the escalator up, I was startled by what I saw in the direction of Shawna's desk. Pulling Maryse to my side, I covered her mouth and dragged her behind an exhibit.

"What are you doing?" she screamed exasperated. "Have you gone mad?"

"Shush!" uncovering her mouth from my hand. She cursed me under her breath as I held her back and peered through the exhibit to a young aboriginal man whom I recognized.

"Uhh!" I groaned as the pain from her stamping on my toe registered. "Maryse, be quiet!" I grabbed her by the arms and squeezed her firmly enough to make her listen. "Remember what we talked about in the car on the way in this morning? Well, I think the guy over there is the fellow who ran into me last Friday at the exhibit in Vancouver." I watched as her eyes gave an indication of recognition.

"Are you sure?"

"Yeah!"

We both peeped from behind the exhibit for several moments while he waited by the desk where Shawna had worked. A door opened beside the desk, not exposing the person behind it, and the young man briskly walked to it and disappeared. Waiting several moments, we crept over hand-in-hand to the door and gently gave it a tug; the door was secure.

"Come on, let's go sit over there and wait till they come out." Taking a seat on a cushioned bench slightly hidden by some foliage, we sat and patiently waited. After fifteen minutes and a call to museum closure, it was obvious they were not coming out.

"Well hun, it doesn't look like they're gonna come."

"Yeah, I think so too."

We looked at each other and slowly got up and walked to the escalator to ride down. Once outside, I put my arm around her and looked around at the rain as it gently fell into puddles dotting the courtyard. Underneath the canopy of the front doors we were protected, but as the rain did not let up after several minutes and the inevitability of the situation was upon us, the crocked umbrella was unleashed.

"Come on, get up!" I sighed arguably after a moments struggle. Maryse and I, arm in arm, walked towards Beaconsfield Park, to take the long way back to the car.

Looking up the alleyway beside the museum, I noticed a motorcycle beside the dumpster halfway to the back. A chime went off in my head and I handed the umbrella to Maryse.

"Wait here hun."

"Why?"

"Wait here!" as I squeezed her arm, persuading her to the brick wall close by, protected from the rain. She said nothing as I crept quietly up the alley staying close to the wall. My footsteps echoed lightly on the pavement, but not above the resounding raindrops hitting the hard surface below. My senses sharpened as I could hear scuffling behind the bin. My ears began to ring as I strained to identify the voices above the raindrops. I could hear slapping and groans and a woman's muffled scream. Squeezing myself between the bin and the wall, I edged forward till I could just see through the vertical crack the figures of four men and a smaller figure, presumably the woman. Watching for a moment, sizing up the situation, I saw a sparkle below the ear of the man who was restraining the woman.

"That son of a bitch," I grunted and lurched forward to attack him, wedging myself further between the bin and the wall! Trapped, but still unnoticed, with all the strength I could muster, I reached back to one of the vertical steel arms of the bin and yanked myself free. When the woman gave another yelp, fearless anger welled up inside me and without a second thought I raced around to the front of the bin, taking a giant leap in the air, feet first. The woman was free, and I landed on top of the earring-clad body and shot out unbalanced toward the other three men. With all my strength, I drove myself into them, knocking them off their feet; they toppled to the ground with the deafening noise of a gunshot. Above the ringing in my ears, I could hear the sound of a small piece of iron hitting the hard ground. Not stopping to look, I scrambled up and kicked and punched aimlessly as if there were a thousand before me. After several moments of sheer exertion and direct hits, two of the men ran away, disappearing further up the alley. One lay slumped against the wall, a green garbage bag by his side. The other lay face down on the pavement, his earring dangling on his cheek.

"I must have landed on his head," I half yelled toward the woman as she went to comfort the man slumped against the wall. She said nothing as she fondled his hair and opened his coat to expose a dark damp patch on his side.

"Is he going to be alright?" I asked crouching low on one knee to assist her.

He grunted as he tried to get to his feet, "We have to get out of here. Those guys will be back!"

"Who are they?"

"Jaguar!"

For the first time, I realized that it was Shawna; and the man propped against the wall exposed in the dim light was my elusive friend from the exhibit.

Blood was starting to pool on the pavement below where he was propped.

"We have to get Peter out of here." she cried frantically. "He will bleed to death in this cold and rain."

"Lets take him to the hospital; he needs help."

"I can't." came Peter's panting voice. They will be waiting for us there. Shawna, we have to go, quickly!"

"Will you help us?" came Shawna's' desperate voice.

"Where?" I asked with a shrug.

"Anywhere but here for now."

"All right, follow me."

"Wait." Peter bent over as best he could and picked up the green bag.

As I reached out to grab the bag from him, he redirected my hand as if to refuse and struggled with the slippery awkward bag close to his chest. Shawna ran to pick up her large purse from the ground by the door. Supporting Peter from both sides, we left the unconscious body behind and returned to the entrance of the alley-way and Maryse shivering in the shadows behind a bush.

"What happened Brian? I heard a gunshot."

"Honey, it's alright. Kind of hard to explain right now, but I have to help these people. Come, we have to get to our car."

In her platform shoes, Maryse struggled to follow us as best she could under the crocked umbrella as we dodged our way through the puddles and mud in front of the Parliament Buildings. From behind, we heard the revving of a car engine and the squeal of tires. With the lights of the building well lighting our way, it was obvious we would also be exposed to the men who had left the alley. Tucking ourselves behind the stone-wall of the front steps, we were out of view. Looking back to the museum courtyard and a black sedan we assumed to be them, we waited for the way to be clear. Seeing a cab waiting in front of the Parliament walkway, I grabbed Maryse by the arm and forcibly ran with her down the curb and opened the door and threw her in.

"Maryse, I love you. And I don't know what is going to happen right now, but I would feel a lot better if you would head home and wait for me to call. Don't worry. I'll be all right. As soon as I get these people out of here, I'll call.

Slamming the door behind her, I rubbed my hand across the wet glass to see her clearly as she drove off. Turning back, I ran up the walkway to Shawna crouched beside the wall and a near fainting Peter, no longer clutching the bag that lay on the ground at his feet.

"Come on! My car is just around the corner."

Continuing along the front of the building, the three of us, with the bag, rounded the corner staying close in the shadows and watched from behind the bushes as the black sedan slowly cruised by. Waiting for it to clear, we edged our way across the street and lifted Peter into the back seat and covered him with an old blanket I used as a throw. The blood was still oozing from the wound and he looked pale as we prepared to drive off. Shawna squeezed into the back to comfort him while the green garbage bag was placed in the passenger's seat in front with me. The square box inside took up half of the area of the seat. Shawna's' woven purse, that looked as if would hold a ton, was placed on top. Starting the car and doing a U-turn, we headed for Government Street, and a way out of the area. Pulling up to the street-light and waiting patiently for it to change, I looked back to Peter and saw Shawna giving the wound direct pressure. She stroked his hair with the other hand in comfort. Clutching the leather grip of the steering wheel, the middle knuckle on my right hand started to throb. I could tell it was badly bruised but not broken. We sat anxiously waiting for the lights to change. The tension began to build at the same rate the pain and swelling around my knuckle did. As I looked up to watch the lights, I came eye to eye with the driver of the sedan directly opposite us, glaring back.

"Wow!" I screamed, my heart racing a mile a minute.

Without waiting for the light to change, I stepped on the gas and squealed my way through the intersection passing them. Glancing in the rear view mirror, I saw the black sedan do a U-turn and follow us in pursuit. Zipping by the bus station, we zoomed our way over to Douglas Street, and headed south toward the park. The rain had cleared the streets of any pedestrians so we were clear to drive at a good pace. In the rear view mirror, I caught a glimpse of weaving headlights several vehicles back and wondered where the best place to try to lose them would be. Feeling the pressure of the moment, with a wounded and bleeding man in the back, my palms began to sweat, and I could feel my skin become clammy from the humidity in the car. The urge to head right for the police station kept tugging at me, but without knowing the consequence of the action along with the uncertainty of the prevailing circumstances; patience. Controlling my fear, and holding back the stress as best I could, I looked in the rear view mirror to Shawna.

"Are you sure there is nowhere to go?"

"These guys have been trying to catch Peter since Friday, and we have had to be very careful where to go here in Victoria. They have already hurt several of our friends trying to locate him. I thought you were one of them till just a few minutes ago. Peter had mentioned you at the museum in Vancouver, but was not all that sure that you weren't one of them."

"Oh!" I replied, a little insulted. "You know, it appears they have been following me as well. I am not sure exactly how long, but I think from before I left Vancouver, to come here. The guy we left back there in the alley was on the ferry ride over and almost ran me off the road near Sydney on the way down town."

'Now there's a thought.' I whispered to myself, wiping the condensation accumulating on the windows. Looking in the side mirror to catch a view of the cars behind us, I was just in time to see the big sedan pulling up beside us. With a quick pull of the steering wheel to the left, the pursuing car veered to avoid the collision and bounced off the curb of the oncoming lane. Stepping on the gas, with tires spinning on the wet road, we did a four-wheel drift around the corner onto Dallas Road. With the car back under control, the road was all clear ahead of us, and a chance to gain some distance. But as I looked in the mirror, the pursuing car had the same advantage and overtook a car that had pulled in behind us as we made the corner. The sedan closed the distance and was again at our tail, nudging us along with no more than several feet between our bumpers. Noticing the entrance to a parking area to the right side overlooking the strait, I prepared to pull to the right giving the car chasing us no option but to straddle the low curb dividers to the individual parking spaces. Timing it just right, I gave a quick pull to the steering, cleared the dividers and watched as sparks flew as the under-carriage and the lower wheel yokes of our pursuer scraped the cement curbs.

"Good! With any luck the car will lose its oil pan and we'll be in the clear relatively soon."

Swerving back onto the main road, I made a quick left up Moss Street and turned at the next corner, and then again at the end of the block, then back onto Dallas Road. Heading further east, Ross Bay to the right was dark and ominous. Tall waves crashed over the beach and smashed against the break-wall sending plumes of water and spray high into the air. The walkway and road had inches of water on them as the waves washed back toward the shore over the pavement. I slowed down to avoid hydroplaning over the surface and hoped we had lost the black car following us. Looking in the rear view mirror, I caught a glimpse of the car quite a distance back and wondered whether it was they; under the well-lit roadway along the shoreline, we were sure to be seen. Once through the wash area and approaching the winding hills of Crescent Road, I speeded up into hopeful obscurity. As we rounded a corner and crested the hill, I slowed down just in time to watch in my rear view mirror as the sedan started to hydro-plane out of control and get hit simultaneously by a wave as it washed over the guard rails and road.

"Yes!" I screamed, slamming my palm on the dash. "Alright! We are free!"

Turning the defrost fan on high to help with the condensation building up on the inside of the windows, I felt a weight lifted from me. Continuing down the dark roads by the shore and further reaches of Beach Drive, we continued out to Oak Bay.

"How's he doing Shawna?"

"I don't know. He is shivering and cold. We really should take him somewhere and get his wound seen to."

She reached up and grabbed me by the shoulder. "Do you know of a doctor we could take him to who would look at him without reporting it?"

Thinking for a moment and wishing to be on the main land where I knew several who would help in a moments notice, I could offer nothing.

As we passed the old Victorian Oak Bay Inn, I could not help but think of Vincent and the fact that he knew of some of the goings on of the First Nations in the area. And I knew he was familiar with the Royal Museum here and worked at the University in Victoria. Perhaps he would be of some help.

"Have you ever heard of the name Vincent DaLima? He lives a short distance from here. He may be able to help us.

Shawna thought for a moment and replied, "The name rings a bell, but I cannot honestly say I have. I don't think I have ever met him."

I glanced in the rear view mirror at her and caught a set of headlights behind us. Feeling slightly panicked, I thought to myself 'It couldn't possibly be them'. Proceeding on at an even pace, we continued along Beach Ave. till we came to Haultain, where I turned left. The car followed behind us as we continued west. The roads were wet, and the reflected lights of oncoming traffic made it difficult to see anything clearly. Becoming frustrated with my foggy side mirror, I rolled down the window to wipe it clean. As we drove by Shelburne Avenue, I got a good look at the car, and sure enough, it was them.

"Well, we have our friends back." I sighed to Shawna, who strained to turn her head and peer through the rear window. "They seem to be content with doing nothing at the moment other than following us. But one thing is for sure, we will have to lose them, and soon. This is starting to bug me."

Easing my foot down on the gas a little more, we quickly made our way to Cedar hill Road, up to Hillside and out to the main highway to the Ferry. Trying to think of the best way to get rid of them safely, with no harm to us, the back roads of Elk Lake seemed the best. I had been there once or twice, and had found it quite delightful, but got lost. Speeding passed the little shack by the lake with the canoes I pulled into the roadway by the gas station to drive around the back. Slowly, I eased the old Beemer around the building and out past the front by the pumps. Sure enough they had followed me around the rear and were now out of sight behind the building. Shutting off my lights, we quickly headed down the small paved highway away from the gas station and the main road. Over the hill and out of sight in the dark, I watched in the mirror as they pulled up and stopped by the edge of the station. Not knowing which way we had gone, they just waited. A little relieved that my trick had worked, I began to wonder where the road was and came to the conclusion that in theory it had worked, but in the pitch dark, it was not at all practical.
"Shit! I have to turn the lights on."

On came the lights and in a flash the sedan was in pursuit once again. But now the roads were not only wet but also narrow and hilly; I had a sports car and a general idea as to where I was going.

The way was dark and foreboding, with little for reference to indicate where the roadside ended and the gravel shoulder began. All that marked the way to success, or sheer disaster was an occasional tuft of grass or bit of rock. After several moments of roller-coaster riding and screeches from the back seat, the road seemed to smooth out to an open stretch with steady rain. The headlights in the rear bobbed up and down as the large sedan followed, but at a safe distance. With the end of the road coming up fast, I had to decide, Beaver Lake, or Prospect. Racking my memory, I tried to remember which would be the more promising. Prospect was a more dismal place at this time of night and would afford a better chance of escape, but more treacherous roads headed back up to Brentwood past Butchart Gardens.

"Prospect Lake it is!" On to the highway and an almost immediate right and we were on our way. As I drove along, I was hoping to see more to facilitate our escape, but every time an idea came to mind, I'd miss the corner almost ending up in the ditch, or sliding past the exit with all fours locked on the wet pavement. Speeding through the hamlet of Brentwood, I remembered a small road we had previously turned off on to go scuba diving in the Bay. By this time the persistence of our pursuers, close behind, was driving me to desperation.

"Hang on Shawna. There is a small road up here that heads down to the water. I remember it from several summers ago."

Locking all fours, I slowed down and allowed our followers to come right up to our rear. Stepping on the gas again, we pulled several hundred feet in front of them.

"If I can time this right, they will be speeding up just as we make our turn. Hang on!"

I cranked the wheel just as they were ready to ram us. Down we flew, only it wasn't as wide a road as I remembered it. Slick with mud and covered with cedar boughs and roots, it was very rough. Unable to stop on the steep mud decline, we shot down bumping up and down till the shocks were hitting bottom. Trying my best to stay in control I got a glimpse of headlights coming after us.

"Idiots! They must be nuts."

"Yeah! You're the one that's nuts. They weren't the ones who turned down here. This isn't a road, it's a walkway."

"Oh God!" I sighed looking ahead as the headlight illuminated the up coming event as if in slow motion. With nowhere to go we sailed down toward two trees that lined the path on either side.

"We're not going to make it." Shawna moaned from the back.

Centering the car in the path as best I could, I took my foot off the brake and let it glide. Squinting my eyes just before impact, I prayed and watched helplessly as the advancing trees got larger and larger. Clutching my hands on the vibrating wheel and pushing my head back till it hit the rest, I took a breath and watched in slow motion as the front of the car bounced and tilted sideways. I heard a ripping noise and watched the mirrors disappear from my doors and a tug as the rubber trim came flying off the rear bumper. In shock, I watched as the bottom of the hill came racing up toward us, and at the last minute slammed on the brake and turned the wheel. Coming to a skidding stop, just feet away from an embankment heading down to the shore, we sat motionless. The sound of a loud thud and crashing thundered down at us from up above. Shaking myself out of my stupor, I opened the door and eased myself from the seat and stood to face the hillside we had just maneuvered. About thirty yards up the slope, remnants of the front of the black sedan were strewn down the hillside with chrome pieces of headlights still bouncing at my feet. One headlight still intact illuminated the muddy path up to the lodged car. The dome-light in the sedan exposed two well-shaken individuals, slowly trying to mobilize inside the crumpled wreck. Turning back to my car, and ripping the remaining rubber from the bumper dangling loose, I climbed back in and started off slowly down the shore road back toward Brentwood. No one said a word as we continued to the other side of the peninsula and Vincent's house. At one moment, I had an uncontrollable urge to laugh at the absurdity of it all, but remembered the plight of Peter in the back.

"Is he OK?"

"I don't know. I think he was the lucky one."

Shawna just stared out of the window as we drove down the back road close to our destination. Pulling into a service road two drives down from Vincent's, it would be far enough away, that they would have a difficult time searching for us should they find the car. Reaching back into the rear seat with my arm around Peter's back, I gently lifted and pulled him from the back seat. Within several moments, with Shawna lifting and pushing him, we were along the dark paved road. I supported Peter over my shoulder and half carried him along the way. He mumbled and staggered along semi-conscious. Shawna carried the green bag.

SEVEN

The driveway leading to the house was well lit from the spotlight mounted beneath the eaves of the garage. Silhouettes of the tree branches overhanging the driveway reached toward us like fingers trying to clutch us and bar our way. The gravel crunched and rustled beneath our feet as we walked further up the drive closer to the light. Shawna struggled to hold onto the slippery, green, garbage bag, while I dragged Peter along holding him beneath his armpits. He had lost a lot of blood and looked deathly beneath the strands of black, wet, hair matted to his forehead. He was delirious and kept mumbling about the bag and how cold he was. Luckily, even with the dreadful trip in the car on the way here, the bleeding had stopped. Without knowing the safest place to go at the time of the night, Vincent's seemed the best. All I'd hoped was that we could find a doctor willing to make a house call at the late hour and in these rainy conditions.

We continued down a darkened path beside the garage to the back of the house and up onto the large, cedar deck. A wooden lattice, and the stringy remains of hanging plants, obscured our view of the walkway for the most part. As we skirted a three-foot, planter box, and stumbled up a second set of steps, the lights came on automatically to light our way. Through the window, we could see Vincent standing beside the fireplace; leafing through a book, he took no notice of the torrent outside. The family room looked warm and inviting compared to the extreme weather-conditions we experienced on the deck. By his feet, Lilly sat patiently, her head tilting from side to side as we approached the back door; even with the loud sound of the rain thundering on the roof, and then running down in torrents onto the deck, she was still able to hear the shuffling of our feet. She barked furiously as the lit doorway exposed us through the glass. Shawna tapped lightly on the pane while Vincent, realizing someone was on the back deck, edged his way past the furniture to the window to view 'the sorrowful threesome' outside. Standing drenched beneath the vine arbor, he recognized me after a few glances and opened the glass door to let us in.

"Brian! What on earth are you?" He stopped short seeing Peter slumped over and semiconscious, his hand upon a pink-stained cloth at his side.

"I know this man. What happened? Come sit him down over here." With a wave of his hand, he directed us toward the couch. Realizing the seriousness of the circumstance as we edged Peter to the couch, "I'll call for a Doctor."

I raised my hand as if to stop him, but he already knew.

"It's alright. He is my neighbor and just lives several houses down."

Nodding my head in approval, as if there was 'a choice' in the matter, I looked around to see what there might be to help Peter get warm. Grabbing a loose blanket folded on the back of the armchair, I gently eased Peter down. Shawna removed his shoes and managed to ease him out of his soaked jacket, then laid him down and lifted his feet up on the couch to wrap them in the blanket. He was holding his side where the bullet had hit him and gave a grunt as we shifted him to wrap him. Lilly sat in the corner peering from beneath her wispy brow; she didn't utter a sound and watched as Vincent donned his coat, raced out the back door and then across the deck and out of sight. Vincent had barely left when June came rushing into the room in her housecoat and slippers, a little dazed at the commotion and the sight of the three of us.

"Where's Vincent?" she asked slightly panicked.

"He has gone to fetch the neighbor." I replied calmly pointing in the direction across the deck he had disappeared to.

"Who? Larry!"

"I would presume so, a doctor." I said with a smile.

"Oh yes! Is there anything I can do to help?" she asked in a bit of a tizzy.

"No June, thank you, everything should be alright."

Embarrassed at the condition of her floor, water lying in pools on the reddish, clay tiles where we had stepped, I watched sheepishly at a diminutive puddle growing beside the plastic bag.

"I am so sorry about all of this. There was nowhere else to go, that we could think of, and I desperately needed to talk to Vincent."

"Oh that is alright, Mr. Alexander. We were sure we would see you again, but not so soon!"

I could feel the color come to my face as she smiled, and I was convinced we had made the right decision. "Thanks, June." I looked to Shawna, who was holding Peter's hand, on his chest.

"You're welcome," June replied. "Now allow me to get you some dry things and we will clean up some of this water." As she cleared the archway to the open kitchen, she turned back, "I'll put the kettle on for a hot drink." Lilly scurried after her. June was back within a moment distributing towel and fleecy, cotton shirts. Multi-colored, shoulder blankets were thrown loosely around our shoulders and she was gone again as if a mini tornado had done a swirl in the room and blown right back out dropping its refuse as it passed.

Shawna, sitting beside Peter, lifted the wet blouse and sweater from her body in one sweeping motion, dropping them to the floor without a notion to her exposed nakedness. I hesitatingly took her wet things that lay at her feet and handed her a large, white sweatshirt and the shoulder wrap. She looked up at me and smiled in appreciation as she slipped the sweater over her head, then turned her attention back to Peter. I turned away, a little embarrassed at her candid indifference and helped with cleaning the water that trickled between the cracks of the tile.

On my hands and knees with rag in hand, I worked my way from the couch toward the door in a sweeping motion to where the green, garbage bag lay. Feeling a little faint from the chill, and still not fully recovered from the near sleepless night previous, I stopping and closed my eyes, right there on all fours. A scene flashed before me of glaring headlights of cars with people milling in circles about them. Tremendous clatter and yelling almost deafened me as I walked through the center of the calamity. I feared for my life.

"Brian! Brian!" June's voice was echoing in my ears. Realizing June was standing patiently above me, I continued mopping the floor, face pale and trying not to show my perplexity.

"Get up dear," she said softly. "Let me finish that. You've had a difficult day and you need to rest." Lilly, still at her feet, perked up and looked in the direction of the door as noises grew louder from the direction of the deck. Vincent entered the terrace door with a stout man in his forties, black bag in hand.

"Hello." he stated looking down at me as he made a direct beeline for the couch. Without a sliver of uncertainty, he grabbed Peter's face between his hands and yelled. "Wake up!"

Rather startled at his action, I watched as Peter slowly came to and stuttered a few nonsensical words and fell back to sleep. Looking at Shawna, the doctor asked for Peter's name.

"Peter, I need you awake for a little while!" he shouted again as Peter groaned and slipped back into sleep. "Peter!" The doctor pulled the blanket back and slapped him lightly across the face. Peter came to with a 'what-did-you-do-that-for look on his face' and stayed awake while the doctor looked in his eyes and then his ears. The bleeding at his side had stopped for what must have been about an hour and as he took the pressure bandage off, I could see the dark purple hole just above the hip. He prodded the tender area around the wound and slowly tried to lift Peter on to his side.

"Excuse me, miss, could you slowly role his hips while I lift his shoulders."

Without hesitation Shawna knelt on the floor and gently rolled Peter's hips toward the back of the couch. The doctor's finger prodded what appeared to be a small mole towards the middle of his back. Peter writhed in pain and gave a grunt.

"You're one lucky, young man." the doctor stated. "If the bullet had hit you at a more direct angle, you might have lost a kidney or even worse. As it is, the bullet traveled under your skin and left your body through the larger hole in the front." He looked around at me and pointed to his bag. "Would you pass me that?" He ripped open a small package and began to swab the small area surrounding the entrance wound. He reached into the bag again and pulled out some gauze and adhesive to cover the wound. Rolling Peter once again, onto his back, he repeated the procedure on the front only taking more care and time. Peter gave a sigh of relief as the doctor put away his syringe after a shot of antibiotic. "You will have to go and have this seen to at the hospital as soon as possible, in case of broken blood vessels. The bleeding has obviously stopped for now and apart from the localized swelling, everything looks alright, but I can't be certain." He looked directly at Shawna. "There will be more swelling, so you must keep your eye on it for infection."

She nodded in agreement, a smile coming to her face in appreciation, "Thank you, Doctor."

We all nodded in assurance and watched as the doctor collected his paraphernalia and coat, and proceeded to the door. Vincent donning his coat, once again, followed him towards the door and left with the doctor.

"Thanks again, Doctor." Shawna piped as she helped prop Peter's hand up in farewell.

The silhouette of the two figures slowly disappeared into the haze of misty light and into the blackness beyond the edge of the deck. The tense atmosphere in the room relaxed as we realized that all would be well, at least for now. Peter began to slump in exhaustion and Shawna eased his head down onto the cushion again. She slid her legs beneath his feet and tucked them up onto her lap to elevate and cover them with the blanket for warmth once again. June, who had stayed in the background all along, brought a warm drink of tea for Peter to sip on. He gratefully took a gulp and slumped back into the cushions and oblivion. Shawna re-wrapped the blanket tightly around him as best she could and eased herself down behind his legs again. I could see she was almost as exhausted as he. They both drifted off into sleep as the previous three hours of mayhem had come to an end. June still standing, teapot in hand, looked over to me and lifted a cup as if to ask whether I was ready. Collapsing back in the large cloth-weave armchair, I smiled and nodded yes. She brought me the tea and touched my hand as if she was aware of the turmoil that had occurred since the early hours of day. Lilly sitting at my feet gave a yelp and scurried along after her as she disappeared out of the family room and into the inner reaches of their home. Finally, being able to relax, I took a sip and looked about the room. The dull lighting and the fire behind the flagstone hearth, imparted an antique, reddish hue to the artifacts and paintings that lined the walls. The tiled floor and the Mexican style print of the couches made me feel as if I were in a different world. For a split second my mind took me back to sitting around the fire on the mesa in my dream, and the weather lined faces of the participants. The feeling of compulsion and emergency came back to me as the periphery shadows on the walls came alive with figures dancing in silhouettes round about me. A black vase with a white, zigzag motif, atop the stone mantel caught my eye, along with a few brightly colored figurines. I eased myself out of the chair and wandered over to inspect the collection. As I gently rolled each piece in the light to view the intricacies of the artwork, the green, plastic bag, and the mysterious box that lay within, grabbed my attention. Looking toward the couch to see the two lying quietly side-by-side, I retraced my steps around the tiled, mosaic, coffee table back to the chair I had been sitting in. Seated on the arm, I wondered whether I had the rite to delve into the personal belongings of these two individuals I barely knew. After a few moments of indecision, I came to the conclusion that yes, since it, the green bag, had almost cost me my life, I was entitled to see the contents. Unscrupulously, I crept across the tiled floor by the back door to the rear of the room, bag in hand, to a large, drafting table with a stool tucked beneath. A swing-arm light off to one side was the appropriate tool for enabling relatively inconspicuousness for close scrutiny. Placing the bag on the floor, I reached inside and eased the box from its hiding place. With apprehension, I placed the square box, approximately a nine inches square, on the table and turned on the light. Looking back to see if my actions had triggered any response from the couch, I continued with the unscrupulous act.

'This is the box that Peter had been carrying when he ran into me at the university museum two days ago.'

Standing back at arms-length, I looked and wondered at the implications. 'This was more than likely the stolen artifact?' There was only one sure way to find out; open the crate. With the anticipation of a three-year-old child at Christmas, I reached out to unfetter the box when, to my disappointment, I heard the faint thudding sound of footsteps on the back deck. Within a moment, Vincent was shaking the wetness from his clothes at the door and wiping his face with one of the towels June had brought. He looked at the two resting peacefully on the couch and then to me in the back corner under the illumination of the extended, drafting light.

"What you doing?" he asked in a playful tone seeing the small, wooden crate on the table.

I raised my index finger to my pursed lips to direct him to quietness and motioned him over to the edge of the table.

"I think this is the box that was stolen from the university museum Friday."

Vincent's eyebrow lifted to one side and he gave an elevated "Oh! What makes you think that?"

"You have heard of the robbery at the Neustadt Exhibit, right?" I asked.

"I haven't read anything in the paper yet, unless it's been kept quiet."

"I believe this is it. 'The Pillars of the Moon'."

Vincent rubbed his chin, looked at the box and then over to Peter. His face became pale as if he had seen a ghost. "If this is so, we could all be in serious trouble."

"What do you mean?" I asked a little startled. "It's no big deal, we can give it back."

"Not likely!" came a reprimand from the direction of the couch. Shawna slowly lifted herself from behind Peter and made her way over to the illuminated corner of the room to face us. "Peter and I have to deliver that to one of the Makah elders, across the Strait tomorrow. He will take it on from there."

"Take it to where?" asked Vincent curiously, his eyes piercing.

Shawna returned the same unnerving look that I had experienced before from her when we had first met. She said nothing.

"I'm afraid this is a bit like Pandora's box," Vincent sighed, turning back to me and grabbing my wrist as I reached out to touch it.

Shawna made a move to grab the box from the table.

"Wait a minute, Shawna. Nobody should do anything right now, especially us, until we decide what the best action to be taken is."

"Excuse me!" she returned emphatically. "This is none of your concern, and as soon as Peter is a little stronger, we are on our way."

"Shawna, as soon as you and this little crate came into my house, it became my concern. You have put me and my family at risk."

"Sorry, Vincent, this is my fault." I interjected drawing his attention toward me. "We should have gone somewhere else, but at the time I could think of nowhere else to go. We were being followed by the people who shot Peter, and had no way of getting away from them apart from driving like madmen down the back roads of Brentwood. Luckily, the motorcyclist from this morning is back in the alley, or at least he was, and their car is totaled in the forest along the bay road."

Not knowing what else to say, I looked back to the crate and rubbed my hand along the binding.

"If this is what you say it is," Vincent continued, his eyes darting back and forth between the two of us, "and we are not careful, all of us could be dead by morning."

Shawna and I stood quiet and looked at the crate sitting innocently on the table.

"For the last fifty years that I know of," Vincent said quietly, "there have been murders, physical threats and attempts to steal this thing. In the light of what has happened to Peter tonight, you should know this to be true."

Without moving, Shawna stood and stared at Vincent.

"The first time I had even heard of the 'Pillars of the Moon'," he began, "was before the war when some members of the Third Reich traveled throughout this area trying to locate 'the bowl' at their leader's request. He had an insatiable appetite for artifacts and talismans that took his people all over the world in their pursuit. Many marvelous, stone carvings from numerous archaeological sites, the Peruvian mountains, Central America, Egypt, Samaria, had all found their way to Berlin and his supposed World Cultural Center. He was ruthless in acquiring some of these pieces for his collections; we need not get into the details, but they usually got what they were looking for, at any cost.

I got the feeling that Vincent had experienced some of the Reich's' determination and without saying more, he pulled the drafting stool over and cocked one thigh upon the seat. "Throughout ancient, American history, there have been many tales and fascinating stories about gods and distant travelers, but there is one tale of an article that has dominated the folklore of this continent as much as the search for the Holy Grail, had Europe, for two thousand years. The Spanish adventurers sought after it under the name 'La Taza de Madre', 'The Cup of the Mother'. Ponce de Leon searched far and wide and found nothing, apart from more illusions. Other explores, Portuguese, English, French all sought after the illusive and fanciful ' Fountain of Youth'.

"Really!" I blurted. "But what does the 'Fountain of Youth' have to do with this?"

"Well, there is little fact and a little speculation." he continued cautiously, getting more comfortable on the stool. "When the explorers and conquistadors of Spain, embarked upon their religious conquests of the Americas, they continually came across folklore tales of eternal life and a story of a miraculous fountain that gave rebirth to those who bathed in its waters. These all have a familiar ring in the biblical phrases of 'the rivers of living waters' and 'one must be born again', to the point of some concern for the church. There is also the related tale of a bearded, fair-skinned man, a Christ-like figure, who lived in the mountains around Lake Titicaca, named Viracocha, who taught the natives of healing, and agriculture, and was later venerated as a god." Vincent smiled with one eyebrow raised. "This was also of some concern to the church. Sound familiar?"

"Yeah, a Christ-like being." I answered.

"The mother church in Spain, was continually being slapped in the face with stories similar to their own Christian faith that, in their minds, reeked of heresy and shrunk their business monopoly in Christ. This," he said looking down to the floor, "began one of the most calculated and gruesome acts of conquest and religious cleansing that the world has ever seen." He took a breath and slowly scanned the crate.

"As far as we can determine, the story of the 'Pillars of the Moon', that surrounds the bowl, is actually a combination of several stories: the one, a Mayan creation concept of the universe, which is found in the story of the moon, named Ixchel, goddess of weaving and childbirth. The story goes something like this:

'In the afternoon of a bright, sunny day, Ixchel, characterized by the moon, weaving a tapestry with her aged father, was stolen by the sun. The irate old man, in anger, fired on sun with his blowgun, and Ixchel, the moon, which shone lightly during the day, was accidentally hit and fell into the sea, shattered. In an attempt to save her and right the terrible wrong that had been perpetrated, the old man ordered millions of tiny fish to join together to form a net and collect all the broken pieces of light and lift her up to her lover, the sun. Their attempt was in vain, and defeated they left moon in the sky at night illuminating bright, to continually chase her lover the sun, shining during the day. On a clear night as you look to moon, over the water, you can still see the millions of little fish reaching to lift Ixchel to the sky in the form of a pillar shimmering on the surface'."

Vincent smiled and looked at Shawna. "The other, equally as obscure, comes from the story of a fabled, antediluvian world that saved the chosen people, the ancestors of the Hopi, from destruction. A firestorm had raged on the surface of the earth, initiated to cleanse the earth from its unfaithful inhabitants, who had fallen away from the ways of the Creator. These 'chosen ones' lived for many generations beneath the surface of the earth without tasting death. They were able to see in their underground domain with the help of silicate sand with luminous properties, not considered too far-fetched since the discovery of light producing, cave-dwelling bacterium. It later resurfaced in another tale, a gift from a prince to his bride-to-be on their wedding day, at a temple site in what is now Guatemala. She jilted him and took the bowl; he pursued her for her heart, and the bowl."

"You're losing me here. What does Hopi mythology have to do with the Fountain of Youth, or the Pillars? Is there any connection with all this?"

"Well, some people think so. They think this little bowl holds the key. The Tewa Indians of the Pueblo district have an antediluvian tale also, but theirs states that the people beneath the waters of Sandy Place Lake, to the north, did not experience death and emerged through a hole in the ground. The Kwakiutl, of upper Vancouver Island, have a similar tale. The Hopi tale also mentions, while in the antediluvian world, crystals found amongst the particles of sand in the caves helped illuminate the darkness during their long stay"

Surprised by his story, I stood motionless trying to grasp all he had mentioned.

"Brian, this is not something I have made up by myself," he chuckled realizing the quandary he had put me in. "Many scholars have labored hard and searched long for the answers to the riddles this bowl has birthed. And it is far from over." He put his hands on his thighs and gave them a rub.

"Quite a history, this little jade box in the likeness of the Mayan," I said notably. "That is, if this is indeed what it is."?

"To be more exact, Olmec, and from approximately one thousand B.C." Vincent stated emphatically. "And it is not so much the bowl but what is alleged to be inside that has caused the intrigue."

"Shawna." Vincent turned directly toward her. "May we open the crate? If it is what you say it is, then we will have to act very quickly. If we do not, it could end up in the hands of one of the unfriendly groups of people who have tried to acquire this bowl, indirectly, for a thousand years."

"I take it you do not mean the Third Reich?" I asked humorlessly.

"No Mr. Alexander." He said dryly looking to Shawna. "Have you ever heard of the 'Cult of the Jaguar', and the 'Feathered Serpent'?"

I felt a bead of sweat form on my forehead and my tongue grow thick and dry. The vision of the young girl mutilated and flayed came to mind and I replied, "Yes."

My knees slowly gave way and I caught myself on the edge of the table.   I couldn't help feeling overpowered with both confusion and apprehension. 'Why me?' Where did the vision come from? Why is it here in my mind? When will it come again? When will it go away? So many questions.

Vincent and Shawna, could see my uneasiness and persuaded me back to the armchair. Shawna reached to the cup on the table and handed me some leftover tea.

The room spun slightly as I sat sipping trying to relax and gather my thoughts.

The subdued lighting, the crackling of the fire, the sound of the wind and subsiding rain outside echoing in my ears, all helped to fuel the confusion I felt. I was a strong-minded person, and up till then had been able to handle any amount of stress, but even the strongest have their limits. Vincent's clear,blue eyes stared at me searching for the moment to interject.

"You've experienced something, haven't you Brian," Vincent asked soberly?

Shawna stood beside him, unnervingly still, and silent. There was nothing compassionate in her eyes, just a cool darkness. I felt she was trying to read me as much as Vincent, but not for the same reasons. I had not realized the contempt she felt for me at the museum. It could have been a racial thing. Lord knows, we as the nation of whites did nothing to nurture the trust and faith our relations with the First Nations deserved. Her need for answers was not the same as Vincent's, but as I gathered my thoughts to try to explain the events of the last few days, I began to know Shawna was as much a part of this as Peter.

Taking another sip of tea, to steady my nerves I began to formulate the words I needed to express what I had experienced.

"Tonight, as you know, was not the first time Peter and I had met. Two nights ago at the University Museum, I was trying to get into the first viewing of the 'Pillars of the Moon'. There was a robbery at the museum while I was waiting to get in. Not knowing this at the time, I went for a walk around the side of the building. Peter, obviously on his way out, ran square into me, knocking me over. He was very much in a hurry and carrying 'that' crate. But of course you knew all that, didn't you Shawna?" I looked squarely at her. She spoke nothing in return. "When the guard questioned me about seeing anyone, I had not told him about Peter. There was no reason for me not tell the policeman of the incident, apart from being very uncomfortable and ambivalent towards him. In retrospect, I am not so sure I did the right thing. Ever since that time I have been having flashbacks, or visions, of people and things happening. The first was behind the museum just after Peter left, of an old, gray-haired native elder. The next was in the Stanley Park, by the totems the following day, I presume the same guy. Later that night, I had a horrendous experience in some desert area where a girl was sacrificed by a group of men."

Looking at Vincent, I strained to swallow as the spit in my mouth dried again. I took another sip of tea. "A half hour ago, I had another, where it was late at night and I was illuminated by car headlights. There was a lot of yelling and banging on the cars and war cries and stones being thrown at me."

'What did the old man look like? Shawna interrupted.

I had drifted off in thought when the question came snapping at me again.

"What did the old man look like?"

"He must have been in his seventies, with long, white hair pulled tight to his temples by a thong holding a ponytail at the back. His hair started low on his forehead above a straight, deeply lined brow. His eyes were clear and bright. Not sure of the color. Piercing, with a sparkle of intensity I have not seen before. He had a small tattoo on his left cheek bone."

Speechless, Shawna nodded her head and turned to go back to where she had been on the couch. Vincent and I watched her as she motioned back, without saying a word, to Peters' side. Lifting his feet, she tucked herself behind his legs. As she put her head down on his lap, she gave us a long glance and closed her eyes.

Vincent, looking back to me with concern in his eyes, spoke, "It sounds like, and you may be familiar with this, a transference of spirit that took place when you ran into Peter."

Looking up, I acknowledged the possibility and after a few moments of collecting my thoughts again, asked, "What's in the bowl that's so important?"

Vincent slumped into the chair opposite me and reached to pour some tea into an empty cup. Gesturing me for more, he leaned forward and refilled my outstretched cup.

"Crystals and sand." he stated, easing himself back into the chair. "Crystals and sand from a very, very long time ago." He took a sip of his tea. The Hopi ancestral heritage goes back thousands of years, perhaps tens of thousands, even hundreds of thousands. There is no way to tell, only their legends. The jade bowl, which I suspect is in that crate, is old, but just predates 1000 BC. The contents in it, the crystals and sand, although there is no way to carbon date them, may go back a long way.

"Then how do they know how old they are?"

"The scientists who were asked to study the piece, scrutinized a sample of the crystals and sand collected through a small hole drilled at the edge of the lid years previous. Along with the sand, adhered to several grains, was a husk of seed. They dated it as best they

113

could, with such a small sample; it went back tens of thousands of years. Wanting to confirm, they tried to get another sample but could not find one. Not wanting to take the chance of damaging the already tampered bowl, they chose not to proceed. And without a second sample of the seed to carbon date a second time, no verification. But with that one husk, of unknown species, they determined the contents predated 30,000 BC. (He ran his fingers through his fine, gray hair and leaned back for a moment to think again.) Several of us have searched far and wide, for years now, looking for evidence of crystals being a part of ceremonial activity. In all of the known native nations of this continent, north and south, there were many references to crystals in various shapes and sizes being used in religious ceremonies and healing practices, but never crystal flakes mixed with silica sand. It was only when I came across the legend of the Hopi and their antediluvian existence beneath the earth, during the fire storm and then the ice-age, that the occurrence of crystal chips and sand become associated with this artifact."

Silently, I listened to what he had to say. There were questions I wanted to ask, but was unable to muster the fortitude. After a few moments of silence, Vincent got up from his chair and walked over to the fireplace to a pipe sitting in a small cradle atop the mantel. Giving it alight tap on the stone hearth, he dug about in the bowl with a small penknife and ejected the remains into the burning ciders and returned to his chair.

"About fifty years ago, I was asked, along with a group of colleagues, to a special showing of an artifact, of unknown origin, to determine its age. It was very hush and we all proceeded to the National Museum under 'silence'. Once there, we were treated with the utmost courtesy, somewhat of a strange experience for someone as young as myself, and were welcomed by an elderly German couple. Some notables in attendance C. Newcomb, W. Duff, G. Linton and others were included, but were unfamiliar with its history. I was the youngest of the group apart from my assistant Daniel, of which Peter has an uncanny resemblance. I had only heard of the likes of these characters of antiquity, and anthropology, so when they appeared, I was awestruck. (He slowly packed some loose tobacco into the pipe from an elongated plastic envelope.) "The elderly couple was relaxed, very pleasant orators and did a wonderful presentation on enlightening us on the responsibility we had for the prosperity of the West Coast Nations, and their heritage, and to do what we could to ensure their physical and spiritual survival. They were the first, and perhaps before their time, to begin a long and unheard of course of action to repatriate artifacts, possessions and the ancestral remains, to their descendants. There was one piece that had been found in a small village on the west coast of the Olympic Peninsula that was the centerpiece of the consortium, (he lit a match and drew its flame into the packed tobacco with a sucking sound; white plums of smoke and a delicious aroma filled the air), a jade, engraved bowl. They did not know how to proceed with its repatriation because of the odd circumstance as to its arrival on the peninsula. The sealed, jade bowel was carved and engraved in the likeness of the Olmec of the Yucatan Peninsula, three thousand years and miles from its resting place, approximately eighty miles from here. It had been unearthed at the turn of the century from a burial site near the old location of the native village of Ozette, thirty miles from Neah Bay around the northern tip of the peninsula. (He took another puff on his pipe.) The Village itself was not rediscovered till the 1970's after a number of artifacts washed up in the surf along the coast and brought attention to the area once again. The Makah village was very active up to the 1500's, till it was buried by a mudslide and left abandoned. The bowl, sealed with a concoction of bees-wax and tree sap, was found wrapped in the leather bag along with the burial belongings of a local Chief, also preserved in the mud from the slide. Luckily, it was brought to the attention of a local archaeologist from the University of Washington State, and eventually found its way to the Nuestadt Foundation for Preservation. Little else was done at the site till rains exposed more of the antiquities and Ossette was marked for rediscovery. Throughout the West Coast, Native folklore had alluded to a sacred, ancestral bowl for all nations being handed down from generation to generation, but no evidence of its existence till then, that is if this is indeed the fore-mentioned bowl. After much soul searching and concern for the First Nations, the Nuestadts thought it best to return it to the descendants of its original owners, or in this case, caretakers. That is where the troubles began. Since they were unable to determine who they might be, and after discussion with some of the world's leading authorities from Central, North and South America, as well as some from Europe, speculation began to rise as to what this artifact truly represented. It became apparent that it was going to be a difficult task, with several groups laying claim to the piece. During the course of the endeavor, several people had been hurt and one killed in a robbery attempt on the piece. It was finally determined that it should be held in the national archives. A young and budding anthropologist and his native assistant were engaged to deliver the piece, first to Shiprock for repatriation rites, and then on to Washington. Tragedy struck along the way and the bowl was lost for several weeks. A number of deaths were directly related to the theft of the bowl, along with disappearances; my young associate was one; he was eventually found."

"You were there, weren't you," I asserted.

Vincent did not reply but continued, "One group claiming authority was the Reich, of course; another, a group of businessmen associated with a consortium of international interests, and yet another, a group from Central American with ties to the Jaguar Cult. All were very ardent suitors but none could come up with the appropriate credentials for the release. Then about twenty years ago it was discovered that the Hopi Indians, of the Four Corners Area of Arizona, had made a claim that never arrived because of the murder of their representative, also my assistant, who was of Hopi descent."

Vincent was quiet and thoughtful for a short while.

"Daniel, my assistant had never mentioned his strong association with his people south of the border, and I was certainly to naïve in my early years in Canada to be aware of the nuances to his associations with the University. His body had been mutilated and thrown down a dry well in northern Arizona. There was little evidence found at the site that could point the investigators in the direction of the murder; the remains of a pair of leather boots, some shreds of denim, a turquoise, silver ring and a small, silver, engraved medallion in the likeness of a jaguar face. Since then, death is a factor to be considered whenever the piece is to be transported, or shown. Ultimately it never was, until now, and has been hidden in an unspecified location for some years. It is obvious the piece still draws as much attention and interest as it ever did. How Peter ever got his hands on it, I'll never know."

"Unless, he had inside help."

Vincent sat back to relax for a moment and relit his pipe.

"Would you like a drink?" he asked.

"No, I still have some tea."

"No, I mean a real drink." He got up from his chair and proceeded to a closed cabinet by the bookcase. "Brandy, beer, wine?"

"Brandy, please. No ice."

"Wouldn't think of it."

I watched as he poured the golden liquid into a couple of brandy snifters, cupped them both in one hand and returned to the chair. I had never noticed before, but he walked with a limp. Handing one of the small glasses to me, he looked back and literally fell back into the comfortable arm chair, feet automatically shooting out to the coffee table to rest upon some magazines stacked high. I could see he was beginning to relax.

Looking over his shoulder to Peter, "He is the spitting image of the friend I lost all those years ago."

I gave him a reassuring nod as he turned to face me again.

"You see, Brian, this story is endless, with much implication that the established academia welcomes, but also wishes would go away. We talked earlier, when we first met, about ethics and the truth. Some people don't want to know the truth. The one claim, for this bowl, supposedly sitting over there, which held all the credibility, was from the Hopi Indians. The name Hopi, which means 'people of peace' had virtually nothing to gain from the return of this article apart from, it seems, their heritage. The bowl repatriated, like their other artifacts, would be kept in hiding, along with their sacred tablets of migration, till the end of this fourth world. Their tales of creation appear to go back hundreds of thousands of years to a time we can't even imagine. They do not consider themselves isolated from the civilized world, but we have fallen away from them. The Hopi believe the Creator chose them to be a remnant to reseed the world after each cataclysm of which there have been three. According to them, we are now in the fourth world and heading straight for the fifth. Each of the worlds destroyed was subject to a calamity brought on by man and his own deviation away from the Creator and His purpose. The first world, as their tale states, was destroyed by the total reforming of the earth by volcanic eruption. The tilting of the axis of the earth and a subsequent ice age created the second cataclysmic event.

Vincent stopped to take a puff and placed his feet on the floor. "After each of these events, a spirit, with the visual aid of a cloud, had guided the remnant Hopi by day, and a star by night, to a shelter in an antediluvian world. The spirit was then to only reappear when the Creator sent His emissary to set them free from their dark confines. Before the third destruction, by water, which the Hebrew Scriptures refer to as the flood, they were directed to build reed boats, not unlike those of Egyptian watercraft. And like Noah, they were ridiculed for their absurd behavior. After being sealed within these reed boats, they traveled across the water to a new world, there to roam on dry land for thousands of years before settling in a permanent spot divulged only by the Creator. Even the ancient Chinese, talk of a flood and subsequent sacrificing of unblemished bulls once a year by a High Priest, similar to the ancient Hebrew. They even talk of a great God with the name of Shang di', similar to the Hebrew God, El Shaddai."

"An emergence from the under world after the ice age, has a parallel in the creation story from tales all over the Americas. In Peru, the Incas, early in their history, have a tale of emergence from Lake Titicaca, high in the mountains, along with the coming of the god-man Viracocha, whom I previously mentioned. The Incas believed that he created man and woman in his own image, and gave them tribal customs and languages. He then sent them into the earth only to emerge at a later time from caves and hills to found new civilizations. The Hopi talk of emergence from the earth as a natural part of their history. The modern-day Tewa, of the same region, and descendants of the Anazazi, who were also believed to be descendants of the ancestors of the Hopi, in their creation stories describe an emergence from the earth and their migration throughout this land."

Vincent stopped to take a puff on his pipe and a sip from his glass. "Brian, this goes way back in time, recorded on cave walls throughout North, Central and South America, long before, by secular standards, the Hebrew Scriptures and their confirmation by the Dead Sea scrolls, as well as the conical clay tablets of the once fabled Nineveh. This continent has an ancient history of its' own, that is just starting to emerge. It goes back literally hundreds of thousands of years."

Vincent took another sip, "Unfortunately, it has been overshadowed by thousands of years of subjective belief in cultures and economic systems that have very little relevance to the ancient culture of this American land."

He took another sip of his brandy and put his glass down on the table. Easing himself out of his chair, he picked up the glass again and approached the hearth. Poking the dying embers with an iron, he stared at the brilliant sparks as they rose up and disappeared into the darkness of the flue. "We need to put more wood on the fire Mr. Alexander."

Looking over to the firebox at the right of the hearth, I saw that it was still full. But then I began to realize he was not talking about the wood but about the need to enlighten a nation, and perhaps the world. I got out of my chair and made my way to his side and looked down at the embers. Within moments, the heat radiating from them caused my damp pant legs to steam. The warmth was soothing; I was more relaxed now than I had been for quite some time. The brandy had done the trick, warming my insides and blunting the edge off the nervousness that had been so much a part of this peculiar weekend.

"Grab another piece 'wood yah'." he chuckled, without taking his eyes from the fire.

As I came back from the corner, I could not help but see the deep lines in his face and his stooped stance. The gold reflecting from the burning coals on his shiny skin reminded me of the vision of the old man at the fire, on the mesa, who had reached out his hands to me and poured the crystals. Placing the log on the fire, I sat down on the hearth and watched as the fire slowly licked at the sides of the new fresh log.

"I'm getting old, Brian," he said with a sigh. "There is still so much to be done."

I could tell there was more for him to say and I gestured him to sit.

"The Christian Messiah has been a light unto this world and is perhaps 'the cloud by day and the star by night' which we are to follow, but there has been so much irreversible damage done over the years to so many nations in the name of Christianity: the inquisitions, the crusades, the conquistadors, the mass murders. It is hard for these assaulted nations to turn and embrace a faith that in their eyes is so contradictory and has caused so much pain and suffering. In the words of a well-known Makah women Elder," 'I am not sorry the missionaries came. I am proud to call myself a Christian. I just wish they had allowed us to change slowly, from the inside, instead of imposing their culture on us, uprooting us from all that we knew was sacred. We have lost so much'."

Vincent continued, "The legacy of this religion, and all religions imposed on innocent cultures, as well as our native culture, has left scars that will not heal. We must help in that healing process as much as humanly possible. Part of that is helping them achieve their spiritual well being through giving back what was not ours to take. Their articles of ancestry and sacred grounds, thousands and thousands of hectares of forest and plains, taken, and allotted to settlers, dating back as far as the Spanish occupation in the 16th century."

He stopped once again and gulped the remainder of the brandy in one swoop. We were both quiet for a few moments until he stirred and looked over to me.

"Well Mr. Alexander, ready for another?"

"No thanks, I still have a little left."

"Ah, come on. We may never see the light of day again." he beamed with an expression of delight.

He grabbed my glass and limped over to the cabinet and poured two more. Instead of returning to the chairs, he motioned me over to the back corner where the crate sat ominous, illuminated by the extension lamp. Placing the glasses gently down on the table, he waited for me to arrive. Taking a screwdriver from the drawer, he gently unscrewed the securing ring around the crate and freed the lid. Inside was a lining of Styrofoam with the lid secured down with tape. Gradually pulling at the corners, he eased the tape up and the lid along with it. Yet another lining, of a leathery material, hid the article from view.

"This is it." he sighed, reaching for a pair of cotton gloves in the drawer. Slipping them on he continued the chore of unraveling the thong that was tied around the mouth of the bag. He eased the bag open and I caught a glimpse of a deep, bluish-green portion of the lid. Carefully reaching around to the bottom of the bag, Vincent lifted the bag, and its contents to the table beneath the light. As he slowly eased the bag from around the bowl, I gave a sigh. It was the most awe-inspiring piece of craftsmanship I had seen in some time. The jade was dark green, with the light accenting it to a brilliant, bluish-green hue. The clarity, that allowed you to look deep into the walls of the inscriptions, was almost flawless. The occasional deep, natural fissure enhanced the carving, as if the piece had been designed by the natural forces that created the ancient stone in the beginning. The pudgy, grotesque face of the Jaguar Child, deity of the underworld, and the ornate figure of a man adorned with a feather headdress, peered at us from two sides. Two stylized snakes coiled their way around the bowl, joining the caricatures together to form an intricate design of faces and obscure symbols. Rolling the piece gently, exposing the intricacies in the light, he looked over to me.

"See the Jaguar deity, guardian of the underworld, and the Creator God Feathered Serpent. And look, on one side, of lesser relief, a Feathered Serpent, and on the other side directly opposite, the Fire Serpent." These were two lesser inscriptions, with the snakes intertwining the four visual deities, in great detail with small feathers and seashells. He picked up a white, cotton cloth from the drawer and wrapped the base of the bowel in it to hand it to me. "Take a close look."

Taking the piece gently in my hands, I rolled the bowel several times to view the intricate interweaving of the snakes. The whole inscription wove itself into a mastered tapestry of the natural forces somewhat less understood in our present times. Scrutinizing every crack and inscription with enthusiasm, I peered at the round lid in the fashion of an Olmec calendar wheel and to the faint white dot near the lid's edge where the extraction must have taken place. A close look in the light exposed a small indentation, and the resin, that sealed the contents of the bowl from exposure to the outside world.

"It is nice to see the piece again," whispered Vincent, under his breath. "I had forgotten how beautiful it is."

Mesmerized by its visual elegance, Vincent nudged me and reached to take the bowl from my hands and put it back into the leather bag and its resting place. Replacing the tape and sealing the crate back up as we had found it, we returned back to the chairs by the coffee table and the warmth of the fire. For several minutes we said nothing as if to digest what we had just had the opportunity to feast upon. A feeling of excitement and concern, mixed together with a little fear, brought the feeling of urgency back, and the visions that had impressed me the last few days.

"The cult of the Jaguar, Vincent, what is it," I asked?

Vincent pensively took another sip from his glass and leaned over to a wood, carved, cedar box on the table to pull out another small pouch of tobacco. Packing a small amount in the ivory-stemmed bowl, he left the remains on the edge of the table and fumbled in the box, once again, for some matches. With a quick flick of his hand and sitting back in the chair he drew the flame into the well which billowed a small puff of smoke. After several draws and a quick snap of his wrist, the match flew through the air toward the fireplace, consumed before it landed amongst the embers of the fire.

"I've heard about it and have read the obvious from studies of the Olmec, Mayan and Aztec. But where did it originate and why?" I asked.

"Can't you ask me a simpler question, like will it rain tomorrow?" He laughed as I gave him a double take surprised at his humor. "You ask a million dollar question Brian. Like the myths and legends, there is a lot of conjecture and little fact. To be quite honest, we just don't know. In our more recent history, thankfully, human sacrifice has appeared to have stopped, at least as a part of our religious ceremonies. The cult of the Jaguar has its early roots in the Andean Mountains. Some of the earliest relics and evidence of ancient civilizations come from the Ecuador Mountains. Not all were centered on the bloodletting that was such a part of the Mayan, Aztec and Zapotec civilizations at later dates. That does not mean it did not happen, there just seems to have been a gentler time when children were given the roles of collecting flowers and heads of maize used in morning sacrifices to a less voracious Creator God. The Aztec god man Quetzalcoatl, was venerated as the Feathered Serpent, and adhered to the wishes of his priests by continuing the act of human sacrifice. Later in his reign, he was betrayed and expelled from Teotihuacan, near Mexico City. He founded a new city called Tula on the coast where he banned human sacrifice and returned to the sacrifice of fruits, flowers and staples. In an uprising by the former priests, he was once again expelled and left Mexico for good, departing from the coast by ship. There have always been sacrifices made to the gods as long as there have been stories told and sung. Down through the ages they have made their way in rhyme, or scratched on cave walls throughout the Americas. Comparatively, not so long ago in Peru, the Incas would take young boys and girls, and leave them on the mountaintops, to freeze, as a sacrifice to the sun god. Treasure seekers and adventurers in recent years have come across frozen remains on virtually every mountain top in the Inca Empire."

He took a drag on his now cool pipe and reached for the matches to relight the fragrant tobacco again. After several puffs, he picked up his glass for another sip.

"In one of my visions I saw a young girl painted blue, killed and flayed."

I picked up my glass and took a quick gulp before I had time to imagine the scene again.

"Well," Vincent sighed, taking another puff on his pipe. "The Mayans would paint themselves blue as a war dress in times of battle, and as an act of revenge, would flay their enemy captives and prance around with their skins as a sign of victory. They would also sometimes cannibalize their enemy captives as a show of superior strength, and to literally embody the spirits of the defeated foe. The Mayans, as well as other civilizations of Mesoamerica, would also continue this practice during their ball games. You think rugby and football have gotten tough? You lose in that ball game and you're dead!" He gave a chuckle at his own candid humor and stopped with a sigh.

I looked out to the deck and the clouds that had begun to clear with the stars peeking through

"Why do you think I saw that girl, and witnessed what had happened to her?"

"I'm not sure Brian, but what I am certain of is that you have been drawn into this by your basic knowledge of the First Nations, not only your good nature and openness, but also your ignorance that has almost cost you your life. The deeper spiritual needs of the people of this land and the desperate need for some type of closure is paramount, but I hope not at your expense. The Creator will use whom He will to get the job done, at any cost, but let us hope and pray, for His grace. I have a den full of a lifetime's study plotting the migration of man on this earth. Some of it you would find surprising and very fascinating. But now," he said easing himself from his chair, "It's time for me to go to bed. Make yourself at home. The kitchens over there, the bathrooms down the hall, first door to the left."

With that he got up, staggered a little to the left and put his hand on the archway to steady himself. Picking up my glass by the stem from the table, I watched as he disappeared down the hall. The information he had imparted clung to my mind like the residuals of Brandy to the sides of the snifter. Taking the last drops in my mouth with a gentle swish, I looked up to a flicker of light catching my eye from outside on the deck. The rain had stopped and the moon was almost full, high above the naked trees. The wind had almost ceased with the bare branches gently swaying back and forth. The planks, still wet from the rain, reflected the moonlight with a twinkle as the light breeze blew over the surface. I sat and watched as the million tiny fishes, in the form of a shimmering pillar on the deck, tried in vain to lift Ixchel to her lover in the sky.

EIGHT

Sleep was fitful for the remainder of the night. With my feet propped up on the coffee table, blanket draped over my body, I tried for hours to get comfortable in the lazy chair. My mind wandered from incident to incident keeping last evening's fight in the alley foremost. Peter's wound and how close we had all come to being killed made me shudder to think of a slightly different scenario. The jade bowl fed my imagination like the faggots I occasionally threw on the fire. The bowl's age and inscriptions shed light on a possible alternative to our past with implications contrary to our conceived perception of North American history. With every thought came new and more troublesome questions. The giddiness I felt from the brandy along with Shawna's nakedness etched in my mind added to the unease and frustration.

Finally, with the faint glow of dawn silhouetting the trees at the rear of the garden, I drifted off into erratic slumber only to find myself in a strange room standing at the foot of a bed. Two figures peacefully sleeping close together beneath the blankets were oblivious to my being there. I also felt a presence beside me, but could not turn to look at what or who it was. Drawn to the window, the willowy trees swaying back and forth pulled me to the rear of the garden. As I looked to the back of the house and deck, the faint lights in the family room and the dimly glowing hearth illuminated a familiar figure reclining in a chair feet outstretched before him. The dried ivy against the stonework of the house and vines dangling from the grape arbor over the rear patio door gave the house an eerie look but no impression of danger. To the left of the deck, another smaller window beside the steps leading up to the landing was almost obscured by the sparse remains hanging in suspended flowerpots. The windows were dark but not dismal and sensed a presence that lay within. I briefly looked down to my feet and then brought my hands up to look at them. Slowly turning them over and looking at my palms, I became aware of the oddity of my predicament. I heard a gentle audible hum as a mild breeze brushed my face and stirred within me a feeling of serenity. In the stillness of time in which I was immersed, I stood motionless watching the world around me as if I were the center of this universe and that all had been orchestrated for my benefit. After what felt like an eternity of being, my attention was drawn back to the house and window. Immediately, I was back in the bedroom where Vincent was sitting up in the bed looking toward the figure beside me. A strong urge to scream gripped me, but, before I could open my mouth the figure of a man with long fair hair and fiery eyes stood directly in front of me. He stared intently into my eyes as if to look deep within me. I awoke with a start and was back in the chair of the family room. Completely alarmed at what I had experienced, I stood up to face the fireplace, heart pounding as if I had run a marathon. Standing motionless not knowing how to handle the experience, I turned and waked through the archway and down the hall to where Lilly was lying by a door slightly ajar. She wagged her tail as I bent to stroke her and peered in the open door. There, lying peacefully beneath the blankets were June and Vincent, all was well. Lilly whimpered a little as I tiptoed back to the family room and the warmth of the fireplace to watch as the last remaining embers died to a dusty white.

The morning horizon silhouetted the trees as the sun began to rise beyond the eastern mountains. Shawna began to stir as the family room brightened to illuminate the furnishings with vibrant color.

"What time is it?" she yawned.

Looking down at my watch, "Quarter after six," I replied.

I sat wearied at the reply and wondered how I was to make it through the day with only several hours of sleep. With my elbows on my knees, I watched, head in hand, as the last plumes of smoke eddied up in wisps into the sooty darkness of the chimney. Peter began to stir but moaned in pain and was unable to move with ease. Shawna fumbled with his blanket to keep him warm and whispered several words to him. It was obvious he was going nowhere for the time being.

"What should we do?" I asked Shawna, slumping back in the chair feet projecting to the footstool.

"I'm not sure, but we will have to move quickly. I was supposed to phone from Port Angeles this morning to find out where to take the crate."

"Why not just phone from here?"

"I have to phone from a specific telephone booth. If I can make it to that spot without hindrance, my people are confident the rest of the journey will be safe for the custodians of the bowl."

"So, it has to go further?" I questioned.

Without saying a word, she gathered her blanket around her and shuffled over to the archway beside the kitchen.

"The bathroom's down to the left, right?" she questioned as she scurried along the narrow hardwood floor of the hall.

"Right," I returned as she shuffled along pulling the tea-shirt tight about her and pointed in the direction with her thumb.

Feeling as if my eyes were full of sand, I sat quietly in the chair, wondering how much more I should become involved. The only real danger so far had been with the jaguar men and hopefully they would forget me as soon as the bowl was no longer in our possession. On the other hand, this could be the chance of a lifetime to look into the sacred aspects of an indigenous North American religion that had been influenced by other cultures in ways yet to be considered. Closing my eyes and drifting off again, I faintly heard the flush of the toilet and the shuffle of feet on the tiled floor beside me. A sharp poke in the shoulder brought me back from rest and a tone of voice that was starting to bother me.

"Come on, let's go."

"Where we going," I asked looking up?

Shawna's fresh face glared down at me, her eyebrow lifted simultaneously as her hand slid to sit upon a hip. A swift hand reached out to caress my face but instead gave a gentle slap, "You look terrible."

"Great!" was all I could return as I tried to pull myself out by the arms of the chair. "You'll have to give me a moment to get myself cleaned up."

I staggered to the washroom beside June and Vincent's room. Trying to be as quiet as I could, I splashed some lukewarm water over my face and rummaged for a razor. Emerging from the room a relatively respectable man, I passed by the entranceway to the kitchen; June gave me a start as she stood in her nightgown preparing cups of fresh coffee.

"Good morning, Mr. Alexander." came her childish voice with just enough sarcasm to show she was not impressed.

"Sorry to wake you June. I have been trying to be quiet, but with very little sleep last night, I am finding it difficult to keep myself together. We have certainly taken enough of your time and hospitality. Shawna wanted to get going as soon as possible."

I came along side her by the coffee pot and said nothing. Reflecting on my dream, "How is Vincent?"

"Oh, he will be all right. He has one of his headaches this morning and thought it best to stay where he is."

Silently, I nodded and took the tray to the table in the family room. Shawna, without hesitation, grabbed a cup and took several gulps as if it were a flagon of beer. Looking back to June leaning in the archway to the room, I gave another gentle nod in appreciation and watched as she disappeared down the hall to her room, Lilly close behind. Turning back to the tray, I prepared myself a cup and waited for Shawna to announce her plan of action. She offered none.

"Well, what are your plans," as if I were not including myself in the scheme?

Looking over to Peter still asleep on the couch, "I have to go; there is no doubt about it. But whether Peter can come with me is another matter." She pensively sipped her coffee. "Could we leave him here?"

A little shocked at her suggestion; I placed my cup down and headed to the couch.

"I don't think so. He doesn't look so good and it sounds as if Vincent is not well either."

Crouching close to the couch, I watched as Peter labored to breath, making the occasional gesture to change his weight favoring his wounded side. "I really don't think Peter is at all up to a trip over to Port Angeles. Could we not just drop him off at a friend's or someplace where he could rest? Besides, he really should go to the hospital as the doctor suggested." She said nothing, as if waiting for an answer to manifest from thin air. As luck would have it, out of thin air it came. I got an idea!!!!'

Vanessa, still half asleep in Vancouver, answered the phone again and before long I had learned that my family had been heading for the Inner Harbor in Victoria by last night.

Once we had decided to move, we had Peter on his feet and were on our way back out onto the deck, green, garbage bag and luggage in tow. As we proceeded down the steps and past the window I had seen in the dream, it dawned on me that in the dim light and rainy conditions of the previous night it would have been impossible for me to see the window. And yet in the dream I had seen all of the rear of the house in its exact proportions and cosmetic disarray. In a way, I was glad to be departing, but leaving Vincent and June gave me a sadness that was hard to explain.

Large puddles of water lay in the worn tire valleys of the drive leaving us to struggle down the narrow center three abreast with Peter propped in the middle again. At the drive entrance, we waited and intently searched for any traffic seen or heard. A hundred or so meters down the road, we came to the large woodpile, my black beauty waiting. Tears came to my eyes as I began to view the damage that had occurred the previous night on our excursion down the mountain trail. Gnarled metal exposed gaping holes where the side mirrors had been attached. The side moldings were gone leaving white and gray scrapes running the length of the sides where the trees had rubbed the outer coatings of paint off. There were no-longer mud flaps except for little stubs still riveted to the wheel wells. All the side rubber and vinyl side dressings to the bumpers were gone. We stopped about ten feet from the car and stood motionless staring as the events of last night began to sink in.

"Wow!" was all that Peter could muster as we edged toward the car.

"Is it going to run?" asked Shawna in a low tone as if to reflect my loss.

"It better."

Luckily, the keyholes were undamaged and I was able to insert the key and open the passenger door. The interior was fine apart from the blood stained blanket Peter had been sitting on. Handing the garbage bag to Shawna, I reached in to the rear and moved Shawna's large purse she had placed in the back. Grabbing the blanket and rolling it up in a ball before Peter had a chance to see, I reached over and pulled the narrow

door lock up on the driver's side and eased myself
back out of the car. Grabbing the garbage bag again, I
returned to the rear and dropped the blanket on the
ground. Shawna was struggling with Peter to get him
into the rear seat and finally decided it best to put him
in the front. Opening the trunk, I straightened a few
things and placed the garbage bag gently down
wrapped with my old sleeping bag, my overnight bag
propped on top kept it secure. Closing the lid, I bent
down and grabbed the flap of the remaining bumper
guard and yanked it free. Wrapping the guard in the
bloodied blanket I found a small cleft amongst the
scattered logs and tucked the blanket far up into the
crevice out of sight. With Shawna squeezed into the
back and Peter now in the front with me, we started off
once again to downtown Victoria, with the hopes of
seeing my sister, not the Jaguar Men.

The weather was trying to clear as we cruised
down the coast road toward downtown. The fog was
being nudged away by a cool, south easterly blowing
up the straight. The distant mountains on mainland
Washington, were hardly visible with a haze of mist
hanging below the snow-capped peaks like a bib below
a baby's chin. The waters of the distant inlets below
sparkled brightly between the intervals of lichen-
covered boughs that harbored remnants of the morning
fog. The pungent, damp, aromatic smell of the upper-
tidal zone drifted throughout and helped to clear the
haze my head. The tour was solemn as it became more
evident that Peter had not recovered to any great
degree. I had not witnessed the beating that he had
taken in the alley, but it must have been severe. A
severe blow in the right area could rupture a spleen or

bruise a kidney; it could be quite agonizing. I could see his face was draining of color again.

"We'd better take Peter to the hospital as soon as possible. Even if the goons spot us, we'll have to get him there and handle the situation as best we can. If need be, we will go to the police."

"No police!" Peter grunted, leaning against the glass on the passenger's side.

The drive down Cadboro Bay Road, was much like the scene out of a movie, three individuals in a beat-up black sedan, trying to stay as inconspicuous as possible and yet sticking out like a painted lady on a Friday night.

I waited patiently in the car as the two of them started up the ramp to the 'Emerge'. Uneasy with our predicament, I scanned the area every few minutes to ease the uncertainty. Hoping the goons of the previous night were nowhere near, I began to realize how absurd and out of control everything had become. My life had always had its dips and spins, but this had taken the cake. Since being run down at the museum a few days ago, it was if a switch had been turned on to start the chain of events and decisions that had brought me to this, near macabre. My skin grew cold and clammy as I sat there forcing myself to stay awake. Taking a few minutes to lean my head on the glass of the side window, I became mesmerized by the moisture collecting into droplets on the exterior of the window glass. From a distance I began to hear a voice calling my name but I was too tired to lift my head. Again, I heard my name and tried to lift my head but couldn't. A jolt in the arm brought me back with Shawna sitting besides glaring at me,

"Get going!!!"

Through the streaks in the window screen, I could see a black sedan in the distance that was sitting idle just around the corner. Taking a second look, I could not see any distinguishing figures in the car. Cautiously pulling the car from the curb, I checked to see that there was no movement to be seen any where on the street and continued downtown.

"What did they say about Peter?"

"Well, from what I gather he is passing a bit of blood so his kidneys were hit last night. They did some blood work, but I couldn't wait around any longer."

"They'll probably make him drink a gallon of this real awful clear fluid and make him hold his pee for several hours."

I couldn't help but smile thinking about the occasion for my barium baptism. I do not envy him at all.

"At least he is in good hands for now."

Continuing down Pandora, the day began to spring to life with cars starting to appear as Monday morning work traffic began. The roads were drying from the night's rain, with steam rising as the sun warmed the pavement.

"We have to locate Rose and Steve, my sister and brother-in-law. They will be able to suggest some alternatives for you and perhaps even get you across the straight. I don't think there is a ferry till later in the morning."

Heading down Cook Street, toward the shore, we veered off to the right down Collinson along the northern tip of Beaconsfield Park. Crossing to Superior, we slowed down to find a parking spot. The streets were still relatively empty of traffic so we were able to find a good place to park within walking distance of the harbour. Pulling the green garbage bag from the trunk, I pushed my overnight bag toward Shawna,

"Carry this."

"Excuse me!" she replied.

"Please, carry that." I rephrased.   "You will appreciate it if we have to make a run for it, my bag is lighter.

With a twisted look on her face, she clutched the bag to her chest and led the way as we headed through the back alleys and parking lots to the waterfront. Passing the promenade of hotels and bed and breakfasts, we cautiously crossed the street just in front of the ferry terminal. Clearing the small Aquarium with the Inner Harbour exposed, I could make out the profile of Steve's twenty-seven foot boat toward the center of the floating maze of docks and wooden walkways.

"Wait a minute Shawna." I cautioned, grabbing her by the arm. "You should wait here out of sight for a little while. Let's put you over there in one of the restaurants while I go see what their plans are. We don't want to jump in unless we are welcome."

With Shawna settled at a table in a small cafe, the green bag by her feet, I jogged across the street with my overnight bag over my shoulder and down the concrete steps beside the Aquarium to the boardwalk. Continuing down the central floating walkway, I finally reached the small blue and white single mast craft named Eventide. The ventilation hatches were open and the sounds of clanging dishes could be heard within.

"Hello down there!" I announced through the open hatch. "Rose! Steve!"

"Hey Bri, we've been expecting yah."

Bounding out from the wooden hatch, came that all-so-familiar sight of a heavyset man with a bush of brown wavy hair stuffed under a baseball cap. Steve's beaming, sunburned face looked over to me as he straddled one of the wooden-slat benches opposite from where I leaned. Immediately after him came a shock of Rose's wind-blown hair dancing in wisps escaping from the mass stuffed up in a makeshift bun. Rose edged up out of the berth with two cups in her hands.

"Coffee?" she smiled.

"Thanks. Could you take this Steve?" handing him my bag. He lightly tossed it on the deck under the bench and stretched his legs across to the seat at the transom beside the rudder arm.

"Vanessa told us that you had called last night when we phoned. We were just on the other side of Salt Spring Island before dusk and got in about eight last night.

"You look like you went moose hunting and got run over by the moose." Steve piped when Rose had finished. "You've been workin' too hard again. But then again so you should."

"Yeah, right" I returned jokingly.

Rose looked directly at me; "You look so god awful."

"Well," I started, climbing in the stern and getting seated. "A lot has happened over the last two days and it looks like there is a lot more to come. I wish I could explain it all to you right now but there is no time. I have to get a friend over to Port Angles as soon as possible and the ferry is not leaving for at least three hours."

"Steve looked over to me, "And you expect us to take you."

"Well not exactly." I continued, quickly scanning the area about us. "I'm not sure how we are going to get there yet. We are being followed.

"By who," Rose asked, a little perturbed?

"The same guys that almost killed us last night."

"What! You were almost killed last night?"

"When Marese and I came out of the museum last night, we saw a guy being beaten up in an alleyway. It turns out it was the same guy that ran into me at the museum. Remember?" I questioned, looking at Rose and pointing to my cheek. "I ran over to give the guy a hand, not knowing who it was and the hit men, or who ever they were, shot this guy and took off. They later came after us when we took Peter, the guy's name, to a friends for help."

"Is he alright? Where is Marese?" Rose's voice was beginning to go to a higher pitch as she realized the danger.

"He is alright. At least I think so, and Marese is at her parents'." Sensing my sister's concern, "I didn't drag her into any of this. I put her in a taxi as soon as we were free."

She sat down beside Steve and looked into her coffee cup.

"Look! I do not have much time before I have to leave. I have to figure out a way to get us out of the harbour without being seen."

"We'll help yah Bri," offered Steve. "If it is as important as you say, then we'll help. This is what we could do."

After about ten minutes of discussion and a second cup of coffee, I headed back toward the restaurant.

Casting off the moorings, Rose headed off in the other direction on foot. Steve was preparing to set sail.

Shawna was sitting as I had left her, behind the table with an empty flask of coffee empty on the table, green garbage bag at her feet.

"I have a way for us to get across. It may be a little slow but we will get there. Of that I am sure."

"Good. How soon do we leave?"

"We will have to wait a few minutes while my sister gets a few things ready."

"Why? What has she got to do?"

"Be patient. Everything should work out fine as long as we don't get caught."

After we had sat for the better part of a half hour, I finally saw my sister in a large motorboat with twin outboards come wheeling into the harbour rocking the sleepy flotilla as she passed by.

"Come on. Let's go!"

Shawna grabbed the bag from the floor as I leafed through my wallet for a fiver to leave on the table. Tossing it as I stood, we scurried out the door, down the steps and raced to cross the road. Taking a quick glance right and then left, I got a flash of a white collar and a pair of sunglasses peering at us from beside a black sedan. At second glance, I recognized who it was. The fellow in the alley, whom I had flattened, was now in a neck brace.

"Great!" I screamed under my breath. Grabbing Shawna by the arm tightly, I pulled her along toward the concrete steps down to the boardwalk.

"Don't turn around. We have company."

Hopping down the steps two by two, without looking back, we quickly shuffled along the walk in front of the brick wall to the central walkway, the Empress Hotel towering high in the background.

'Ping'

"What was that?"

Another few seconds and I heard a loud whiz and a pop with wood splintering at our feet.

"They're shooting at us! Run!"

Pulling Shawna as hard as I could, we had made it half way down the walkway when Shawna tripped on a cleat and went flying, almost landing in the water. The green bag and her purse went flying through the air landing a few feet from us. Stopping as fast as I could to help her to her feet, I heard another whiz and a ka-thunk as another bullet came close and hit the water spraying us. Now, only twenty feet from Rose in the boat, and the green bag lying just several feet behind us, there was another whiz and a crack as wood splintered between us. Frozen, not sure which way to go, my heart pounded in my ears, my throat almost closed from the tension, I looked to the bag, and then to Rose and back to the bag. Shawna stretched out her hand toward the bag just as another bullet hit in the same spot. The rifleman had found his mark and was letting us know that the next bullet would be for one of us. Pulling Shawna away from the bag, I took a quick glance over to the ferry terminal and the trees that hedged its' walkway. Well camouflage and almost undetectable was the marksman. Still holding his silenced rifle, he knelt unmoving waiting for his next target. Sensing our defeat, I tugged Shawna by the arm and pulled her to the boat, Rose nervously waited to whisk us away. Defeated, but alive, we slowly toured out of the harbour toward open water and watched as they raced down to the walkway to the green bag.

Carefully unraveling the wrappings, they pulled out the box and threw the small wooden crate along with all my shaving gear into the water.

"Damn. I liked that razor."

"You'd better step on it, Rose, they're really pissed now."

The last we saw as we rounded the spit to the break-wall was several of the guys running from boat to boat trying to persuade their unwilling owners to muster for a quick trip.

As we rounded the corner out of sight of the main harbour, Steve waved us over to where he was anchored just in the lee of the break-wall before the open water. Shawna threw a line to him while he desperately placed some bumpers along the starboard side of the craft. Steve held the line tight as we leapt onto the boat, and releasing it, slowly left Rose behind. With a wave of her hand and a kiss in Steve's direction, she pushed the throttle to full. She sped around the corner and up the southern coast, her mane of red hair flowing behind her. Sydney Harbor's a good twenty minutes away and a fair jaunt for any able seaman in a sailboat. Without a doubt she will have no problem evading them should they follow.

Steve pulled anchor and we edged our way around Lighthouse Point distancing us from the break-wall. Sure enough, a few short minutes later, with Rose almost out of sight, an old wooden cabin cruiser came out of the harbour. Radio aerial swaying high in the air, the boat oscillated and labored to crest the growing waves of the open straight. Shawna and I waited out of sight in the hold wondering whether the ruse would be successful. Once they were by and well out of range, we clambered out from below to watched with glee as they labored to navigate the turbulent seas. The cruiser slowly made its' way up the coast and out of range while we edged further out into the open strait.

"Well, we did it." I sighed, giving Shawna a hug around the shoulders.

Shawna not so pleased did not respond to my embrace. She had not noticed my plastic, shaving kit floating on the water as we pulled away from the harbour, or heard my sorrow for the passing of a good and faithful friend.

"Come here, I want to show you something."

Taking her hand, I led her to sit down on the stern bench, back to bulwark, and reached below to my overnight bag. I slowly unzipped the black bag and handed it to her. On top was my camera, and beneath wrapped in the old oily rag she was familiar with was the article she had sworn to protect and deliver. Exposing the Styrofoam that protected the bowl, a smile came to her face as she realized what I had done. Without saying a word, she sat quietly and held the bag by the handles and let it dangle between her knees.

I watched without saying a word as tears slowly slid the length of her nose and on to the wooden slats of the deck, "You know Brian, last night when you described the old man's face in your dream, I knew who you had seen. I was not all that sure what to make of you and your involvement and did not trust. This is difficult for us as no white man has ever been involved with the things that you have seen. The man you saw was a kachina, a guide from our clan, part of our holy ceremony. Even I have not seen all things and been a part of the full ceremony of the kiva. But now I know. You have been chosen."

"Chosen for what," I asked with a half chuckle? She said nothing. "Please Shawna; I am trying to make some kind of sense of it all. I did not ask for any of this."

"It appears you have had no choice."

"What do you mean?"

Without a word, she sat expressionless and looked at me. The look in her dark eyes at first startled me' but slowly began to soften my turbulent mind. I noticed a sparkle of appreciation.

Steve, getting a little anxious, began to ready the rigging for full sail.

"Come on, Bri, we'd better get under sail. It looks a little rough."

"Got any Gravol?" I yelled as I slid the rudder arm under my elbow against my ribs.

"Sure, down below."

Shawna nodded to me and disappeared back down into the hold, emerging a few minutes later with some floater jackets and the much-needed Gravol.

"I just hope it isn't too late." I yelled in Steve's direction.

Steve unraveled the main sail and headed forward. Zipping up my jacket tight, I pulled my toque down snug over my ears and watched as Shawna slipped into her jacket. I noticed a bit of attitude as she prepared herself, but saw a lot of confidence. Overhearing one of her conversations with Peter that she had been with Makah elders, I wondered at that point whether she was indeed Makah, I had presumed she was Haida. If so, we had with us the embodied ancestry of the world's most proficient West Coast whalers and sea fairing peoples that this continent has ever known. We had little to fear should the spirits of her ancestors be guiding us this day. She disappeared with the bag down the hatch, closing it behind her. I tied myself down and within seconds we were bouncing with the rolling waves. Spray, arching high over the bow as we crashed down into the oncoming swells, hit me hard in the face. Steve, after tightening everything down, came to my side and grabbed the rudder arm and took over. I watched, amazed as he looked straight into the wind and spray, wet curls of hair streaking back from his tightly secured hood. After ten minutes of steady rolling, I could feel the sensation of lead in my belly and felt the color slowly drain from my face. My tongue got thick and my mouth dry and I knew 'this was not going to be easy'. I stood up for a moment but realized the boom would be swinging soon from the tack, so I sat down again. Keeping my eyes focused on the distant shore, I was determined not to throw up. I began to feel better as I concentrated on the horizon and the distant mountains of the Olympic Range. As I looked back at Steve, he smiled and I could tell he was having the time of his life. With my stomach temporarily in control, I began to think of my will and last testament and whether I had made everything clear enough. I began to pray that if I made it through all this, I would settle down and get married. After a few more moments my jaw went slack and I knew this was it. Over the side I leaned.

After a few heaves, the coffee and remainder of the piece of toast floated away into oblivion and I felt a little better. The bitterness from the Gravol was detestable.

"You got any water?" I yelled at Steve.

"Yeah, below."

As I looked briefly up over the undulating bow of the Eventide, the distant shore was getting closer and closer, but oh so painfully slow! I couldn't help thinking as I looked back at him, full faced in the wind, enjoying every minute of the journey, 'you're nuts!!'

NINE

Shawna had slept soundly in the forward berth on the crossing. I, not so fortunate, sat at the galley table, head down, listening to the saltshaker roll back and forth, back and forth with the listing of the boat. The rolling motion kept a firm grip on my equilibrial concentration, while I did the same with my half digested toast. Able to doze from time to time, the crossing time was painfully slow, and seemed to take forever. Steve eventually called me topside to help prepare for a change of sail. I was more than willing to oblige, and stumbled up the steps to a face full of fresh, salty spray.

As we motored past the jetty, the rolling subsided, the sun came out, and my stomach was able to settle. Shawna, up from her nap, gave a hand by tossing the bumpers over the side and prepared the bowline for docking. As we moored, the thought of firm ground, and a chance to sleep was more than I could bear. Tripping over a clove hook and flopping down lazily on the boardwalk, I waved my hand to be left alone. Thankfully, the motion in my head slowly subsided while I clung to the dock. Within minutes, I was drifting off to sleep, the waves slapping methodically on the underside of the dock. Shawna and Steve secured the lines.

For the better part of an hour, I lay warm in the sun while Shawna continued to prepare for her meeting. With a change of hairstyle, and borrowed t-shirt tied in a knot at her hip, she bounded up the dock ramp to the telephone booth alongside the marina parking lot. Slow to rise, I remained on my back to watch the cloud formations far above me. Almost fully recovered and feeling hungry, I gathered a few things and headed off to the harbor master's office for a snack and information about ferry sailing times. Still staggering slightly from indolent sea motion, I wandered, camera over shoulder, to the ramp at the far end of the maze of board-walks. Flipping my cell phone open to see about reception, I made the slow and steady climb up the ramp's steep incline to street level. Heading back along Marine Drive toward town, I tried texting Marese, but with no luck. The Eventide sat idle apart from Steve working at a slow pace, getting ready to set sail again. Through the haze of my sickness, I had noticed his unease; he obviously preferred (even though we had not talked about it) to leave the bowl, and Shawna, to their own ends and have me set sail with him. I, on the other hand, with my eagerness to sail diminished, would prefer to stay ashore.

On the way back from the office, schedule in hand and munching on a chocolate bar, I caught a glimpse of Shawna sitting on a bench with her bags by her side. The restaurant frontage, feet from the main road and just off to the side of the lot, was the only liquor bar in the marina area. Unknowingly, she sat framed by the flashing neon sign of a half dozen popular beers; with the word 'Destiny' illuminating the mansard six feet above her head, I couldn't resist a photo that insinuated a rhyme of false impression. Cross-legged and out of the sun, her toe bobbing up and down with impatience, she looked from this way to that, taking in whatever visual stimulation this bland excuse for a social arena had to offer. A vision of exceptional extra-ordination, her native beauty was striking, I moved to center her figure in the only splash of color and shadow the building had to offer. Trying to be nonchalant, but unable to fool her, she slowly reached up and took her sunglasses from her face to expose a glaring reprimand. With tongue poked out, and a hand assault on the air in front of her, she spirited me to carry on 'away'. Aware of the compromising predicament that I placed her in, I quickly packed up and headed further along the parking lot.

The government boathouse and ramp at the end of the lot were vacant and dwarfed by the massive mound of cedar chips behind it. The whole dock area and the marina were not the most attractive I had ever seen, and if the truth be known, a bit of an eyesore. Sheet metal boathouses strewn in irregular fashion up and down the lines of wooden walkways gave the impression of a city slum. The inspiring view of the southern coast of Vancouver Island, in my opinion, was the only redeeming feature the panorama had to offer. To make matters slightly less depressive, from a distance, I could see Steve, outstretched on the deck enjoying himself basking in the fleeting moments of sun. A lovely character shot, he will be pleased.

As I approached the down ramp, the gentle squeaking of brakes came from an old cream-colored pick-up truck stopping in front of the bar. Snapping a picture from the hip, I continued toward the ramp, clicking additional pictures every few steps. After Shawna's eventual acceptance to enter the pick-up truck, I stopped and watched as they slowly pulled out of the parking lot with Shawna in the passenger seat. I took an exposure of the license plate as the truck pulled away. A little black and white dog frolicked in the truck bed and yelped at me in curious disapproval.

I rejoined Steve waiting patiently and snacking on a few stale chips. We continued to nap for the better part of an hour until we finally heard footsteps on the boardwalk. Shawna came striding up portside, almost happy to see us again. Her huge bag fell forward as she climbed over the guardrails, dumping some of its contents onto the deck. Lunging forward with my hand, I was able to save it from tumbling into the water. Embarrassed, she scurried to pick up her things and gather them together as if she were assembling a deck of cards. Reaching over, I picked up a laminated card embossed with the figure of a black bird, its wings outstretched and pointing down at the ends, surrounded by writing and symbols. On the other side, her picture with her credentials, and a swastika-like cross in the corner. A bell went off in my head as I remembered what Vincent had told me about the Third Reich and their antics years back. Not letting my apprehension show, I handed the card to her and smiled.

"Thanks." she responded, as she took my hand to lead me forward to where Steve had retreated.

"Well?" Steve sighed, as he tossed a half smoked cigarette into a rusty soup can hanging from the wire rail. He lifted his head to peer from beneath the rim of his 'A's' baseball cap.

With a wave of my hand to silence him, Shawna and I seated ourselves beside him to form a semi-circle. We all proceeded to look at each other and waited for the other to begin. After several moments of silence, Steve put his head back down with exhalation, and pulled his cap over his eyes. After several more moments of gathering her thoughts, Shawna looked over to me and tried to say something. With hesitancy in her voice she stuttered and fumbled for more words.

"Spit it out, Shawna. Tell me what it is they want you to do."

"The Elders are very grateful for your help Brian, but are split down the middle as to how to proceed. What we have brought, and presented to the council, is not such an easy responsibility to be passed on. Even though the council has been waiting for decades in preparation and anticipation for this day, there are spiritual ramifications and forces that must be considered. You have been a guide in the journey of the ancient that some do not feel has been completed yet. For the most part they would like you to continue on your path with us and have asked me to encourage you to do so. But some of the younger members of the council are against it."

I propped myself up on both arms behind me and crossed legs flat out before me, "I've been pushed, bullied and dragged, and I still don't completely understand how and why this is happening. In some ways I'm glad to be able to help, and for the experience, but this is not a conscious contrivance of mine. I seem to be, 'just coming along for the ride'."

She gave a nod and said nothing, reflecting on what I had said. Sitting motionless, I watched the light dancing on the water, reflecting its motif on the hulls of the other vessels. Below the tide line, mussels and white-crusted barnacles clung on to wood trusses adorned with green algae streaming like tresses of hair beneath the surface.

"This experience, as you call it," she continued, "is reflective and cognizant of the history of my ancestors for thousands of years. I do not understand it all either. The experiences you've had are repeated time and time again throughout the stories and history of my people. It is much greater than either one of us can realize, implications point to the spiritual rebirth and survival of my people, and perhaps, of all mankind."

My eyebrow lifted, as I looked back at her with that numb and furry feeling that arises when you sense that the truth has been spoken, but have nothing to say. I began to remember what Vincent had said about the contents of the bowl, and the mysterious crystals from an antediluvian world, and wondered at its significance.

"All right, I will stick with you for a while longer, as long as there are no more sea voyages. But you have to be up front with me, on all accounts."

Shawna nodded with a half-smile that curled the side of her lip. "I will try. After what we left behind in Victoria, we'll be safer here anyway."

"Yes," I replied. "It appears that would be the case."

Shawna peered down at her watch hardly noticeable amid a collection of turquoise and silver ornamental wristbands. "But they would like to talk to you."

"Who, the jaguar men," I replied jokingly, "or the elders?"

"The elders feel that you have been used for a purpose, and chosen to help us. Some don't want you to be allowed to go any further, to experience our sacred ceremony."

"Experience! Sacred! What ceremony?"

As I threw the bowline onto the deck and gently shoved the Eventide on her way, Steve's face conveyed a dis-ease. He was thankful to be on his way, but I sensed reservation. It had been a restful stopover and a diversion for him, but I knew there would be questions when I got back. As I watched him ferry out of the marina, I couldn't help but think of how lucky we were to have been rid of our adversaries in Victoria. Hopefully, the 'town of angels' has guardians over-watching us.

The bow of the Eventide bobbed up and down as she vaulted homeward out into the swells of the straight. I was relieved not to be heading back into the tempest of the strait, and the galley. With my overnight bag slung over my shoulder, and camera in hand, we followed the boardwalk up and proceeded to the phone by the bar. Feeling hungry again, I grabbed a snack inside the restaurant while Shawna made the appropriate call. Our rendezvous was out front on the bench again by the neon signs. We waited.

Between bites of steak sandwich, I took snaps of the fishers strolling up from the waterfront below; characters of all shapes, sizes, and nationalities. Natives, blacks, whites, with a seasoning of the Orient mixed in. Some went one way to their vehicles, others passed by us on their way to rinse the salt from their throats.

It did not take long before the cream pick-up pulled up and I was motioned into the back with a sardonic smile and the wag of a six-inch tail. With the squeal of tires and a cloud of dust, we were heading out of town with me crouched in the corner behind the cab, sharing the remains of my sandwich with the dog. For more than an hour of winding road cutting through some of the most magnificent scenery on the west coast, we continued our journey through the valleys of the great Olympics.

The geology of these glorious mountains, along with the Rockies, was created from huge oceanic volcanoes along the border of the colliding tectonics of the Pacific and North American plates. Expelled and thrown up, the range became a fertile and rich expanse of a changing environment. Clothed with a vast and dense rain forest, the mountains stand formidable, maturing some of the largest trees the world has birthed, the giant Red Cedars. Seeming to hold up the sky, these trees like spires of an ancient cathedral help to purify waters that flow from the mountains. Cascading waterfalls, deep crystal clear potholes and hot springs dot the area, bringing forth their own unique, individual biology already diverse in this lush environment.

With the truck slowing slightly, and sensing we were nearing the end of the coastal highway, Shawna peered through the sliding window and shouted the encouragement, "Hang on, just a little while longer."

The continual rock and bump of the pickup had frazzled me to near exhaustion as the mutt and I had cuddled close beneath a well-worn hair-covered blanket. Although the weather had cleared and warmed, the relentless wind in the open back had beaten me numb. Between the boat ride over and the roller-coaster express that got us thus far, I was feeling rather spent.

As we slowed to a tolerable pace to cruise down the main street, I was impressed to see how neat and tidy the town appeared. There was not the flamboyance of a commercial strip, nor garish billboards marring the mountainous view that surrounded the village, but it seemed adequately furnished. Neah Bay did not appear to be a typical reservation-fishing village. Even though there were vacant storefronts and buildings, the sidewalks were kept clean and free from debris. The Makah Cultural Center, at the very gate to the town, was a neat and shining example of the reborn heritage of a community fighting back from near extinction. With a population of several thousand people it had grown from just hundreds over the last two decades. Now was obviously not the best time of year to visit this area and other towns along the coast. This was perhaps one of the wettest places on the North American continent, influenced by the rising clouds dumping hundreds of inches of rainfall every year. With spring on the way, the wet weather would ease up and people more visible preparing for the new season. Summertime is quite the opposite, full of activity, with festivals highlighting Makah culture and fishing. The area bustles with tourists visiting the western-most point of the continental USA, along with the curious, looking for truth in the artifacts of the long-ago culture.

A number of fishing trawlers sat idle in the harbor, waiting for the sun to set far enough into dusk before venturing out again into the straight for an evening catch. A collection of iron relics from the bustling days of logging still marked the shores, influencing the layout of the marina.

A scan of the dock and marina reflecting the commerce of the area showed the absence of the usual paraphernalia and regalia that accompanied more modern urban marinas. The perimeter of beaches lined with black volcanic rock rolled smooth by the pounding surf, did little to brighten this sleepy fishing village. As I watched and passed the many stores and houses in the foreground, an inauspicious feeling clung to them like the mist that hung amid the cedars out toward the point. With a welcomed warm Pacific wind, all the stagnation could blow away to reveal the beauty that lay beating above the surf.

A remnant of loggers, as I would learn later, had remained behind to add too the melancholia of years of near desperation. Alcoholic abuses, and even murder, were not uncommon to these rocky, weather beaten shores, which only added to the off-season desolation. The affluence of more developed times had parted, but the usual merchant frontage, lining the board-walk streets, gave hope to those who had remained to build a future with fishing and tourism. With the changing facade and renewed awakening of the native peoples, it had become the homestead of the Makah Nation, the greatest whalers the world has ever known.

Not long after, we were seated around a coffee table at the 'Maidens Locker', a local bar and restaurant. All of us stared mindfully into our glasses of beer, while a half-dozen or so local men stared back. Eager to talk, these leather-faced, toothless seafarers began boasting of their local history and legends, which centered on the old loggers, sunken Japanese vessels, and several murders happening years back. Everyone had his own version of the bride who had been betrothed to another man, further down the coast that had been stolen causing homicidal retribution. Another oratorically, embellished tale was of a long-outstanding feud involving a stolen knife and fishing gear, resulting in another furry of uncontrollable rage and kidnapping. It became obvious these were issues of questionable proportion, stoking the fires of imagination with much smoke that would not blow away. As the beer began to flow, so did more stories. Feats of courage and strength, bridled with prowess that engaged all but the elderly of this exuberant, male, dominant society, were all that we heard for the better part of an hour. I'm sure the women had their equal say in matters, but sensed in this braggartorium, the only ostentatious female to be heard, was the bar maid bellowing orders from across the room. From all appearances these men were uncomplicated with a great sense of tradition. Strong ties to the sea and the mountainous land that surrounded them, forged these men rugged and strong, and without a doubt a challenge for those who chose to deal adversely with them. As I listened intently to more of the older tales of the sea going Makah, it became obvious the broken image of a once flourishing nation, was still missing pieces.

After a great mudslide influenced the deterioration of their existence along the coast, an epidemic of smallpox, brought on by European explorers, scattered the remaining inhabitants to many locations throughout the Olympic northwest. A few short decades ago a larger remnant slowly gathered together in Neah Bay after artifacts from the ruins of Ossette were discovered, washed up along the beach a few miles south west. An effort launched by several courageous souls, started a movement and a discovery that ultimately ended in the prized Cultural Center. It helped to revive and enlighten, the almost extinct Makah, to a need that would revitalize their heritage and almost irrevocable history.

The stale cigarette smoke hung in the air of the bar like a fog in the coastal cedars. The noisy atmosphere, along with smell of charcoal-broiled burgers and beer, reminded me of social evenings in my college years. A familiarity and sordid reminiscence rolled into one. It lent some comfort for me, as I sipped my draft and listened, somewhat separated from the joviality of the table. The ambience of the bar was not one that I was now accustomed; rather austere and undone, with a scattering of arbourite and wood tables. The accompaniment of vinyl and chrome kitchen chairs gave the look of a 'forties kitchenette'.

Shawna seemed to fit right in with the crowd, and held her own against several young men competing for her attention. It was a relief to see her smile and carry on with a sense of humor that until now was nonexistent. Plates of nacho chips and cheese came to the table and were devoured even quicker than the jugs of beer that began to stack the table.

Looking around the rest of the room brought to focus a table of four unpleasant looking fellows, noticeably irritated by our jovial antics. Continually looking over to us, it was becoming apparent of their disapproval to our, or perhaps my, presence in the bar. There was a chance it could have been someone else at the table that they knew, or perhaps they had just eaten bad burgers, but I didn't think so. A little unnerved in these unacquainted surroundings, I started to look toward the exit. The fact that the gruesome foursome were left unattended by the barmaid and totally ignored by the rest of our group was only adding to my agitation.

As the conversations and interactions around our table deepened with familiarity, the men who had finished with their own versions of local history were curious to know what brought me to Neah Bay. As I began to explain my vocation and interest in West Coast First Nations to them, my uneasiness began to melt away. After a few tall tales of my own, with much reference to my photography and filmmaking, they were fascinated to no end and interested once again in my inquiries' to the murders and how I could make a movie.

After another glass of suds, the effects of the last two nights of near sleeplessness became too difficult to combat. With my attentiveness slipping, and the half finished beer becoming as flat as my attention span, I started to nod.

Finally, a tribal elder came in and approached the table. The small crowd's liveliness went quiet as one by one each of the men nodded in respect to the gray haired man that stood impassive at the end of the table. He was not a large man, but there was something about him that affected the mood in the bar and made his presence felt. After looking about the table, his eyes finally rested on me, and I knew it was time to go.

Shawna gathered her things to go and lightly patted one of the young men on the top of his head in jest as she passed. He blushed and turned to watch her walk away, while the others laughed and made fun of him at her reproach.

Once outside, I took a deep breath and shook the lethargy from my body. It lifted my spirits to be out in the fresh air again. The sun began to peek through the clouds and light up the wooded encroachments close to the parking lot. The dusting of gnats and flies, dancing through the shafts of light, were making their early springtime debut. The sparse, but busy clouds of insects disappeared as we moved slowly into another angle of light chancing us to the possibility of unsavory inhalation.

The wind direction changed bringing damp, cool, wintry air down from the north and the Queen Charlotte Islands. This area of the coast, being further west on the peninsula than Victoria, across the strait, was more susceptible to the erratic changes in wind direction. Some of the natives throughout the area could read the upcoming winds and cloud formations as easily as their ancestors could read the waves and currents of the water while fishing in dense fog.

As we slowly crossed the lot, I considered the meeting with the concerned elders. Shawna had not mentioned a word in regards to what they were expecting of me. My visions and descriptions were intriguing to some of the elders, as conveyed by Shawna, but I had no control over the apparitions, and wondered what they expected of me. Most native ceremonial ways were unfamiliar to me and I was not sure I could accommodate them. Conversations with Vincent, from the night before about Native American ceremony, came to mind and it would have been nice to be able to talk to him again. He had a great familiarity with the ways and customs of the surrounding nations. I would have to be patient; my mind wanted to wander wild with my imagination. I tried to keep focused on the upcoming meeting.

As I climbed into the back of the late model '4X4' that had been waiting for us, I sank down into the cozy seat, placing my bag on the seat beside me. Surprisingly, there had been little attention paid to the bag, which I would presume, was obviously the holding place for the artifact.

The native man that came to pick us up, said virtually nothing. Introduced by Shawna as Daniel, he smiled and nodded his head, looked about, then prepared to drive away. He spoke several times to Shawna sitting beside him in the front seat in a language I was not familiar. There were a lot of clicks and guttural sounds to the phonetics that were similar to some native languages and dialects of the west coast but for the most part, unfamiliar to me. As we drove from the parking lot, the four men, who had been sitting in the back corner of the bar, walked from the front entrance and watched as we drove off.

Shawna looked back to me, "Those are the guys who do not think you should be involved."

"That's reassuring, but how serious are they in making sure that I don't."

"They will leave us alone. My people are not always the easiest to get along with, but once they have agreed to something, they stick to it. We will be alright," she replied.

A few miles out of town, we turned up a bumpy gravel road and headed inland into the foothills. The jogging and gentle rocking of the truck made me relax and before to long I was drifting off to sleep. Before I had much of a chance to doze, I was jerked forward by the breaking action of the SUV; before us stood several braves, sporting rifles and sun-glasses. In the middle of the road, about ten feet in front of the truck, the two barred the way.

Daniel, who until now had only spoken a few words to Shawna, without moving his head, focused his eyes on me in the rear view mirror, "Don't move! And say nothing."

As I sat and watched without moving, the braves, in army teagues, approached the car cautiously. The hand of Daniel, slowly slid down to between the two seats in front of me and remained motionless on the butt of a hidden sawed-off rifle I had not noticed. My mouth became dry and I could feel the blood drain from my face. It was an odd feeling of sweat and coolness with a slightly elevated heart rate which gave way to my light headiness. Everything became crystal clear, and almost in slow motion, as the two separated, one to one side of the vehicle, and the other to the other. Shawna did not move either and could tell by the stone cold look on her face, she was as alarmed as I. Daniel opened his window further to greet the fellow as he approached the driver's side. The brave peered through the window at me and then back to Daniel. He took a long look at Shawna but did not make a move to direct us out of the car. The brave took a slow walk around the vehicle and back to the window and Daniel. He asked a couple of questions in native tongue, while the other watched through the glass on the opposite side. I could tell by the actions of the subordinate that he was trying to rile Shawna and get her attention.

Shawna, without taking notice sat motionless and tried to concentrate on the brave opposite asking the questions. I could not understand, but got the gist of introductions and the purpose for our journey. Shawna, spoke a few curt words announcing her obvious displeasure and the brave backed up from the car. For a split second there was hesitancy where he was going to lift his rifle, but to my astonishment and relief, he laughed and waved us to continue. The fellow, on Shawnas', side gently tapped the window with his hand and yelled, "Go ahead little sister."

There was no mention of the conversation after, so I presumed with great pleasure that Daniel had managed to appease the curiosity of me to the sentinels. As I turned my head to take a quick glance, the two lit cigarettes as we pulled away. I snapped a couple of pictures and watched, as they grew small in the distance and less threatening. Considering the situation, I was astonished as to how Shawna was able to handle the lewd attention, and comment. With her striking looks and strong, determined persona, she must have become seasoned at holding her own and enduring the riles the native men threw at her. She never seemed to be overly upset by them, and probably knew most of braves by name.

As I turned back to Shawna, the sun highlighted her profile and I watched, for a while, as her eyes flitted back and forth from the road to the palisade of trees. What role in the community did she play? Her immovable emotion and demeanor as the men surrounded the car, alluded to an air of confidence the surpassed her years of age. Then, there was always the swastika on the card in her purse. Who were these men? Were they working for the same group of people as she, or a different organization I was not yet aware?

Sitting in the back seat, I was overcome with fatigue and the thoughts that ran through my head. Was this the area in which Shawna had spent her early years as a young girl growing up? Did she mature here, and acquire her higher standing in the tribe? Were my perceptions about her real, or was I being over imaginative? This whole situation was beginning to wear on me. My mind was preoccupied to the point of distraction. The deeper into the rain forest we drove, and further from civilization we travelled, I was convinced, without a shadow of a doubt, I would not come out alive. It had not been a good day.

Eventually, we pulled off into a clearing by the side of the road. We were met once again by the man who I recognized as driving the cream pick-up truck. My hairy four legged acquaintance of the ride in the open air to Neah Bay came bounding in my direction.

It was nice to get out of the 4x4 and stretched our legs. My little friend came and sniffed at my feet and licked my hand in welcome. The sandwich morsel had won me a comrade indeed. Kneeling down and stroking the back of his head, I looked around at the expanse of the open lot. Several people with some measure of hospitality greeted us for the first time. An elderly woman came to welcome us with a smile and open arms. She must have been in her seventies and when she reached out to Shawna, Shawna put the palm of her hand in hers and gently lifted the back of the old woman's hand and touched it to her forehead; a touching warm moment as she embraced the old woman and nodded to an elderly man standing by the edge of the clearing.

The greeting had reminded me of my trip to Malaysia, where I had seen the hand gesture before at a special occasion where the elders were being greeted by subordinates. It had struck me as odd, and gave the impression of lordship over the individual doing the act. I later began to understand that it was a form of a blessing for both parties. One for the showing of respect and willing submission to the elder, the other, an acceptance and accolades from the younger and their family. Shelter and hospitality, from the respected elders and their families in return, were forthright as long as the stay required. Hospitality, I imagine, in the same spirit of the outlawed, North American native potlatch. It would appear that in most countries in the world, other than North America, elder people are held in respect, and reverence, to their years of experience and are considered assets, instead of liabilities.

After a smile and a short conversation, the old woman turned from Shawna and came to greet me. Not quite knowing how to approach her appropriately, I lifted my hand to offer it in a shake, which she took. I told her my name. The procedure felt a little awkward for me, in comparison to the greeting I had just witnessed, but after a smile and a laugh, my gestures were met with approval.

After our cordialities, I gathered my meager belongings along with the over-night bag and followed Shawna. She was walking off with her arm around the old woman's shoulders like a youngster with her favorite grandma. The old man, with Shawna's purse bag over his shoulder, looked a little awkward but followed in the direction of a wooded area just visible over the crest of the hill.

'I just couldn't believe she was a Nazi,' thinking to myself as I followed along. With my hairy friend at my feet, I looked across the small parking area, showing signs of construction, and wondered at the number of utility sheds with WSU (Washington State University) stenciled on the sides. In the distance, a young boy attempted to hide in the bushes, keeping his eye on us as we went.

"Nothing out of the ordinary about this place, 'little guy'," I spoke in the direction of the lad. "No swastikas here."

Over the top of the hill, a light breeze and the crashing of distant waves welcomed us. Awash with distinct aromas of surf and tidal zone biology, the wind added to the quaintness of the area. My stomach filled with butterflies as my thoughts turned to a family outing, many years ago, on a pebbly beach at Warner's End, England. I thought of the boy in the bushes and envied the wealth of memories and experiences he too will have when he's old enough to appreciate them.

A small, roughly maintained house, half way down the slope to the waterfront, came to view. Rows of tall racks, made from branch poles and slats that I recognized as drying racks for fish and whale meat, bordered the dirt walkway. A small roofed stand for cleaning fish, down by the wharf, looked to be in good shape and still in use. A fair size skiff with canopy and down riggers was tied up beside the stand along with rubber boots and coolers that were left ready for the next excursion.

Walking down the path was like walking back in time. Under foot, the dull thud of the bare ground bordered by uncut, tall grass, along with the noisy din of wind and birds from the close surrounding forest.

The moisture-laden air that blew from the shore carried with it the gentle shushing of the pebbles in the surf and the cackles of plump seagulls foraging in the tidal zone. An open shed revealed a large, cedar log being chipped and shaped into what appeared to be a canoe. Tell-tale signs of woodcarvings, with half finished figurines and animal caricatures, lay strewn around the clearing and beneath trees. A smoke house lay off to the edge of the clearing down toward the waterfront. Up into the hills, back toward the forest, wooden crates tucked beneath the canopy of alder trees, showed a bee apiary of moderate size. It was obvious, there was a lot to be seen and done in this little coppice in the woods.

Once inside the small cabin, the old woman immediately busied herself with food preparations. Over to the left, was an open hearth with a small caldron hanging from a leather thong and a ceiling hook. The blazing fire within the open-faced clay brick and stone, reminded me more of a pottery kiln than a cooking oven. The rich aroma of wood and animal skins was delightful and I began to relax and feel more at ease. The walls were invariably a museum of antiquated hunting and fishing paraphernalia still usable. As I looked more closely, the old hand tools were quite intricate and were adorned with carvings that depicted little persons and creatures. These little caricatures were obviously important to the society and history of these superstitious peoples of the sea.

As we stood just inside the door, the old man took our coats and gestured us to warm by the hearth. After a few moments of coddling myself, I viewed the humble surroundings and couldn't help but revere the simplicity and practicality of it all. I felt strangely accustomed to the smells and wonderful ambiance.

After getting somewhat settled, I questioned Shawna, "The language that you speak with these people, what is it?"

"It is the language of my ancestors, the Quidicca-atx. (Kwee-ditch-chuh-aht) It is a dialect similar to some of the other tribes about here, but our family heritage also comes from the central plains of centuries ago. There is talk of our great ancestor coming from the plains and following the great Columbia River, stopping in many places and finally resting on these shores. His horned image is carved, along with his dog, in a sacred place along the great river and is there to this day."

Shawna reached over and took a cup from the mantle and dipped it in the broth pot that boiled over the fire and offered it to me. I took a sip, got comfortable again and watched as she did the same.

"Shawna. There is something that has been bothering me, and I would like to ask you of it. "

She nodded and took another sip of broth, barely taking her eyes off of the embers of the fire.

"The card I handed you from your purse that fell out on the deck, what is it?"

"Which? This one?" as she reached down into her purse to retrieve the laminated, identity card."

"Yeah, the bird, what is it?"

"It is a symbol that most native peoples recognize as hope. You have heard of the phoenix."

I nodded in agreement.

"Out from the ashes, after thousands of years of war, hatred and oppression, a spirit, a remnant of our people, will rise to show mankind a new way that is as old as mankind itself. The Firebird represents an embodiment of people from the Bird Clan, and the Fire

Clan, both instrumental in the birthing of the new world."

"What about the cross on the back, or should I say, swastika?"

Shawna gave me a side-glance and pondered the implications that might have alluded to the quarry.

"It is not a swastika. It is a cross that symbolizes the migrations of our ancestors to the four corners of this land after their emergence from the world under the ground and across the sea."

"Under the ground, what do you mean, 'under the ground'?"

"Do you remember what your friend Vincent spoke about, in regards to the Hopi legends last night? Well, his story is similar to what our people believe. Our ancestors tell us of a time we spent under the ground as protection from a great time of ice, and then later, with encouragement of the Katchina of this age, a voyage, in grass boats on a great sea. Our ancestors landed, after much time, on the shores of this land, and were encouraged by the Katchina to continue. But shortly before he left, he gave us direction to migrate four times around this great land before we would find our resting place, the center of our universe. The Creator then provided us with guidance, via a cloud by day and a star by night. A great many of my forefathers tried to complete their migrations and created great civilizations in the process, but all failed save a small remnant."

Shawna stopped for a while and stared into the fire. The conversation was complete and I felt I had come full circle. I said nothing. She got up to help the old lady prepare the food for supper and left me to sit warm and sedate. I had been given another piece to the mystery puzzle that had befallen me over the last few days. It was becoming more apparent, the story was in actuality, millennia old.

Dozing off for several moments, Shawna gently nudged my shoulder to rouse me. Straightening up, and out of the chair, I turned to face a wooden table adorned with candles, and a feast of fish, sweet potatoes and types of vegetables that I had never seen before. The old woman motioned me to sit at the table, and the four of us sat together, in silence, while the old man gave a little song of chants and blessing to the fish and spirits that took care of us that day. Looking over to Shawna with head slightly bowed, I could see a glow that radiated from her. I was sure these were her grand parents. As I looked into her eyes, she transformed into a little girl with long, silken, black hair, and a laugh that brought butterflies to my stomach. I could see the love in the old woman's eyes as she recognized the joy that Shawna felt at the moment. She was home.

After much talk and a dessert of a sweet fruit cooked in a large leaf, Shawna and I returned to the hearth to sit and drink a concoction of herbs and leaves.

"Shawna, what are we doing? Not that I mind because I am really enjoying this, but are we going to stay here for a while?"

She thought for a few moments, "There is much indecision as to how to proceed, so they have decided to hold a prayer ceremony and decide on an initiation."

"Initiation, who's being initiated?" I asked.

"You are."

There was not a lot said by the old man and woman for most of the evening. Occasionally, Shawna would go and help with odd chores, and converse with them in their native tongue. They did not seem to be put out by my being there, and appeared to carry on as if nothing was out of the ordinary. Within several hours, just after sunset, two men came to the door and greeted our hosts with warmth and friendship. A quick glance and smile to Shawna and I, acknowledged our presence, but also initiated a desire for us to go for a walk. We donned our coats and headed down to the shore to watch as the waves crashed endlessly on the pebbles and out-cropping of rocks. We sat on the dock and huddled close for warmth. The moon up in the sky just beyond the treetops, lit the surroundings of the protected little cove with its' reflective hue. There was not much said, but our intimacy grew with the closeness and shared body heat.

"What will happen tomorrow?" I asked in a whisper just audible over the swishing of the pebbles.

"I am not sure." she replied. "Nothing to be afraid of, and not near as dramatic as you've experienced over the last twenty-four hours.

Shawna did not look at me, but I sensed she was beginning to feel the magnetism we held for each other as strongly as I; at least I hoped so. We sat for the better part of an hour, huddled close and making small talk, listening to the sounds of the night that encompassed us.

After walking the perimeter of the cleared property for another short while, when we entered the cabin, all was quiet and the fireplace was ablaze with several new logs. In the loft, somewhere out of sight, the snores of the old man, or woman, could be heard like the steady beat of a distant drum.

"You can sleep there, close to the fire," she whispered pointing me to a bed of blankets, furs and pillows. "I'll be right over here."

There was a small cot tucked in the corner, close to the fire, but slightly in the shadows. She turned and disappeared out of sight behind a partition in the kitchen area while I undressed. Emptying my keys and phone on the small rough hewn table to one side, I tucked myself under the covers and watched and listened, to the crackling of the fire barely three feet away. The day had worn me out, and I began to feel the relaxed, sensational prelude to sleep. A rustling noise directed my attention to Shawna in the corner by the cot. The firelight danced about the room, and illuminated her as she undressed out of her day clothes. Naked, she slipped under the covers and rolled over to watch the fire. From opposite sides of the hearth, we could see each other in the flickering light. Neither one of us said anything. The flames reflected in her dark eyes and highlighted the smooth, satin skin of her face and shoulders. We laid for what seemed an eternity, staring at each other. Scenes of her, throughout the day, played on my mind like the shadows on the wall. Wishing the opposite, I found myself thinking of her grandparents upstairs, and rolled over with my back to the fire, and Shawna.

My heart had just settled, when I felt her nakedness slip in beside me under the blankets. Without turning, I lifted my arm and placed it over her waist to run my hand along the small of her back and down her thigh. I could feel her breasts push hard into my back as she reached around my chest to hug me. Her hand caressed the length of my stomach and found its way between my legs. Rolling on my back to face her, our eyes met and we kissed passionately. Slipping on top of me she straddled my leg rubbing herself against my thigh, the wetness felt cool against my warm skin. Slipping her to one side I reached down to remove my under garments. Her head moved down to caress me and I laid in ecstasy while the room danced and swooned to the rhythms of her motion. Her skin was hot and moist and the smell of the wood burning along with the animal skins brought me to heights of pleasure I had never experienced. Turning Shawna over on her back I kissed the length of her body, feeling the response of her flesh beneath each precious touch. Rolling over on top of me again, we kissed and caressed. The inner reaches of her body gave way to my advance. The night was like no other I had experienced. I dozed on and off, for the next several hours, watching Shawna sleep.

I could not help but wonder at her childhood, and how she must have looked with her fine features and olive, satin skin. A thin line of black highlighted her brow, and the line of eyelashes was long and fanned up slightly toward her temple in perfect proportion. Her black hair lay limp against her cheek and over the pillow to cross my inner shoulder, as if drained from the activities of the last hour and before. The fires' still flickering embers danced in highlights on her bare shoulders and breast, as if to reflect the passion still smoldering within. Closing my eyes, I drifted into semi-sleep and the vision of a place along a well-worn path in the forest.

Looking down to the ground, the cedar needles covered the path, cushioning my bare feet against the roots that protruded, gnarled, from the dirt. Skinny, little feet, and ankles scissored back and forth, in unison with mine. A shock of black hair danced above the shoulders of a little, dark skinned girl running along beside me. The smile on her face enforced the feeling of oneness I had as we scurried along together toward the rocks, and the crashing of the waves in the distant. I sensed we were running from something, perhaps another person that had followed us into the bush. Without fear, we stopped at the cliffs edge and peered over to the turquoise and emerald sea below. Froth and foam squirted up in plumes as the waves oscillated back and forth in the narrow channels between the crevices of cliff and rock below. Leaning over to watch more intently, I felt the tug of the hand, and short nails digging into my palm. Breaking free, I leaned over further to view the interior of the caves that were hidden, only truly visible by boat away from the shore. My footing let go, and I felt myself tumble from the cliff-face and fall toward the beautiful color and waves of the tidal surge. I could hear the scream of the little girl as I plunged into the cold depths of the water. Without fear, I watched as the seaweed danced back and forth to the rhythms of the current. Suspended, neither up nor down, I floated neutrally below the surface. The cold made my body tense, and I began to sink to the bottom amid the starfish and anenomi. *anemones* Eventually, the cold gave way to warm numbness, and I opened my mouth to call for my mother. Within a moment, a little boy came, swimming down to meet me. Almost face-to-face, we stared at each other and smiled, and waited. My face began to feel fuzzy, and tingly, along with a loud buzzing in my ears. His face was calm while he watched me as I struggled with my surroundings. With another attempted call, a gulp of water passed my throat to close it permanently. A peaceful, numbness overtook and the loud buzzing became a warm vibration. My throat squeezed out my last groan as I struggled toward my young companion. I blacked out. Traveling through a dark tunnel, I found myself back on the fur lined bed, with Shawna peacefully lying in my arms.

The crackling of the logs was faint, and the light had dimmed to a glow. All that was left of the effulgence were the smoldering embers that illuminated the small area around the oven. The even, monotone sounds of snoring in the loft were all that kept me calm as I tried to reason with the dream, and the tugging in my heart for this creature that lay beside me. The petro-glyph of the 'Drowning Man' came to mind, perhaps it was not a drowning man after all, but a drowning boy.

TEN

I awoke as the first rays of dawn were streaming in
through the small window above the table just right of
the doorway. The illumined sitting area brought alive
the many ornaments and colorful trinkets littering the
shelves and tables. The cabin was light and busy, quite
different in appearance from the previous evening. The
archaic, fishing utensils that hung on the walls
transformed the romantic ambience of the preceding
night into the reality and true purpose of this little
cabin. Bone fishhooks, mussel-shell jewelry and woven
baskets, along with many other ornaments I did not
recognize, began to spring forth as I studied the room.
Perched on the shelf that skirted the perimeter of the
room just below the upper floor joists was a variety of
colorful clay and wooden bowls of all shapes and sizes.

My eyes eventually came to rest on the most
precious ornament of all, hidden beneath a wool
blanket. Sometime during the early morning hours,
Shawna had slipped from my bed unnoticed, back to
her cot on the opposite side of the hearth. As I turned to

get comfortable, her eyes opened to greet me with a sparkle. Her form rolled to a stretch beneath the blanket, teasing me to a responsive smile. The urge to go and be with her again was almost uncontrollable but quickly subsided with the thoughts of her grandmother already preparing for the day. The cocks had been crowing, from before dawn, and the stirrings in the attic had started shortly thereafter. Tucking my forearm up under my head as a pillow, I watched as Shawna teased me with her poking tongue and tucked her pillow beneath the covers clasping it firmly between her thighs. We lay in silence and watched each other, relishing the warmth and physical hum of the night before.

The dampness of the night air had slowly crept in as the fire began dying down over the early morning hours. From the comfort of the fur-lined cot, it was going to be difficult to get motivated for the day. This was the best I had felt in days and the relaxing atmosphere of the cabin was going to be hard to shake off. With the warmth beneath the covers, and my body feeling great, I could quite easily spend the whole day lounging, reading and sharing with Shawna, possibly not even setting a foot outside.

With Shawna still opposite, napping, my eyes and thoughts wandered to the workmanship of the floorboards above and the construction of the little house. The planks were rough-hewn and showed the chaffing of the adze used to chip the edges and bark away. It had been constructed over a period of years, and from the variety of aged timbers, possibly centuries. Lowering my eyes, I came across something so alien to my natural surroundings that I had to think twice; I reached for my cell phone.

Stirrings from above the boards in the loft began to creak and thump as grandma prepared to descend down the ladder once again. I wondered why they chose to sleep in the loft, but of course it was the warmth from the fire below that rose to the rafters. By the time her foot hit the floor, her mouth had spewed reams of sentences, and the two of us were out of bed and hopping to get our belongings gathered up. The morning then filled with chores of chopping wood, preparing food and getting water. We had heard the grandfather leave just before dawn, to go fishing, and would only return before lunch. It turned out to be 'some morning'.

In the middle of the afternoon, Shawna, her father and I, traveled up the hill again, over-shoulder bags in tow. Instead of turning into the parking lot, we headed in the opposite direction to a trail through the woods leading further south and inland from the coast. Within ten minutes, the little boy from the previous day was following us at a distance parallel to the path, but always ducking out of sight when I tried to draw attention to him.

"We have a visitor." I piped up trying to make conversation as we plodded along.

"Oh, do we. And who might that be?" asked Shawna jokingly.

"A little boy, a real scruffy, little, half naked boy."

Shawna looked at me in amazement. "There are no other families living in this area. Are you sure?"

"Yeah, he keeps following us where-ever we go."

"Oh!" she mused, "must be Kwuwati!"

"Kwuwati, odd name. Who is Kwuwati?"

"A little friend." she continued. "Kwuwati is a boy in a fairytale told to us as children by my ancestors. He helped my people in times of hardship by teaching us how to build drying racks for fish, and smoke houses for salmon. He was mischievous, but imparted wisdom to my people.' She continued down the path, looking back every few moments with an impish grin on her face. "No one knows if he was indeed a real person or a fanciful story to interest the children."

I thought to myself of the oddity and watched in amazement as he emerged, and retreated over the next hour, amid the foliage and trees. Every once-in-a-while, I heard a faint whistled laugh as he taunted me at a distance. To my dismay he remained out of sight to the others and began to understand this was evidently 'our thing'.

As we continued on with our journey, I felt a sense of familiarity traipsing along with Shawna, following in the same way as my dream of the previous night. The ground underfoot was spongy from the cedar needles and presumably more comfortable and quicker than the rocky paths by the shoreline. The skittish, resident wildlife of chipmunks and pheasants, alarmed by our presence would entreat us away from their nesting grounds with squawks and flamboyant displays of behavior. A rustling in the bush off to the right, to our astonishment and delight was an elk with calf, feeding and keeping their distance. Our intrusive presence eventually startled them and they scurried away after the subtle click of my camera. Off to the sides of the path, the beginnings of new plant life sprouted from the occasional peak of black, moist, forest peat. Vanilla- leaf sprouted beneath a stand of Sword-ferns, while the Bead-ruby strained leaning in the direction of the afternoon sun. Turkey-tail fungus, jutted precariously from the trunks of trees, perched above the upholstery of moss-covered roots. It was a botanist's cornucopia of earthly floral delight.

The three of us plodded along at a steady pace enjoying the fresh scent, and scenery of the rain forest undergrowth illumed by the shafts of sunlight piercing the upper canopy. The mid-afternoon air had warmed considerably, and reversed its journey from the interior back out to the sea. The treetops gently swayed in rhythmic harmony of wind and music as the branches urged us on at their steady pace.

Eventually, we came to an open clearing on high ground overlooking a small bay breaching to open water. To the left of the clearing, a fire had been lit in a shallow pit, a natural indentation in the rock. Almost obscured by large boulders that protected the flat stone area from the elements, was a unique little enclosed area where a short, elderly native man stood by the fire. He welcomed us as we came close and stood by an outer circle of uncut stones. The circle was approximately twelve feet across, and flat with a bedding of packed earth and dried cedar needles bordering the inside perimeter. The occasional crown of a large, smooth boulder peeped through the dirt suggesting previous use and occupation.

As I crossed the boundary of stone to shake his hand, I looked off to the right taking note of the shapes far below in the shadows that lay open to the rocky beach and ocean. The upper portion of the tidal-zone sported the remains of pits and what appeared to be archaeological digs. The overgrown foliage, and lack of current signs of excavation, gave the impression they were years old. As I turned back to face the elder, he greeted me with a warm smile, but did not offer a hand in gesture. Returning the smile and replacing my hand by my side, I watched him and realized I recognized him. His eyes were deep brown, and sparkled brightly from the reflection of the fire as he turned to see that the others had not crossed the circle of stones. A gray ponytail swung on his shoulder as he turned, and it was then that I remembered him as the man sitting with me in my vision by the totems in Stanley Park. Shawna and her grandfather had not moved, and stood beyond the periphery of stones, conducting a short conversation from where they stood with the elder. They spoke in the same tongue I had heard earlier with the guards as we drove inland from Neah Bay. After their greetings and welcoming gestures, the mood became sober and the elder turned back to me.

"Our ancestors welcome you to their home with open hearts. What you have done and offered in friendship can never be repaid. You have entered our circle of friendship and are welcome. Come sit and we will talk."

He motioned me over to several large stones alongside a woven mat placed on the ground. A steaming pot sat by the fire, with two small bowls placed beside. As I eased myself down on one of the rocks, he reached forward to fill the two bowls from the kettle. After giving me one, he sat down, half facing me on another boulder, and began sipping his tea. Watching him for a while, without taking a sip of my own, I began to wonder who he was and how he was able to visit me in the park. What part did he play in this vision quest?

"Relax!" he sighed, taking another sip of tea. "You have nothing to fear. I take it you have been told a little of our customs."

"Well no." I replied, looking over to Shawna and her grandfather. They both smiled and turned to head down to the shore.

"What you are about to partake in is a ceremony that we give to our young men as they come of age. Nothing fearful will happen to you, as the only person you will face is yourself. Take some tea before it gets cold."

I put the cup to my lips and took a sip. "A little bitter, but not bad!"

"Just herbs, spices and a little honey." he replied. "Our ancestors have offered us a great gift, of which you have been a part. A gift, that in itself has no power, except from that which men wish to give."

With that he reached from behind the rock and pulled the leather bag that housed the bowl and placed it between his feet on the ground.

"You have seen this," he nodded, "but you have also seen many other things."

I nodded not sure of what to say; I took another sip, the tea's warmth filling my belly.

"The bowl is just an object, like this stone or this pot, and has no value to anyone else apart from the person who created it through craft. It is human desire that has brought such false value to material possessions that man is so incensed to acquire and take from those who have always been so willing to give. It is your own heart that you will test tonight."

An uneasy feeling started to rise within me until his smile and warm gaze brought reassurance and a wholesome feeling back to the meeting.

"You will do well," and he got up to leave. He unraveled the bag exposing the bowl and placed it on the opposite side of the fire. A shaft of light from the setting sun caught the edge of the bowl at such an angle that the bowl appeared to illuminate from within.

"Where are you going?" I asked, slightly bewildered.

"No where. This circle was created for you. No one else can be a part of the intimacy that you will experience. You will see others, but they will only come at your beckoning."

"Experience!"

"I will be right here." He pointed to the cleft of two large boulders just beyond the circle. "I will place wood on the fire from time to time to keep you warm, and you have a blanket.

I looked down to the woven mat that seemed much too thin to be of any value. Picking it up, I clasped it to my chest and inhaled the scent of cedar boughs. Exhaling, I felt a fresh ticklish sensation in my lungs as if I had taken a breath of mint for the first time. 'It had begun'!

As the sun set over the watery horizon, the canopy of stars began to sparkle and crackle from the eastern sky. The bands of electrified light danced and chattered as if to mock the distant setting sun. The fire was slowly burning and I had placed several small logs on it myself, more out of boredom than necessity. It was almost dark, and I had been within the circle for over an hour. I wondered what I was supposed to do, and tried to think of how I was to meet myself. I knew nothing of the custom or what this ceremony was about. I had heard of sacred ceremonies of honor, where braves hung themselves from hooks, by their skin, until they went into a trance. 'Thank God there were no hooks dangling about'. My mind wandered to another ceremony of which I had heard with the circle of rocks, not unlike this circle, but there were no poisonous snakes that I could see, to bite me and put me into a trance. 'At least I hope not'. Scanning the perimeter of the rocks in anticipation, I grabbed the fire poking stick just in case.

Beyond the edge of the firelight, I saw the elder's feet tucked beneath his outspread knees; his face was obscure in the shadows. Having him there was an assurance, but I had my doubts as to anything happening apart from a lousy night's sleep. Feeling a little more at ease with the predicament, I leaned back and began to reflect on the dreams and visions of late. The popping of the coals in the fire drew my concentration to the scarlet, molten core. This experience, I decided now relaxed, was worth a go. Finishing off the pot of tea, I snuggled down on the mat and covered myself as best I could. The hum of machinery in the background, and the buzz of the crickets, kept me conscious of activity surrounding this desolate place. It was soothing being close to the fire with the radiating heat absorbed by the woven mat wrapped tightly around me. I drifted off into a light sleep, but after a short while found the ground uncomfortable and the noise of the crickets getting louder to the point of annoyance. Rolling on my back, I tried to get comfortable again only to notice the elder had disappeared. Not being all that concerned, I closed my eyes and covered my ears while the warmth of sleep began to overtake me again.

Tea Time:

Drifting for a short while, I was aroused by a buzzing noise so loud that I could feel the effects on my face. Uncomfortable with the intensity, I became aware the buzzing was inside my head. A slight shock wave of fear gripped my body as my comprehension of reality was beginning to change. The fear then began a wave motion within my nervous system from my toes that ran the length of my body to the top of my head. Not wishing to fight the fear, but to go with it, I let go and tried to relax with the sensations permeating my system. Wave after wave intensified till after only a few moments, they became one steady stream of energy. Fear slowly disappeared as I allowed my consciousness to drift with the sensation. The waves became pleasurable intervals of light that ran up my body like one steady stream of electricity along my nervous system. Within moments, the stream was so intense that my whole body glowed, and I found I was no longer contained within my body. With every wave of electricity came a flash of light before my eyes till it appeared as a strobe. My inner being moved upward, and after what seemed an eternity of lights and sounds, I was out of my body standing in a fertile field of grass with a faint breeze blowing in my face. The short grass swayed in a wave motion, like a gentle sea that was touched by the breeze. Warmth caressed my skin as the air's motion enveloped me.

The buzzing in my head had subsided and was replaced by the mild hum of the machinery I had heard earlier. The softness of the audio tone seemed to permeate my being and somehow, visually, be a part of all that surrounded me. The environment was soft, greenish in color and not with out form and substance. There were various colors, but all seemed to be translucent, less vibrant. I did not feel doubt or fear, only a sense of belonging.

The stars were above me, as they had been before, sparkling and bright. Below me, at the bottom of a huge grass-covered funnel was my body as it appeared in silhouette. Wondering where I was, I looked down at my hands and noticed the veins and their bluish color. A tug came to my consciousness, and I felt jolts of pleasure bolt through my body once again; flashes of light, like leafy-pages of a book, fluttered before my eyes.

After what felt like an eternity, a strong jolt brought me back to consciousness and I found myself alone, atop a high four-tiered stone building. Many stone steps led down a centered staircase to a courtyard. Many people surrounded me with torches fluttering mystically in the haze of the smoky plateau. The air felt moist and warm, while the full moonlight reflected off the treetops above the stratum of smoke. On the next landing, immediately below me, a group of people was seated looking up to where I was standing. I sensed a familiarity and a kinship, but was not overly concerned. A warm, excited numb feeling surged through me, as I stood high above the large courtyard. The people milled about and shouted, as if witness to a game about to begin. Behind me in the shadows stood a man I did not know, but sensed a coldness and authority. As I turned to look to the shadows, a man stepped forward. He was adorned with a colorful headdress of feathers, while his face was covered with the mask of a cat. Others, naked to the waist, also with headdress, danced and sang, as if to celebrate the coming sport. A flash of light caught my eye as two men grabbed my arms and led me to a stone table fashioned in the likeness of a seated man with his knees and hands facing the sky. A last glimpse of the people below brought me in contact with a youthful woman decorated with feathers and paint. Tears ran down her cheeks, and my heart gave a tug at seeing her face. The first pangs of fear of what was about to transpire raced through my body. Forcibly, they laid me down backwards across the flat-topped statue. The stars began to sing, as I looked up recognizing them from the few precious moments before. Waves of electricity and light began to flood my body once again, as my consciousness began to ebb away. The priest lifted a green bowl that I strangely recognized. From the contents, he sprinkled white sand from between his fingers. Watching as it slowly blew away in the wind, he paused for a moment to reflect on the crowd below. Turning my head to the left, with the cold stone against my cheek, I watched as the moon reflected blue light on the particles that had landed on my outstretched arm. He replaced the lid on the now visible, small, blue-green-jade bowl, and gave it to another standing off to the side. He approached me again, with a large, golden, carved bowl and black obsidian knife. As the fear mounted within me, unbearably loud buzzing in my ears became so overwhelming and I found myself surrounded by light; the word, 'Chocmol' echoed in my ears.

Once again, on the hard ground, back at the fire at Ozette, I began trying to orient myself. My face felt swollen, as if the blood were trying to force itself out of the pores in my skin. Unable to grasp my predicament entirely, I saw a strange-looking individual sitting just in front of where the old Chief had tucked himself away. Unable to move, or take my eyes from him, I lay still and watched as he watched me. Motionless on the rock, with hands resting on his knees, he sat like a king, foreboding and gruesome. Upon his head, two large, curling horns protruded from a headdress perched on his forehead, like those of a buck antelope. Long, dark hair hung loose down the sides of his temples, cascading over his shoulders. His skin was very dark and shiny, almost black. An animal-skin cloak draped his shoulders, and from what I could see, he wore a loincloth of some sort. From his large toes and up the front of his shins, white dots ran the length and ended just below his knees where a leather thong was tied with feathers dangling loose. He was motionless except for his eyes that, from time to time, sparkled in the firelight. I got the impression of Pueblo Indian decent.

Helpless, I lay and watched. My heart pounded a steady relentless beat in my chest and echoed to my ears. Looking about the fire to see what might have caused him to be there, my eyes came to rest on three round-faced, flat-nosed individuals. They were as dark as he, but felt they were no threat. They were naked with fat tummies and lean legs. Their eyes flashed in the firelight, and somehow that strangely gave me comfort to know they were there; their fluffy, curly, white hair blowing in the breeze. All adorned long beards except for one who sported braids down the front mingling with his chest hairs. A younger man and a woman, seated to his right, were almost motionless. A gentle tapping sound began echoing in my ears; the woman held two sticks in her hands tucked between her knees, which she periodically struck together. The young man responded, and got to his feet to kick the ground and dance to the rhythm of the tapping. His dance became more heated as he spun circles and stomped the ground stirring what little dust was there atop the rocky clearing. His body was now dusted, with accents of white dots and lines along his arms and legs. Feathers, tied to his upper arms and ankles, danced up and down with his jerky, almost erratic movement. The old man's attire had changed as well. He too was now adorned in the same attire, with dots and lines painted on his face along with his body dusted white. A low, deep and hollow sound could be heard, in the background, just audible above the crackling of the fire. The tapping and the barrage of sound they made became more frenzied and amplified the buzzing and wave motion within my body. I found myself overwhelmed and eased myself over on to my back hoping to resist the drawing away sensation from this surrealism. Closing my eyes from all that was encompassing me, I tried to concentrate on strong and vivid scenes of my childhood to gain control of my thoughts. It was an impossible task, and I began to slip as the buzzing and waves of light overtook me again. I had no idea how much time was passing, or what was happening to me, but I was at the dream's mercy.

Drifting down a tunnel toward a flicker of light, within seconds I was back into the world, seated in a car looking out the passenger side window to the lush roadside scenery beyond. In the reflection of the glass, a face stared back at me that was not unlike my own, only younger. Beside it, in the near distance came the familiar face of Vincent, only younger. Turning quickly, I came to face him and smiled as his hands tightly gripping the steering wheel.

"Hello! Did you have a good sleep?"

"Yes." I replied startled at his presence. "Thank you!"

We spoke very little, and when we did, it was light conversation of no consequence. We proceeded up the valley on a windy highway toward the interior away from the ocean. A great river was off to my left that I recognized as the Columbia. We drove past a great huge natural stone overpass that the river had carved centuries before.

"The Bridge of the Gods," I shouted to Vincent, as we passed the monumental, stone overpass. He was intent on driving, commenting on nothing.

As I thought of the wonderment of the formation, it came to me that it had collapsed many years previous and that all that remained were legends and drawings of the great bridge. Wondering at how that had come to be, a loud audible snap in my head brought me walking, following Vincent up a narrow, shadowed riverbed with high walls either side. A crystal clear trickle of water washed over the smooth rocks and moss that covered the creek's bed. Moisture dripped from my nose and puffs of mist billowed with every breath as I panted after him. A gallery of ferns and plant life clung to the cliff face, as delicate as I had seen anywhere. Beneath their roost, water dripped from cracks in the layers of sedimentary rock, slowly making its way down to mingle with the waters that flowed beneath our feet.

Vincent stopped before a large boulder outcropping, staring at it without saying a word. As I approached the spot, an excited feeling began to well up within me. Before me were petroglyphs of a stick man and the likeness of a dog jumping at his side. The headdress of the man was high and gave the impression of horns and feathers. It could have been the headdress of a hundred or so native cultures from Peru to southern New Mexico, and it was here! What was it doing so far north, thousands of miles from its southern kin? Vincent turned to me and smiled, then looked away to several men approaching along the path from whence we'd come.

"We must go," he suggested quickly with no elevation to his voice. He gave me a reassuring nod as he disappeared into the nothingness we had emerged from.

With the familiarity of the petroglyph resonating in my mind, another loud snap brought me back to Ossette.

Lifting myself to one elbow to view the fire, I could see that new logs had been placed on the embers, but no one-else was to be seen. The surroundings looked equally as surrealistic only furry, as if all had a coating of clear, liquid goo. The hum, that I had heard earlier, was barely audible over the pounding of my heart in my ears. I reached for the stick by the fire in slow motion as if time itself had slowed to a near standstill. Lying back down, I closed my eyes trying to get self-control. My tongue was thick and dry making it impossible to swallow. Struggling desperately to hold onto the prospective reality, I lay with the only thing anchoring me to it firm, my heartbeat.

Looking up to the stars again, an intense flash shot across the sky leaving a brilliant trail behind it. Following its arching path, my attention was drawn to the other side of the circle. Just beyond the stones, to my dismay, the little scruff of a boy I recognized from earlier stood looking at me. Surprised by his appearance at the fire, I tried to raise myself to speak with him. He was still half-naked as I had seen him before, but now he had a blanket, not unlike mine, draped around his shoulders. His face was dark with a band of soot across his eyes like a raccoon. In his hands was the leather bag and bowl that had been left by the fire in the safekeeping of the circle. A toothless grin came to his face as he watched me from outside the circle, struggling to get to my feet. Staggering, half stooped, I skirted the fire to go after the boy and reclaim the precious bag. He turned to face me, and with a taunting, whistled laugh, disappeared into the darkness of the surrounding forest.

"No!" I shouted after him.

Without thought, I left the perimeter of the circle and bounded after him into the blackness of the Olympic rain forest. The rest was darkness.

Dream Time:

Coming to again, the sun was just rising above the line of hills on the horizon. The scenery had changed dramatically and I was no longer at the fire or in the lush rain forest of the Pacific Northwest. It was cold and dusty, and I was lying in a heap on the hard ground. My legs felt cramped as I straightened from the fetal position and remained prone on the ground. How did I get here, and what had happened that had caused Vincent to leave me in a place like this? Had Vincent just dumped me off here? All were good questions, but there were no answers.

Fortunately, the sun was on the rise and I could tell by its warmth on my face that I would not be cold for long. My mouth was dry, my tongue felt thick as I ran it across the cracked surface of my lips. Resting on one elbow, I began looking for relief from the dryness. Nothing was available. No flask of water, no overnight bag, just, to my thankful dismay, the little, leather bag that housed the bowl. Frustrated by the cold and my situation, I sat up, wrapping my arms around my knees. Facing the sun, I pondered my options and what my responses should be. The countryside looked somewhat familiar and it made good sense to head east and find a settlement. Thinking that the sun rose in the east, I looked toward the south and an expansive plain between two humps on the horizon. Making an effort to get up, I noticed my leather boots were different than I had last remembered, well worn, and more of a riding boot than the hikers. My jean jacket was a favorite I had worn years ago, as a teen. My hands were well tanned and I still recognized them vaguely as my own; a small turquoise ring adorned my middle finger. As I ran my fingers through my hair, it felt long, matted and wind-blown, something I was not used to. My jeans were bleached and dusty, caked with debris and remnants of the trip.

"When did I last eat?" I asked the sky as my stomach groaned. "What did I eat?"

Getting to my feet, I dusted my legs and continued to look about, trying to find clues that might enlighten me to my circumstance. I searched the area for my knapsack and camera, but they were nowhere to be found. It appeared all I had was the leather bag, the clothes on my back, and a felt cowboy hat that was as weathered as I. The brown, leather bag sat conspicuously in the center of my vision on the ground. Taking stock of my pockets, I found nothing more than my wallet and a book of half used matches. In my upper pocket I found a pocketknife and a piece of paper with the names, Moon Rising and Flagstaff scribbled in pencil. A light wind coming from the south pushed aside the strands of hair from my eyes. As I raised my head to take note, the sun broke the horizon over the low ridge of distant mountains. A slight band of green could be seen at the base of one of the distant hills, just this side of the range. A canyon promised a chance of water, and with water, a river; and with the river, a farm; and with a farm, people. I was all right for now, but knew if I did not get water soon, I would be in trouble. My natural instinct was to dig for roots, but all that were available were the prickly tumbleweeds and a few cacti, a typical scene straight out of the old west. After a short walk, I found a small, round cactus-like plant tucked by the side of a boulder sticking up from the parched ground. Plucking it up with my knife, I peeled back the leathery, spinney skin to expose the fleshy moist heart of the plant, I sucked and chewed the moisture from the core, spitting out the remaining fiber like a wad of spent gum. The taste was slightly bitter, but all that was being offered a-la-carte; unless a snake or lizard came my way, it was all that I would be eating for some time.

The sun rose high in the sky, and the distant, green belt slowly came closer and more into focus. The air was not all that warm, but waves of heat came up off the distant rocks giving the mirage of movement. The appearance of water, suspended several feet above the ground, gave me a false sense of hope and only added to the stress of no water. The distant hills beyond the thin, green belt became hazy with mist. The heat of the rising sun was evaporating the available water out of the soil, lifting it to suspend this side of the low mountain range as haze. That moist air, unfortunately, would never lift high enough to condense into rain and relieve the surrounding area of drought. The air mass would continue, relentless, across the plains, leeching whatever moisture it could from the exposed terrain.

From the rock formations and the outcropping of shoved up and tumble down sedimentary layers, it was becoming obvious I was in the Badlands of the mid west. Without knowing for certain, the Colorado River, or one of its many tributaries, was the most likely course to follow. There was no way of knowing for sure, but since I was heading east, with a large mountain range behind me in the distance, the foot hills, and two peaks south to my right, I seemed to be heading in the right direction; the Grand Canyon was likely, but had no idea which side I could possibly be on.

Sweat dripping down my legs began to pool in my boots. My socks had slowly worked themselves down to a band below my ankles and were very uncomfortable. It was now high noon, and I imagined I'd been walking for five or more hours. I would need to stop and rest soon, and get my socks dried out. No problem in the heat built up in the ravines, but finding shade from the high sun to rest in would take some doing. As I plodded along with my jacket tied around my waist, and sleeves rolled up as high as they would go, my mind wandered in a dream back to my studies back in Vancouver and how my photography had really gone nowhere. There had been good opportunities, but none seemed to pan out successfully. In the present, the only audience that seemed to appreciate my circumstance was the birds circling overhead. 'You are never really alone', I thought to myself. My mortality began slapping me in the face when I realized that lack of water was becoming as deadly as a loaded gun. The heat became unbearable, beating down on me, while below my hat my head was sore and wet. Somehow, I mustered the will to plod on and continue down the dried tributary. The imaginary river at the end of this wadi kept me focused while the memory of how nice it was going to be to fall head-first and lie beneath the cool surface till I could hold my breath no longer kept me moving.

The bluffs that surrounded me must have been over twenty feet tall and afforded very little, if any, shade this time of day. There were no large logs, nor small trees, only the occasional outcropping of rock that gave a foot or so of shade at its very base.

Feeling the need to rest, with desperation setting in, I took a large piece of flat stone and crawled to the base of one of the overhangs. Starting to dig at the undercut, I slowly worked away with little energy, till there was enough room for my body to lie prone in the crevice. The coolness of the newly exposed earth was short-lived, but a blessing all the same.

Slipping my boots off, I wrung out my socks and let them hang on the sides of my boots to dry in the sun. The foulest things I'd smelt for a while guarded the leather bag and its contents which I shoved hard down into my boot. The smell must have attracted someone for the next thing I recall, was staring at the ground rocking to and fro, on my belly across the back of a mule.

"Uh!" was all I could grunt. My jacket had been draped over my back and head, and I was baked.

"Whoa!" came the yell of a fellow from in front of the mule.

The mule came to a stop and I felt a tug at my belt, and my feet touching the ground, with excruciating pain.

"Uh!!" escaped me once again. I collapsed to the dry ground and looked at my feet. They were swollen and almost twice their normal size.

"You should never have left your boots off, Amigo. You cannot walk."

I looked at my boots, tied with my socks through the loops, draped over the neck of the mule.

"Yeah," I sighed, acknowledging my predicament. "Where am I?"

The dark, Indian fellow said nothing as he reached for the water flask over his shoulder. He cautioned me, with his thumb and index finger to denote a small amount, and waited.

Getting to my feet as best I could, I leaned against the mule that looked back at me with a big black eye. It gave the impression he was not impressed with his duty. The short, dark man draped in a light shawl and large woven hat, waited patiently while I struggled to walk. He also had no shoes.

Without saying a word I took a sip winching as it burned my tongue and throat. I went to take another sip when he grabbed the flask from my hand.

His eyes were kind, and set deep in a well-lined face that gave the appearance of soft leather. His shoulder leaned into me to prop me up as I climbed atop the mule again. The sun had moved a fair distance across the sky and could only guess that another four hours had passed since I lay down. How soon after my Indian friend had found me, I have no idea, but I was thankful he had. With the discomfort of the mule's spine keeping me from drifting off to sleep, we started again down the dry creek bed.

We did not travel for too long before the faint smell of fire smoke stung my nostrils like a mild acid. In the distance, a thin, straight pillar of white smoke rose unimpeded within the confines of the bluffs, only to dissipate several hundred feet up when it cleared the summit. Plants had started to appear along the parched lines of the dirt below us. The mule became more alert and lively as we entered a small, flat, delta area that opened up into the small river a half a mile or so in front of us. The smell of the air changed from a dry nothingness to the faint, sweet aroma of grass and foliage. It was becoming ever so difficult to coax the mule further than the tufts of greens that looked appetizing even to me.

We stopped short of the river by several hundred feet and the small Indian fellow helped me down from the mule. Winching from the pain, I stood half bent wondering why we had stopped. I could see we were not far from the smoke and reasoned we were just around the bend. He handed me the water jug and let me have a drink. Taking it back, he turned and started to walk away toward the turquoise ribbon with my boots still draped over the mule.

"Wait!"

He kept on walking without turning back but behind the mule this time. The mule, dusty and scraggy, had sensed the end of the journey and forged on ahead. I slowly hobbled after them and subsequently, after several very painful minutes, came to the edge of the shallow, fast running river. By the time I had got there, the two had already crossed and were almost out of sight around the bend.

Pebbles were visible through the clear water that had a bluish-green hue at its depths, and looked delightful. As I stuck my aching feet into it, a rush of tingles and relief ran up my body in the form of sheer ecstasy. The coolness gripped my ankles and it was all I could do to keep myself from plunging headlong into its shallow depths. Slowly easing myself down onto my belly I began to crawl out into the middle where it could have been barely over my waist. Assured, I would not lose consciousness, I dipped my head under and drank its delight

The sun was almost setting when I crossed the river and around the bend to the little adobe house that stood in the open on the opposite side of the clearing. The low, clay building was surrounded with small, wooden lean-tos with a collection of farm equipment scattered in the open; the area was dwarfed beneath the towering cliffs of the surrounding mesas. A small dog began to bark and ran from behind a chicken coop off to the side. He barked continuously until the curiosity got the better of him and he came to me for a sniff. The saint, who had found me earlier, came walking from the hut. Two small, naked children ran up from behind me, giggling as they passed. I sensed that they had watched me in the river, while I too ran naked, playing in its freshness. They looked as if they could have been twins. The girl with long, black hair was slightly smaller than the boy who was darker, stocky with curly hair. Both seemed charming, but a little wild. Their hair danced in the wind as they ran past to their father. The dog, that had been rather persistent in his alert, came to distraction with the children and quieted down. A goat, tied to a post at the farm's perimeter, looked up to take note but continued to graze lazily. All came to ignore me apart from the man, who waited at his distance till I had crossed the small yard.

It appeared that this area was a flood plain with noticeable watermarks several yards up the sides of the cliffs. A trail meandered hundreds of feet up the distant cliff to higher ground and possibly winter quarters. I had known Pueblo Indians lived under these conditions, but to have the opportunity to see first hand, was appreciated. The habitat was rough, but not unpleasant. As I walked across the yard, I began to reflect on how we have become accustomed to our way of doing things, and presume that ours, in the western culture, is the best. Perhaps it is the struggle of life that is the gift of life. Obviously, under these conditions, conventional farmers could not survive, nor would they want to.

Impressed with the sheltered location, a good combination of sun and shade, I looked at the condition of the crops. An immature crop of maize, small and stunted grew haphazard lining the terraced hill down to the river. A small field of what appeared to be squash covered a flat and dusty area away from the vibrant moist soil of the river basin. I presumed, they planted their crops after the flooding of the winter thaw and spring rains were over.

As we came close, a smile blossomed on his face, "Are you feeling better?" he asked with a strong, broken accent.

"Yes, fine. I must thank you for your help. You probably saved my life."

He returned a gaze, then looked down to the ground. "You would have done the same for me."

Without saying more, he turned to the elevated doorway of the adobe. A beautiful, small woman, I presumed his wife, smiled and walked from there motioning the two of us to sit by an open pit where the smoke had previously emanated. Below, smoldering coals and a small kettle had been prepared and waited for my arrival. Clay bowls and a small hook, to hang the vessel, appeared from the opposite side of the hearth. She gently poured the steaming liquid into the bowls, offered the first to me and then to her husband. She did not drink with the two of us.

We sipped the delightful liquid that reminded me of Sake' and watched as she slowly prepared the pit with meat, yams and vegetables. After loading the bottom, she placed some branches of wood over the ingredients and covered all with a leather blanket. I was told later that the blanket starved the fire of just enough oxygen to smolder the new branches into a smoke filled oven. The food slowly baked and was left with the savory flavor of the particular wood that was included. They used three or four different varieties of wood to help enhance the flavor of their food.

Just before we sat down to eat in the open air, the children became more bold leaving their 'look outs' and 'hiding places' to come within several feet of me. They seemed always very polite, not saying anything but giggling and teasing me as they became more accustomed to my presence. I would guess to say, I was one of the very few people to drop by that these children had seen. We spoke little during the meal, but I made sure the taste and quantity of the food eaten was appreciated.

After dinner, with the moon and stars now visible overhead, the wife and children busied themselves with bedtime preparations. Wrapped in loose-woven shawls tied about the middle, the children were kind enough to carry my boots from the anterior of one of the lean-tos. I nodded in gratitude as they sheepishly brought the boots to where I sat in the firelight. Each, in their turn, went to sit on their dads lap and watched the fire as it peeked above the rim of the fire pit. Looking into each boot for the leather bag, I caught the two looking toward me and shift with discomfort in their father's lap.

"Uh hum!" I blurted, clearing my throat and watching them.

They each stirred, not sure of their next move. Carlos looked up from the fire sensing my admonishment. He looked at each of them and spoke to them in their native tongue. Shyly, they looked over to me and the boy got up from his fathers lap and scurried off into the darkness toward the lean-to. In a short few moments he returned to the fire and stood in front of me with the leather bag open in his hands. The green bowl peaked out from the folds and I could tell that the lad had not seen anything like it before, very few had. Carlos paid more attention to the fact his son had been disobedient and gave him a light scolding then sent them both into the hut with their mother. The doorway to their home was well lit and showed the stucco of the interior walls. The faint sounds of explanations and arguments to bedtime duties could be heard above the crickets and crackling of the fire. Within moments after the children had climbed into bed, the hut was dim and quiet.

We sat by the fire and finished our bowls of tea, saying little. Boldly trying to make conversation, I asked, "What nation are you?"

Without taking his eyes from the fire he answered with very broken English. "I am mixed, with my ancestors Hopi, and Hohoakim from the south of here. Many years ago Spanish raided my family and they had to head further north to escape their assaults. My Hohoakim family joined with the Hopi at the time the ancestors of the Navajo came from the north. My mother, six generations with many children and much land, married a Hohoakim man. Her husband had been killed in a Navajo harvest raid."

Without any questions, I sat with him for a while and watched the fire also.

"I am Canadian. My ancestors came from England and France. I was born in Canada but have traveled to many places and seen many things. I am here on a trip to deliver a package."

In the quietness and the light of the fire, I handed Carlos the little package, which he unfolded and held within the palm of his hand. He slowly turned it this way and that as if to read its inscription.

After several minutes of close scrutiny he gave a sigh, "Very beautiful. I have seen something like this before." He gave it some thought and then asked, "Where did you get this? This is very familiar to me."

He handed it back to me and without saying more, he continued to look into the fire.

"I am to deliver this to a man in Shiprock. His name is Moon Rising." showing him the paper.

Shifting slightly, without taking his eyes from the fire, he cautioned softly, "We have to be careful."

"Why?" I asked. "No one knows I am here."

He turned to face me directly. "They have been waiting. They know you are coming."

ELEVEN

The cock crowing from the other side of the mud-packed wall shocked me from a sound sleep. The smell of hay mingled with animal droppings woke me like smelling salts to a faint victim. Lying prone on a small pile of hay with my hands propped behind my head, I felt confused. Was I in a dream? If so, why did it feel so real?

Light peeking through the cracks of the log and branch walls displayed the dusty condition of my surroundings and quadruped companions. Free-floating, dust particles were illuminated in the shafts of light, dancing on the eddying currents of air in the enclosure. Two mules, a ram, and a mother goat and her baby, stared back at me from their tethered posts. The little dog, my close companion for the night, lay at my feet and wagged his tail at my sudden arousal.

Considering my good fortune of the previous day's events and how lucky I had been to be found by my host, I could only conclude all was as it should be. My feet were still sore and swollen, but were one hundred percent better after being rubbed with a concoction of oil and herbs; Carlos and his family had been very kind to me. I had not plied him with questions, but was curious about his last comment before we settled in for the night. The language was a barrier, but with patience and much hand illustration, I was able to understand more of these private and complacent people. Strengthened by last evening's meal, I felt strong enough to continue on.

Sweeping aside the colorful, zigzag patterned, woven blanket, I attempted to brush away the refuse that covered my back. Easing myself from the mouth of the small structure, I stood to gaze the sheltered little valley. In one quick flicking motion of the blanket, the dust and grass scattered in clouds suspended in the air and dissipated in the gentle breeze; I folded the woven piece into a neat square. The river's chatter was inviting me from its short distance away. My small companion, who had been so unsure of me the previous night, strode fearlessly along-side me, jumping, trying to snatch the blanket from beneath my arm.

Mist slowly rolling over the grass on the opposite bank gave the area a still, mystical look. The air, in these early days of spring, was still cool at night and the warmth of the morning sun was slow to heat the earth beneath. In the distance, from whence I'd come, a light crown of snow appeared as white lace adorning the high mesas and mountain to the south. The warm temperatures in the lower areas along the riverbeds were still severe and the small patches of winter wheat had yet to be reaped. From the appearance of the stunted foliage and the shallowness of the river within its banks, the rainy season had not started.

I knelt precariously, balanced on a large, smooth

stone and recovered from the shock of splashing the river's coolness over my face. Not noticing the sudden snoop of the little boy coming up from behind, I slipped off the stone.

"Good morning," I sighed.

He grabbed my wet hand and pulled me back in the direction of the house where his family had spent the night. The uncomfortable, cold water-soaked cloth of my pant leg stuck to my knee.

Startled by his persuasiveness, I reached for the blanket and played along after him. As we entered the hut and closed the door, I could sense something was amiss. Carlos' wife sat on the cot with her little girl while the other fellow directed me to sit at the wooden table built for the four of them.

"Hola. Me llamo, uhhh." I stopped short trying to remember my name. Unable to roll it off the tip of my tongue, I smiled at the boy. "Y tu, como te llamos?

Nothing, he smiled back at me with a huge grin from ear to ear. Asking his name in my broken Spanish wasn't going to work.

As I looked over to the cot, the woman slowly lifted her finger to her lips in a gesture to quiet me. Within a moment, I heard horse's hooves and a conversation going on between the visitors and Carlos. Getting up from the table, I crept to the ripped plastic sheeting that covered one of the windows and peered out to see three natives on horseback. Carlos was at the head of the horses keeping them calm while he talked to the riders. Not able to catch a familiar word in any of it, I quietly returned to the table to wait with the others. After a brief conversation that ended in a heated discussion, the three left and Carlos returned to the chores. After several more moments, a knock came to the rear of the hut and the face of Carlos appeared in the back window. He gave me a nod in recognition and after speaking to his wife, the atmosphere lifted slightly and the children began to move about.

"I will be back soon." he said and disappeared as quickly as he had come.

His wife started to move about preparing a breakfast. The children disappeared outside again in loose T-shirts and bare feet. Several times I made a motion to the door, but she stopped me short. I would have to wait.

"Do you speak English," trying to make conversation?

She smiled shyly and spoke blushingly in her own tongue. We began in sign, as she busied herself with the fire and making dough. Annoyed with my fidgeting, she handed me a knife and I started cutting vegetables and pretending all was normal till I accidently sliced myself. She called her daughter in and once again I was left to fidget. She was very adept at using the small pizza spatula-like pan to flip the flat cooking dough. A golden stack of tortillas began to build quickly. Eventually, the girl and boy took over the cooking while she busily prepared some fish along with various roots.

Before she was finished, Carlos had returned to beside the oven-pit with an elder adorned with long flowing black hair. Unsure whether I was to present myself, I waited inside the threshold of the door. Shortly, Carlos came to the house and took my hand.

"Good morning," Carlos said with reserve. "We had visitors you should not meet. The Navajo have been looking for travelers on foot heading this way. I told them I had seen no one and that they were on our ancestral land; some do not like to be told."

The Navajo had come on to transitional land leased from the Hopi. This land has been in dispute for many years with no determination made by the Government. The Hopi had claimed this as their ancestral land defined by the stone records of their migrations and stone markers of a thousand years. Between what they (the Navajo) had taken, and the government has given them, the Hopi are left with a small portion of what their homeland originally was.

With that, Carlos gathered a shawl-like poncho and put it over my shoulders, and then placed a woven hat over my head to hide my features. Even with a good tan, there was no way I could compare to the almost black complexions of these native farmers. Stooping slightly, I made my way over to the outside oven and sat down as if to eat the morning meal.

"Good morning." I directed to the old man as I made myself comfortable.

He nodded in recognition and peered at me from behind deep-set eyes of sparkling coal. His skin was well lined and looked as if he had spent every day of his long life in the sun. He sat across from me and said nothing.

Throughout the meal he watched me as I ate and how I handled myself. I was aware that in some cultures to sit across from someone was a great honor and had great spiritual significance. Whether this was one of those instances I had no idea. The scrutiny felt odd.

After our breakfast, the old man got to his feet, nodded to Carlos and disappeared up the trail to the high ground beyond. Carlos had always treated me with respect, but after this brief meeting, he seemed to hold me in reverence. Even the children changed in temperament and were more aloof than they had been before. Sitting for a while after, we spoke little and finished the final crumbs of tortillas and fish.

"We need to travel," Carlos finally said to me. "The man you seek will meet us soon. Too many have seen your arrival and will come to seek you."

A little startled at his accusation I stretched my legs out before me. "How do you know this?"

"The same way I knew where to find you yesterday."

I thought about it for several minutes and understood that in thousands of square miles of deadly terrain, fissures and canyons there is no such thing as chance meetings.

"From now on, when we are with my people, you may hear me called 'Morning Moon'." He stood and gathered some cutting utensils and looked toward me. "And what do they call you?"

I tried once again to think of what my name was, but it did not come. It was somewhere there, illusive, like the details of my past.

He nodded directly to me, "We will call you 'Ikwatsi', friend."

Returning his gaze in acknowledgement, I too got to my feet and I headed in the direction of my lodging. Once inside the lean-to, I gathered my boots along with the leather bag stuffed inside. Still unable to adorn my boots, I gave my feet a rub. Removing my clean but discolored, gray socks, I lay back on the hay and wondered about travelling with such feet. The bowl which now lay among the loose strands of grass seemed at that instant less of a problem.

With thoughts of the three native travelers, a pang

of caution came to mind; it would be prudent not to carry the bowl for a while. Reaching for a miniature hoe that leaned against the wall, I cleared a section of dirt from beneath the small haystack; a hole about twelve inches round and deep, and after placing the bowl tightly wrapped in the bag within, I lightly packed the earth over top and replaced the hay. Certain everything looked undisturbed, boots in hand, I ventured from the open structure back to the oven-like heat outside the hut.

Morning Moon had been speaking with his wife and prepared a few things to go on a trip; the mules were being loaded with bundles and woven baskets. The children ran around excited as if something special were being enacted. The young boy approached me carrying a floppy bundle in his hand. He smiled and dropped a pair of woven sandals at my feet. Smiling and looking down to the ground, I noticed he too had donned sandals of the same design.

"Thank you." I smiled appreciatively.

"You're welcome." Astonished at his English, I chased after him a few steps to acknowledge he had fooled me these last few hours. He giggled and ran off to his mother who continued with the preparations.

Within the hour Morning Moon's wife and one mule, with the children perched on top, headed up one trail to the south while we followed the trail of the old man to the east. Traveling at this time of day was not good but the circumstance deemed it.

Walking to keep up with my partner who guided the mule became quite a chore. Even though the thongs were a great relief for my feet to walk in, Carlos moved as fast up the cliffs as he did on the flats. He had a slight build but was very muscular and obviously fit.

There were no 'burger stands' out here to clog your arteries and slow the blood flow. The native diet is fairly simple and nutritious, but with the damming of the Colorado River and some of her tributaries, the nutrient rich flood silts that nurtured their crops were no longer bathing the shores once a year, replenishing the soils. The best farms, save for a precious few, were forced to move from the river valleys to higher ground, to allow for the conversion to hydroelectric dams. Irrigation became a necessity and with the high evaporation rate, an abundance of minerals were left behind causing an imbalance in the fragile, wind and sunbaked soils of the flat-topped mesas. It was a true paradox for the Ministry of the Interior to deal with, but for these soil-dependent First Nations, it has become a travesty.

Lagging behind after several hours, it became obvious I had not fully recovered from the previous day's ordeal and followed along as best I could. Carlos would turn from time to time to view my progress and was always patient while I labored to keep up. Luckily, the terrain before us was becoming less severe as we traveled east, but the sun was still hot on our backs as we traveled with it setting behind us. Fortunately, the air had remained cool throughout our trek, but I knew once the sun had gone down it would be cold. Carlos must have sensed my concern and told me we would stop soon. Within an hour, we made our way down into a tree-ranked valley. We pushed our way through some underbrush and came to a crevice between two high bluffs. Squeezing through behind Carlos and the mule, I was surprised to find a sheltered small, hollow clearing with budding trees scattered about the area. Tamarisk trees and a splattering of light foliage marked a corridor of damp soil that leaked from the opposite side across the clearing's floor. A crevice, in the stratum several feet up the marble-like-layered wall, was wet and culprit.

My spirits escalated as my scrutiny brought to life the unique wonders within the obscure confine. A mini ecosystem had evolved within the boundaries of this small enclosure that flourished independent of the harshness outside the small valley. As I found out later, the sun beating down from above warmed the surrounding rock that in turn retained the heat that was slowly released throughout the night. Sheltered from the wind and the elements, this little coppice proved a blessing to all who knew of its whereabouts.

"This is quite cozy." I commented to Carlos as we gathered wood.

"Yes, this is a very special spot for our people. It is well hidden and, until today, is visited by no-one but our tribe." He placed a small armful of kindling by an overhang that he had chosen for us to sleep.

The last golden rays of the sun reflecting off the opposite wall were lighting the sheltered spot. I sat down beside the pile with my back against the warm sandstone wall and watched as Carlos dug in the moist earth in the center of the clearing for roots and whatever else he might find. I knew better than to ask what was to be eaten and accepted whatever was provided. We worked together to get a fire going and within minutes had our dinner of beans and roots cooking away on stones placed in and around the fire.

"Come with me."

Carlos led me to the far corner of the clearing, and while there was barely enough light, he showed me a group of wall carvings that looked to be centuries old. I could make out animals and birds, corn stalks with separate cobs of different sizes. People etched in the sandstone, milling about, with feathers and unrecognizable objects in their hands. Circles and spirals heading in different directions, adorned the walls of this obscure niche, sheltered in the walls of a small canyon tucked in the middle of no-where.

As if to read my thoughts, "For me and my people, *who speaks?* this is the center of the universe. We have been coming to this place since the completion of our migration. My people have traveled south, east, west and north and have fathered many nations from the beginning of time. We have always chosen solitude when the creator was no longer reflected in the lives and purpose of those who lived alongside us. We moved on until we were brought to this place, and have gone no further." He looked long at the inscriptions and said no more. We headed back to the fire.

After the meal, we sat for a while and talked of his children and why he had chosen to live off the reserve. He spoke of a time when the Hopi traveled for days in one direction to come to a place where a village had thrived hundreds of years previous, and was part of their home, but now occupied by foreign people. He spoke in length as to why his people had chosen not to embrace our modern culture, and how, in a previous world lead by a different clan, they had acquired great knowledge and achieved great technology, far superior to ours today, with flying machines and medicine, and how it was destroyed through greed and power. People now think this nation, adhering to simple ways, is backwards, but in fact they have chosen, by will, not to repeat the mistakes of their past and live to honor and worship the Creator. They still have great power, and will be called upon again to act at a time of travail and a great gathering of 'the people'.

Burying ourselves, as best we could, with sand, leaves and whatever was available, we snuggled down for the night. The glowing embers of the fire lit up the cut back in the cliff as we slept with our backs tight to the wall. I slept surprisingly sound with no disturbance and only vaguely remembered a dream of ribbons of colored lights reflecting on the rippling waters of a bay. The rustling of trees woke the two of us just as the sun was beginning to lighten the sky. As we got to our feet and dusted ourselves off, the old fellow from the breakfast of the day previous sauntered to greet us. He carried nothing and looked eager, and spry, and walked up to me without hesitation.

"Good morning," he said with a broad grin. It was almost opposite from the previous morning. "I am 'Sees Dawn Rising", he continued without lifting his gaze. "You may call me Don." I nodded in agreement and retreated to the cleft in the damp wall to refresh myself in the small pool on the ledge. It was sweet and cool, hardly like I had thought it would have tasted. Taking another sip, I splashed the water over my face and wiped it dry with my shirt. Carlos and Don were speaking in their own language and offered no conversation in my direction. The two of them seemed lighthearted as they worked away burying any visual remains of our being here the night before. When all was complete, Carlos sauntered to the water ledge and refreshed himself as well. He then filled the water bag that he had carried all along. Without any words of direction or plans offered my way, we headed toward the opening and squeezed from the vertical fissure out into the country beyond. Don took the lead and we followed in single file, me behind the mule, down the trail to the valley and mesas beyond.

"We are now entering the lands which the government has given my people as peace offering. We believe it is in retribution for them not being able to mediate on our behalf the lands which were taken from us." There seemed no animosity in Carlos' voice and he spoke rather matter of factly

Continuing on in almost complete silence, we forged through the underbrush in the low areas and climbed undaunted the cliff faces. Looking back after several hours, I tried to place where we had been, and without difficulty was able to recognize an almost straight path, up and down cliffs and along the plains. We had walked as if someone had drawn a straight line. With the sun rising into the morning sky and without anything to eat, I slowly became tired again. My mind began to wander to the images I had seen on the wall the previous night.

Boredom, and curiosity, got the better of me
"Carlos," I shouted to him. "I know that you have sacred sites and the place at which we stayed last night was one, but why was I allowed to see it? I am honored, but why me, and why now?"

He looked at me strangely as if I had asked an unanswerable question, "Even though you have some Indian blood, no man other than the tribal elders have seen the drawings of my people," he replied. "You are Kachina. You are spirit come to visit us."

"What do you mean?" I asked, bewildered.

"You are here in a body, and we see you and you believe you are here, but your spirit is from elsewhere."

"What!" I replied, trying to understand what he meant. "How do you know?"

"I don't, but he does," he replied, looking straight ahead to Don.

It made little sense to me at the time, and only left more questions.

After some contemplation on what he had said, I found myself confused, but unafraid. I felt no sense of detachment, only a knowing, somewhere within me, that knew of what he spoke. Watching my sandal clad feet, scissoring back and forth in the sand and rock below for several seconds, I looked at my boots slung over my shoulder with my socks tied through the loops.

'Why am I carrying these' I questioned the wind? Thinking of no good reason, I slung them behind a boulder out of sight and continued on without a second thought unencumbered.

Another two hours went by without incident till Don, who walked ten paces in front of us, put up his hand in a motion to stop. Without hesitation, we stopped and stood. His eyes looked far to the east where we could see the great plateau of the third mesa and the location of Oraibi, the town we were presumably going. He made a visual panorama of the east swinging south to the west, and then stopped to watch the distance behind us. Without moving, he stood and watched. Carlos and I turned to watch whatever it was to transpire, but were on slightly lower ground and not able to see until they were almost on top of us.

Four men on horseback came over the crest of the hill behind us from whence we had come. They all stopped within feet behind us; their horses snorting warm air and mucus from their nostrils on our sun baked necks and hair. The leader directed his horse around us throwing my discarded boots at me as he passed, hitting me in the chest. Recognizing him from the previous day, I could feel my pulse raising and a slight twinge of fear tug at my belly. Able to control it, I watched as he continued on to Don and got down from his horse. The rider walked up to him, and with one motion knocked Don to the ground with a punch, and stood over him, yelling. I felt my body tense up and adrenalin course through me. My legs, which coiled ready to spring to action, turned to lead. A hand gripped my arm and gave it a gentle squeeze. At the same time I heard the clicking snap of a rifle being cocked. Motionless, we stood and watched as Don was repeatedly beaten and kicked. He lay motionless and bleeding on the dusty path ten paces before us. Without mounting his horse, the attacker strode back to us, faced us and spit into Carlos face. Punching him in the stomach, Carlos doubled over on his knees. There was no gasp for air but just a moan of exhaustion as he keeled on the ground. Watching for a moment to see whether Carlos would move, the assailant came and stood in front of me to look into my eyes. With disgust, I peered back deep into the coal, black eyes and a soul of anger. He rolled his jaw in attempt to procure the moisture to ejaculate when a gasp of inhalation came from beside us.

"Go!" escaped from Carlo's prone being.

A deafening crack split the air as a rifle fired. The ringing deafened my ears as I watched Carlo's body jump into the air from the shock of his body being pierced. Trauma and fear gripped me as I witnessed the horrid scene before me. Immediately, waves of light flashed through my body and the loud buzzing in my head that seemed it would shear it in two. Not willing to let it overtake me, I fought to stay grounded and not leave. The visual panorama of the murder scene around me appeared to be running in reverse motion. The voices of those, our assailants, spoke backwards in slow and then fast motion as if someone had his finger on the turntable of the recording. There were only the four of them, with Carlos lying at their feet.

I was now no longer with them, but stood on higher ground looking down at the five frozen in time. Turning to the direction from which we had come, I thought of the farm and within a moment I was standing in the burnt out, smoldering ruins of the lean-to where I had slept. The adobe house was smoking and still on fire in places. None of the animals could be seen and the stunted crops of the terraces were trampled and broken. The remains of a wooden fence lay in a heap at one end of the yard, its obvious use, left crumpled, after being dragged repeatedly over the crops. Sadness overtook me as I looked about. Still struggling with the alignment of my soul to the space and time about me, I tried to comprehend what had transpired. Exhausted, with the need to get protected foremost in my mind, an old blanket, probably used for the mule was left untouched hanging on the stump of tree not far distant. Wrapping it around me, I struggled up the cliff to a protected area where I could take full advantage of the rays and heat of the sun.

Sitting wrapped for the better part of an hour, dozing lightly, warmth and wholeness came back to me. The scene below me was disturbing, and concluded there was little I could do to stop any of the injustice. Whatever was happening was far out of my control, and the little I could do was to follow my instincts, wherever they might lead.

Digging in the remains of the lean-to, the ~~chard~~ charred

PILLARS OF THE MOON

earth slowly gave up its sacred possession still intact and undamaged. Leaving the mule's blanket where I had found it, I tucked the precious package beneath my poncho; the one Carlos had given me days before. Going down to the riverfront, I knelt down and cupped my now almost black hands and took a drink. Standing tall, I took a long hard look at the surrounding harsh countryside and pondered the family, now fatherless and divided, that had been so peaceful till I had arrived.

"What about his wife and children?" I shouted, as if to question the sky that canopied this wilderness of extremes?

Troubled, I strolling back up to the path that led up and over to the east, I pulled my straw hat tight over my head and started, once again, to Flagstaff and a man called 'Moon Rising'.

The next day was a blur and it seemed that luckily, the only unbearably hot day that I was to experience was the one three days earlier when Carlos had found me. My diet had once again returned to the delectable desert fare of cactus and roots. I watched a snake pass, but thought of what Carlos had told me and decided that if I was who I was, I shouldn't have to eat.

As the day wore on, my weakness became more obvious and the thought of the snake, roasting over a fire, started to play on my mind. In desperation looking at the many forks in the dirt pathways that led in different directions, I tried to find traces of the path we had taken the day before. All, but the weeds and the scars in my mind left from the assault of the previous day, had blown away in the wind. With the sun was beginning to set, it was obvious I was not going to find protection from the elements that evening.   Gathering up a few twigs and small bits of wood, I crouched low

221

in a protected area behind some large boulders and started a small fire. Within an hour, I had found some larger pieces of wood and was sitting protected and warm. There was a deep layer of sand and dust that had collected in a hollow between two boulders allowing me to sit comfortably. With hunger gnawing at my insides, I began to wonder why I could not use these strange abilities I had, to travel through space and time to get to Shiprock. As I laid back and started to concentrate on the process, I realized I had no idea what Shiprock looked like. It was only possible for me to go back to the little farm because I knew what to envision. But then again, I did not know how I got to this area from wherever I was from. None of this was making any sense?

"I will concentrate on the sandstone courtyard of the previous night," I suggested to the stars as if they could hear. They appeared one by one in the ever-darkening pool above me. Standing up, I looked west to the orange ribbon of the setting sun as it dropped below the horizon. The infinite shades and hues of red, purple, blue, painted the sky. Blackness, the absence of all light, squeezed the last traces of the day. Apart from the twinkling stars, beacons of the endless hopes of mankind, there was nothing but darkness.

I remembered the cool emptiness in the shadow behind the eyes of the bandit that stared back at me. Carlo's fatality flashed through my mind, and I was left with the stark reality, I would be next. Returning my gaze to the fire, I tried to concentrate, but could think of no other than 'Morning Moon' and 'Sees Dawn Rising'. Carlos, and Don, would not be forgotten.

The frosty air was nipping at my legs when I awoke several hours later. Barely able to move, I knew that if I did not get warm soon I might not survive. Stumbling around in the dark for more wood, I remembered of the oven that Carlo's wife had used to cook. Digging an oblong pit in the sand to the base rock as best I could, I lined the bottom with as many of the coals from the fire that were left aglow and covered them with the newfound branches and leaves. Burying the whole lot with a layer of sand, I laid on top hoping to absorb whatever heat would make its way up to the top. Eventually, I fell asleep with the poncho spread from my shoulders down to my knees. I was able to survive the night wishing I hadn't thrown my boots away.

A new day dawned with my lips cracked once again. The heat from the rising sun on my face, gave me enough courage to start the day. Facing south, I headed off down an obvious path, hopefully, in the direction of Flagstaff. By mid-day, I was near exhaustion again and wondered how I was going to continue. Skirting the imaginary boundary of the Hopi reserve, I had no idea who or what, I was going to encounter. The only ones I certainly did not want see were the four riders of two days earlier.

Coming to a juncture in the path, I sat for a while and pondered the likely-hood of me choosing the right one. Highly unlikely under normal circumstances, perhaps, under these conditions, things would be different. Walking to the highest point within close proximity, I looked to the south and saw, in the far distance, a large town with subtle terrain feeding down to the area. I took the creek-bed to the left. I had not walked more than fifteen minutes when a light brown bay horse crossed my path and disappeared around the bend. A few moments later, tire tracks of a vehicle appeared from the along the banks and followed the path in the same direction. A whistling sound pierced the air and the horse whinnied.

"People," I shouted to the open air and quickened my pace.

Stopping short in my tracks, ahead of me, not more than a hundred yards, were three other horses and the four riders of the days previous. An old, green pickup truck lay unattended just beyond the bend of the pathway behind them. I couldn't believe my fortune. Trying to console myself, I figured with any better luck, I could disappear as before out of harm's way. Knowing I could not outrun them and with no-where else to go, I walked passing them to continue on my journey. Bridling the brown bay, the leader followed after me with the others close behind. Within several moments, they had surrounded me and were walking with me down the broad path. They started to laugh and spit on me as I tried my best to ignore them and proceed. Stopping directly in front of me, one of the others put out his arm almost hitting me. There was nowhere else for me to go except stop. One came from behind and started to frisk me. The heavy leather bag fell from inside my poncho landing with a thud between my feet. As I looked at the fellow in front of me, I felt a strange compassion. He was short and stocky and his eyes were red as if burnt from the sun, or 'high' on something. His round face came to glow as the precious gift fell to the ground. A blow to the back of my head brought his face within inches of my own and I fell in slow motion as my vision shrank to a hollow tube of light surrounded by darkness.

Next, as I came to, my face was flat against the plywood floor of the box of the pickup. I had been breathing dust and grass, scooping it up like vacuum cleaner for who knows how long. Trying to understand what was happening to me, I looked about with my one good eye facing upward to the back. My head throbbed and my half-naked body ached from being tossed, shoved and abused. Not moving, I tried to listen for activity round about. There was none. My arms felt burned from exposure to the sun until I saw that they were bleeding and raw with scrapes from being dragged across the ground. Bits of gravel and splinters of wood protruded from the pink raw flesh. Without any energy to do much else, I lay there falling in and out of consciousness till someone came by and banged the side of the truck. An unfamiliar face appeared over the tailgate.

"It's your lucky day. They are actually going to get money for you."

He threw a blanket over me, and I lay there while he got into the cab and drove down the path in the same direction I had previously come. I was not going to Flagstaff.

The ride was excruciatingly painful. With arms tied behind my back, there was no way to keep myself upright and braced against the rocky motion of the truck. Tumbling and rolling, with only my legs and feet able to stabilize me, the ride was almost as damaging as the abuse I had suffered earlier. Why was I not able to disappear in times of stress, as before? I was certainly in distress now, and I would say in great danger of my life. These fellows had little or no regard for life and I did not expect to be an exception.

After fifteen minutes, of the ride from hell, I was helped from the back of the truck by two guys twice my size. Each had long, silky, black hair down passed their shoulders. One had his tied back in a ponytail, while the other's was loose under a headband. Each had a leather thong tied about the upper portion of their biceps, which were the size of my legs. One was leaner and mean, with veins popping beneath the skin of his arms; he kind of tossed me in the direction he wanted me to go. The black Hudson car sitting idle beside the entranceway was vaguely familiar. Once inside a large warehouse with board and baton siding around its perimeter walls, the goon pushed and pulled me, as if I was a rag doll. The coolness within the building was somewhat of a relief, and soothing to my burning skin. Out of the bright sunlight, my head started to ease from the throbbing. I was forcibly set down at the table and left with one of the goons standing over me. 'As if I was in any shape to go anywhere', he stood, while I sat for several minutes until two well-dressed men came in and sat down across from me.

"Hola amigo! Como estas."

Without a word I sat, and watched, as they shuffled paper into neat stacks before them. From a wooden crate, which he had carried in, the leather bag along with a revolver, were also placed before me. A tall glass of water was placed within my reach. All three of them looked at me with sardonic gratitude in their eyes.

Overwhelmed with their sense of well-being, I took the opportunity to inquire. "Do we know each other?" He shook his head 'no'.

"You are pleased, I take it."

"Si." The man stated with a grin. "You have done bueno."

"Then why do you treat me with such contempt and disrespect?"

"This bag has a habit of disappearing into thin air," came the reply from an elderly man just out of sight. He continued in his thick, European accent, "but we have always been able to hunt it down." He proceeded to the table and gently inverted the bag exposing the bowl and a small dusting of sand. Pulling a white cloth from his breast pocket, adorned with a small, embroidered swastika in the corner, he placed the bowl upon it and retreated a short distance.

It was then that I noticed the insignia on his ring. The small, golden face of a jaguar embossed on black, glittering from the ring table. A twinge of recognition came to my memory, but I was not able to grasp where I had seen its likeness.

He studied the bowl and its inscriptions with glee. Taking a small box from his pocket and placing its contents, an eyepiece, to his eye, he studied the inscriptions on the top of the lid.

"You see, Senor," the interrogator noted, "I have only seen this once before and have waited a long time for this moment. How apt, that it should happen in the middle of the dessert so close to the people who have claimed it for their own? This treasure belongs to no man, apart from the highest bidder. It should be taken back to where its presence shall be most appreciated, in a collection in Linz. This," he sighed with a glint in his eye, "represents the key to all life as we know it."

He slowly spun the bowl and scrutinized the perimeter of the lid. The older man watched intently from a guarded distance. Taking photos of the proceedings, an assistant moved the box camera and tripod closer to the bowl, the rest of the men stood quietly, waiting for further direction from the man opposite me.

"It seems rather ironic, doesn't it," he sighed leaning back into the chair. "We have something so priceless in one sense," looking at the bowl, "but so useless in another." Waving his hand toward the bowl "It is obvious, the mystery of its contents, that has made this bowl so precious will have to wait until we have it secured in the Motherland." He sat and contemplated for several moments. "We need to tie up all the loose-ends before we proceed to the shipping location."

In bewilderment, he turned to the man behind the camera "We shall do nothing. The bowl holds nothing for us apart from the inscriptions on the outer surface of the bowl and lid which we shall photograph." He rested his hands on the table before him, "We must erase everything! The Furor will be pleased," and then placed the jade bowl back into the bag, leaving a small pile of desert sand on the cloth in the center of the table.

"Leave it to me," the older man demanded.

"We have a date to keep, and a trade," the younger said angrily. "Take him."

Without even knowing his name, the man, revolver and the bowl, disappeared out the back door. It would appear that this is the person responsible for my busy, few days.

The goon lifted me hard by my arms tied behind my back and pulled me away.

"Don't move." he shouted in my ear and left me to fold the sand in the cloth, bringing it to me. He smiled as he shoved it down into my pocket, then took the cool glass of water and drank it in front of me. "You might as well take it and give it to your God; at least the trade will be worth something."

Without any consideration, I was dragged outside and thrown in the back of the truck again. He loosened my hands and shouted, "You've got nowhere to go. Don't get out of this truck."

My shirt and poncho were lying in a bundle behind the cab of the truck. I had rolled over them several times previously, but was unable to do anything with them to protect myself from the sun. My Shirt, when I placed it over my chafe skin, began to stick instantaneously to my open wounds. With the sun setting and the coolness in the air, I had little choice but to bear the pain for the sake of warmth. As I leaned over the side of the box to see in what direction we were headed, I came face to face, in the side view mirror, with the battered and bloody face of a young Native American. Barely older than twenty-four, the face was vaguely familiar.

Within the hour, the sun had set once again and we were bouncing along a dirt pathway into the rocky, mesa regions of the Arizona Territory. We slowed right down and came to a narrow corridor of high cliffs. Stopping just beyond the perimeter of a long line of parked cars, facing up into a narrow ravine, I was told to get out and start walking. I could not help but feel the serenity of the moment as I looked up at the stars, possibly for the last time. The shadow of death put its arms around me and lifted me above my buckling legs. Cars, several meters apart, faced each other with their headlights on.

"Walk!" someone barked from behind me.

As I slowly began to walk, the disembodied voices, behind the lights, began to chant, bang their cars with sticks and honk their car horns. Every once-in-a-while, a rock or a stick would fly through the air barely missing me. Several times I was struck, once in the leg, with a rock, paralyzing me momentarily. Struggling in pain, I had no choice but to keep going. Another struck me in the side of my head, deafening my right ear. With loud buzzing in my head, and blood streaming from a gash behind my ear, a warm feeling came over my body. I sensed that regardless of my pain and circumstance I would be all right. After several timeless minutes of struggle, I saw the end of the ravine, a sheer rock face. The lights of the cars faded behind me the closer I came to the cliff. In a protected area at the very end, I suddenly faced a small group of men. They were different, in stature and dress, from the previous group. All stood back in the shadows for some time without moving, till all the clamor of the gauntlet I had passed through had become quiet. Inside my head, I heard the familiar sound of machinery gently humming, something I had not heard for a while. A further peace and feeling of familiarity came upon me. A white-haired man, short in stature, came forward from the shadows. Bathed in the bluish moonlight that came from above, he could have stood barely five feet tall. But as he got closer, I began to recognize him as the man who had visited me in my visions. Unable to hold myself up any longer, I fell to my knees. Exhausted, and broken, I cried like a child.

"I do not have what you sent me to deliver to you," I sobbed.

Without saying a word, he turned my palms to face upward towards the sky. He placed his palms flat upon mine and I felt the warmth of his touch run through me.

"It is the essence I sent you to retrieve."

With that he took his down-turned hands from

mine and placed them in cup formation below mine. In an instant I understood what he meant. Taking the cloth from my pocket I carefully poured the sand crystals from the cloth into his cupped hands. He gracefully poured the sand from one palm to the other while I watched in amazement. The crystals reflected the blue light of the moon with such intensity that once again, still in his hands, they sent faint pillars of light upward into the sky. We sat motionless, facing each other for some time, bathed in the light that surrounded us. Nothing was said, only felt.

While in his presence I felt absolute acceptance of what I was able to do. It was impressed upon me that the bowl, like the skin of man, is not important. It is only God who sees the spirit within man, 'the sand'. The spirit is the gift to all mankind. We far too often look to God for guidance for what He has already shown by revelation, through His Spirit, within our hearts.

After sitting on the ground for a long time, face to face, he nodded to me, 'It was time to go'.

His hands placed on my wounds brought a warmth and partial healing; enough to get me back to my feet. With no more to be done, and nowhere to go except back to where I had just come, I turned and faced the clatter behind me. Walking slowly back through the gauntlet, a sense of well-being became so intense that I no longer felt I was walking on the ground. A loud crack in the air burst through the clamor of noise, culminating in a stab of energy in my belly; I doubled over to the ground and lay there overwhelmed by the intense energy. I sensed I had been shot but felt no pain. I became bathed in total light.

TWELVE

Startled by cold droplets of rain hitting my eyelids, I awoke lying flat on my back looking up at the sky. My clothes were soaked, absorbing the water from the soil and humus below. Apparently myself again, I tried to turn over and right myself. A sharp pain in my stomach reflected the last moments of the previous night, or was it moments ago? I lifted the soaking cloth of my shirt and separated the torn, blood-soaked folds of my under-garments to reveal a gash just to the right of my navel. It bled slightly and looked relatively fresh with very little coagulation at the edges. Not looking like a gunshot wound, it appeared more like a tear, as if I had fallen on something. Replacing the torn shirt as best I could, I held it close and struggled to get to my feet. My joints were stiff from the cold; my legs would not bend without help from my free hand. On my knees and one elbow, I rocked myself to balance and slowly stood. Dizzy and shivering, I staggered down the incline toward a clearing where a brook flowed freely.

Bending low, as best I could, I scooped a handful of water and brought it to my lips. Swishing the fluid around in my mouth, rinsing the film that had caked my teeth and tongue, I spit the water back into the stream and watched the frothy remains float and disappear into a crevasse.

"What on earth has happened to me?"

My bones were aching and I shook uncontrollably. I knew that if I did not get help soon, I would not last the day. From the moss on the trees, I knew the direction north was down the slope and with the stream running close by, I was sure to reach the coast eventually, but how long?

After what seemed like an hour of following its direction, slipping and sliding between the wet stones and decaying logs, the stream disappeared beneath a huge timber and fell over a low cliff vanishing into dense under-brush. Hanging on to the log and leaning over as far as I could, I caught a glimpse to the right out of the corner of my eye of tall ferns swaying to and fro as if disturbed. Struggling to push the log out of the way, I slipped and slid down the muddy decline. Gaining composure and checking the tear on my stomach, I scanned the area to determine the cause of the movement. Seeing no trace of the culprit, I concluded it must have been a small animal alarmed by my presence.

Proceeding down the slippery path, I could not help the despair that gnawed at me like the cold that already soaked to my bones. Out of breathe and exhausted, I found a sheltered spot beside a tree to rest. Leaning with my back against a trunk, I looked up to the tree canopy and the mist that hung in the boughs like a low cloud. Closing my eyes, I doubled myself up to fetal position trying to retain body heat. Dazed, I listening to the sounds of the forest and slowly became entranced by the symphony. Perhaps, I was slipping into euphoria, that allusive state so often associated with extreme exposure to the elements. It didn't matter anymore; I just wanted to sleep.

The snap of a twig brought me to. Unable to move, I slowly opened my eyes to see a scruffy, little, waif of a boy not twenty yards in front of me. Half way up the facing incline, he just stood and stared at me without sound or motion. With little strength, I lifted my arm to wave him closer, but with the motion he turned and strode up the rest of the incline, over the crest and out of sight.

"Where are you going?" I strained from my tight throat.

He was gone. Slumping back in exasperation, I closed my eyes and wondered at his attitude.

"Little bastards leaving me here to die!"

Disturbed by my lack of resolve, what little strength the declaration had brought on, I got to my feet, determined to catch the little beggar. Staggering to follow through the shallow ravine, I followed up the other side to the summit. Observing a tuft of jet black hair bouncing through the air, the boy made off running to the next clearing beyond. Without the strength to yell, I followed after him in the hopes he would stop and give me direction. After what seemed like forever, I entered the clearing which declined and widened into the shoreline of a large lake. Well hidden from where I had just come, there would have been no way for me to notice this lake from the ravine covered in the dense brush and foliage. In fact from this vantage point, the ravine would have taken me further into the interior away from this hopeful spot.   Down by the shore, close to a clump of alder brush, the young boy had taken to skipping stones on the water. Angered at his obstinacy, I staggered awkwardly on the stony shore and came to within ten yards of the boy who appeared to ignore me.   It was then that I recognized him from the other day as we walked through the forest on our way to Ossette. My mind briefly wandered to the story Shawna had told me of the mischievous boy stranger who had helped her nation during times of strife.

I realized we must be close to Ossette and where we had gone for the fire and tea, but the scenery and the lay of the land were quite different. Then I remembered the boys face teasing me at the perimeter of the fire last night and how I had bolted after him.

"Why you little," I started, and turned to scold him, but he was gone!

Looking around, then out across the still lake nestled in the valley of at least four small mountains, I could make out a thin line of smoke reaching up into the sky at the northern end of the lake. With renewed hope, but little strength, I headed in the direction of the ribbon of hope.

Night was falling fast, and the temperature dropping, when I entered the one room cabin by the shore's edge. I remembered little of the occupants apart from wild beards, the smell of wet, wood burning and a cot that appeared to fly up to meet me in the air.

The next was all very confusing. There was a lot of yelling; the feeling of me being bundled up and strapped into another cot, then carried away in noisy thunder.

When I awoke next, I was in a hospital bed with an

IV in my hand and a native sitting in the chair opposite me.

"Hello." he grunted.

"Hello," I replied slowly. "Where am I?"

"Port Angeles Hospital."

"How long?"

"Twelve hours."

"Who are you?"

"A friend."

"Oh," I sighed. "Good!" I looked away and then back again, "Where are my things?"

"Being washed. They will bring them back in a while. The rest, keys, wallet, are in the drawer."

"I know you, don't I?"

"We have met."

I was beginning to sense this man was not of many words. His sober stare made me a little uneasy, but not fearful. He would not have been here if he did not care in some way. I recognized him as one of the fellows at Shawna's parents. On the bedside table, within arm's reach, and close to the chief, I could see my camera covered in mud and a few of my personal belongings. Looking back to my friend, I could tell he was sizing me up. After several minutes he got to his feet.
"I will be back tomorrow."

"Ok!" giving him a nod.

The nurse came by after several minutes, "Hi, sleepy!"

With a half grin I returned the greeting. She busied herself with my chart at the end of the bed, and went to refresh the water jug at the edge of the table that I had not noticed being there. She brought it back with several paper-wrapped glasses and a plastic cup of apple juice.

"Here, drink these. You are dehydrated." She stuck a straw through the tin foil lid and handed it to me immediately.

"How long will I have to stay?"

"We will have to wait and see how you do tonight. You are all stitched up."

I took a look down at the gauze covering the area next to my navel.

"You were running a bit of a fever, so you will have to be a patient patient." She smiled.

"Has anyone else been in to see me since I've been here?" thinking of Shawna.

"No, only the Chief"

At that, she rushed out the room as fast as she had blown in. I could not help but wonder what had happened to Shawna. The last I remember was her cool smile and still gaze as she stood at the perimeter of the stone circle at Ossette. Her eyes sparkled as they reflected flames in the fire, a portent to the spirit she held within. She had turned back to give me a smile in reassurance, but I now wondered if that had not been her good-bye.

The next day just after lunch, the chief strode back in the room. "Feeling better?"

"Yes, much," I replied finishing off the remains of a carton of milk.

He sat back in the chair facing me and said nothing. After several moments of silence he asked, "Do you need anything?"

"No, not really, just for you to answer a couple of questions."

He nodded in approval and continued to look at me.

"Do you know where Shawna is?"

"Gone."

"Do you know where?"

"No."

Wondering at his answer, it was hard to tell if he were telling the truth or not. His demeanor was stoic. My mind wandered to the bowl and then to the last time I had seen it just before the little boy whisked it away.

"The bowl. Did you get the bowl back?"

He paused for a moment. "All your belongings and what we were able to find as we tracked you for the two days, are right here."

"No! The leather bag with the jade bowl inside that the boy stole. Did you get them back?"

"Nothing was taken. I'm not sure I can help you with your bag.

I sensed I would get no answer from him. "Why are you here? I asked with doubt in my voice.

"I am here to help you? You went through many difficulties during your dreamtime. We were not quite prepared when you took off from the circle out into the dark. We could not start searching for you till the next morning."

"The tea was a little strong, was it?"

"No, you white folks have no stamina for spiritual matters unless you agree with them, regardless of the truth."

"Is that what I experienced, the truth?"

"I cannot say." He replied. "It was your dream."

With that the day nurse came in and busied herself with the few dishes left behind. "You are free to get dressed and go, Mister Alexander. Your bill has been paid and your discharge papers await you at the nurses' station." She smiled acknowledging the chief, and carried the tray out of the room.

"You paid for this? I asked startled.

With a shrug and a nod the chief indicated, yes.

"Why?"

"It is our way," he replied. "You help us, we help you."

"But how did I help you?"

"More than you will ever know. Now get dressed; you have a ferry to catch."

The chief waited till I was on board and the ferry weighing anchor before he left the dock. He and the others must have been anxious to be rid of me. They had paid for my ticket along with all the costs of my evacuation from Ossette Lake. It must have been quite a sum. I had some money left in my wallet, but it was wrinkled and mud caked almost beyond recognition. After a stroll around the deck, I made my way to the seats at the front of the boat, just behind the glass. Putting my feet up and checking the pockets of my jean jacket, I tried to relax and give my stomach muscles and skin a rest from pulling at the stitches of my wound.

The scenes and occurrences of the last days, from leaving Vancouver, till now, played across my mind. Remembering Peter being shot, and how I could now relate to the pain, and where he had been shot; the exit point that was positioned almost identical to mine. It felt like ages since the night at Vincent's, and the thought of going to see him and June again gave a boost to my spirits; it could be a short visit, on the way back to the Schwartz Bay ferry terminal. Shawna's face floated beautiful before me too; could I find her back at work?

It was Sunday afternoon again, and a week had

gone by since we'd first met at the museum. My feelings for her were confusingly passionate, yet cautious. 'Perhaps, I should try not to think of her so much; there was still Marese to consider.' Marese and I had been dating a long time and were expected to marry.' I will need to see her right away and get things sorted out'. My feelings and emotions for her were very mixed up.

As I looked down at my fine leather boots that were now scarred and misshapen from the water and abuse of the last week, I could not help but consider how I must have looked on the whole. 'Not a pleasant sight I should imagine. Not to mention my car, that may or may not be parked where I had left it.' My camera was a mess. The bag with all the accessories was gone, thrown overboard into the ocean during our mad getaway in the harbor. How could I ever get my life back in order? At the moment, it seemed impossible, overwhelming and much too great a task for my disordered mind. My head had finally stopped hurting and the ringing in my ears ceased. The ferry ride was painfully slow.

The clanging of the bow ramp hitting the dock woke me from slumber. All the passengers began lining up prematurely at the exits as if it would expedite the disembarkment; it had always been a twenty-minute wait to hit the pavement. Perhaps it was my own impatience that made me feel a certain animosity towards them. 'Everyone seems to be in such a hurry to go nowhere.' Perhaps, I should have been the first in line with everything I needed to get done. Feeling totally undone, I slung my loose camera over my shoulder and joined the line of patrons waiting patiently to disembark.

Looking to the left, up Bellville Street, I could see the museum tower and the main doors to the exhibits. The urge was to immediately head that way and see whether Shawna was there, but with so many questions and knowing that she had many of the answers, it would be sensible to choose another time and place. Glancing up the familiarity of Menzies Street towards my car, I started to experience a sense of ease. As I topped the hill, I could see my black BMW sitting faithfully at the far end of the parking lot, waiting for its master's return. A horse-drawn carriage sat idle in the center of the lot's huge expanse; its blonde and shapely coachman, anticipating my approach, sat at the reins. She followed me with her eyes as I slowly strode by, intent on getting to my car.

"Is that yours?" she inquired with a half chuckle.

"Why, yes." I replied with a smile. "Beautiful isn't she!"

"Yep," she smirked, eyeing the dents and lack of rear bumper and then down to my messy appearance, "a lot of character; just like you."

Without another word, I skirted the hood to the driver's side and tried the door. It was still locked and apart from the bruising on the exterior, the interior looked fine. No one had broken in. Reaching for the key in my upper pocket, I opened the door and climbed in. Saying a little prayer as I put the key into the ignition, I turned it.

"Vroom!!!" Black responded with one try.

"Great! I'm on my way."

Backing out and on to the street, I slowly passed the carriage and coachman with a young couple now cuddled in the back. Overtaking her on the left, she gave me a side-glance and a smile as I sped by. Passing the carillon in the Museum Square, my heart gave a tug as I thought of who might be upstairs and then passed Beaconsfield Park. I drove along Dallas Road, and remembered the chase of the days before and turned up Cooke, and then over to Leonard Avenue and Maryse' home. Sitting outside, a good five minutes, trying to muster the courage to knock on the door, I could not help but feel great reluctance at the prospect and mood of Maryse. We were very close, but I had not contacted her for days. She deserved more, but I was at a loss as to how to explain the events of the last six days, not all that sure I should. The inside of the house was well lit as dusk was heavily descending. Maryse's mother came to the door as I knocked and opened it with a startled look on her face.

"Are you alright, Brian? Come in! Come in!"

"Thanks, Mrs. Beauregard. I think I'd better wait outside. Is Maryse here?"

"Yes, I'll get her," she replied bewildered.

Within moments Maryse shuffled to the door in her slippers. "Brian! Where have you been? I've been waiting to hear from you for days."

"Yeah, I know. I'm sorry; there is nothing I could do."

"What do you mean? I've been worried for you."

"Look Maryse, I dropped by to tell you I would not be coming back for a while."

Her faced dropped. "What do you mean?"

"A lot has happened to me over the last week, and I feel it is only fair to you that I take some time to figure things out"

After pausing for several seconds, she looked up at me puzzled, "Can I help you?"

"No Maryse, I need time to think. I have been

through more than I can tell you and have to put it all in perspective."

"Sort what things out?" she asked sharply. "I need to sort some things out too. You should help me to understand what has happened. You are the one who disappeared."

"I know, Maryse, it is very difficult to explain. It's me. This is my problem and I have to sort it out, alone."

"Do you want to come in and talk? You look tired."

"No. I really have to go."

'Please stay," she asked, tenderly.

"I'll call in a couple of days when I am feeling better."

With teary eyes, she watched as I returned down the path toward the street and into the darkness that had fallen over Victoria.

THIRTEEN

There were very few cars traveling the road on my way to the Swartz Bay terminal. Hungry and tired from the trip over the straight, I mindlessly drove the darkened highway north. Scenes from the past week danced in my mind, but did little to alleviate the dullness of the drive. I felt hollow, emotionless, as if all the experiences I'd had over the last days had completely drained me, leaving only a vacuum. The questions and memories that usually roused me to attentiveness, Shawna, the bowl, my dreams, the wound and the circumstances of its infliction, my concussion; all seemed frustratingly inconclusive. There were only two people who could provide answers. One, I had no idea where she was, and the second, lived only a kilometer away. Looking at the dashboard clock, there was an hour and a half before the last ferry left for Vancouver; just enough time for me to go and visit Vincent.

The driveway to their house was spectral; the

motion detectors had obviously not set off the lights. Walking the shadows to the front steps, I could see illumination through the glass side-panels of the front door. The sound from the brass knocker echoed through the foyer and awakened the guardian from within, Lilly's' nails click on the ceramic floor. She did not bark, but sat quietly until I heard the footsteps coming to the door. The door slowly opened to reveal June in her dressing gown and slippers.

"Hi June! I hope I am not disturbing you and Vincent this late, but I was driving by and thought I would drop in and say thank you for the other evening."

"Yes, Brian, come in." she said in a low monotone voice. "I am afraid I have some sad news for you. Vincent passed away several days ago."

Shocked, I fell back against the mirrored wall almost sending it to the floor. Breathless and gathering my emotions to enquire, "What happened?"

"He died of a stroke." She grabbed my arm in reassurance. "Come in and I will make a cup of tea."

I followed her to the family room where we had spent the previous Sunday night. Everything appeared as it had been before except for several bags of knitting utensils and patterns that lay on the table where I had rested my feet.

"Put some more wood on the fire, would you, while I get the tea."

The wood box by the hearth was near empty and I took the remaining faggots and placed them on the fire. Pueblo pottery vases highlighted the mantel as they had formerly but now kindled a passion that I had not felt before. Their presence triggered the memory of the talk Vincent and I had had and the urgency the situation with the jade bowl had sparked. It slowly became apparent that it would not be so easy to get the information that I needed to bring some understanding to the events of the last week, now that Vincent was gone. I went out onto the deck to retrieve some wood for the fire-box.

After several minutes, June brought a tray with tea and biscuits, as she had done before, and placed them on the small table in front of the couch. She looked fine and in good spirits. Lilly on the other hand sat motionless in the corner on a cushion, her little dark eyes darting back and forth following June's movements.

"You will have to excuse me June, I am beside myself with the news of your husband. On top of having one of the most horrendous weeks I have ever experienced. I am quite overwhelmed."

"I understand Brian. You can sit and relax here for a while." She poured our tea. "It has been a very busy week here too. I had lots of help from our neighbors and friends getting the funeral arrangements taken care of. We had most things prepared years ago when we became aware of Vincent's arterial weakness. It is still very difficult," she sighed looking down at her teacup. "No matter how much you think you are ready for the inevitable, it still knocks the stuffing from you."

"Yes, I can imagine."

We sat for a while sipping our tea and saying nothing.

"Is there anything I can do for you June, to help out over the next week? I can always come back for a few days later if you like."

"I am fine for now, but I will let you know. There is something you could do for Vincent though. He left a lot of papers in his study to do with his research. He seemed to have been very interested in the things you and he had talked about, and spent his last day in his study looking through lots of his books and papers. He was very excited about your find and said he had found some related material."

I could feel my spirits lift a little at the mention. "Would you mind sometime if I come back and take a look at the material?"

"As a matter of fact, he left a letter for you with the hopes you would return. After our tea, I'll take you to his study and you can have a read and take a look. Normally, he was very private with his work material, but for some reason he liked you."

Not able to reply except for a smile, I returned to my tea.

Vincent's' study was as I remembered. His high back leather chair was eschewed, as if he left in a hurry and not returned. Straightening the chair and wheeling it to its rightful place, I took a seat behind the great mahogany inlaid desk. Rubbed its smooth, shiny, cool surface and wondering at its origin gave me a sense of anticipation. It was a fine piece of furniture, strong to support the personality and the work of a great man with noble purpose. Overcome by my feelings of uncertainty and impotence, I sat among the life achievements of a man who was immensely purposeful and sagacious. A white envelope with my name written along its breadth, leaned conspicuously against the base of the antique, banker's lamp. Flipping it end for end pensively between my fingers, I took several minutes to wonder at its contents. It was not lengthy by any means and read as such:

Mr. Alexander,

If you are reading this letter, it is because we did not have the good fortune of meeting once again. I have instructed my wife to allow you time to review some of the material that I was able to locate in your absence in regard to the bowl of jade. It is probably long gone by now and heading back to some private collection, or worse still, deep in the jungles of Central America. My concern, which I wish to impress on you, is that it does not fall into the wrong hands. In itself, it is just a bowl; but as I stated before, it is the implications of its origin and the power it represents to some. Should it fall into the wrong hands, they could use it as a powerful tool to unite and resurrect the darkness of an era that for the most part, is gone. Read the material I have placed in the folder marked 'Belmopan'. There is a small trust fund put aside for research, which my wife and our attorney will administer, should you choose to pursue this further. I only wish that I could be there with both of you, to help you to unravel the mystery set before you. Brian, you are welcome to use my study and all its resources to fulfill this quest. My wife will assist you should you need anything.

With trust, and in the hands that formed us all, fondest regards, Vincent

I laid the paper upon the desk and sat back to rest my eyes. My body still ached from my ordeal of the last week and I felt lightheaded. In my lethargy, I was not able to figure out whether this be blessing or curse. If there is one thing that has become apparent along life's way, it is that most things happen for a reason. The irony being of such gifts, is figuring out when these morsels are to be used, ignored, and if pursue, gathered into what form and used when? Belmopan,

Belize, was beside Mexico, and I was not all that sure I wanted to be in that close a vicinity to Mexico since Steve's and my last foray to paradise lost. Did I have the strength, let alone the desire, to take on such an endeavor? The urgency was not immediate, but knew the longer that I waited the more distant the opportunity of resolution to Shawna's where-abouts would be.

Lilly's' nails clicking on the floor and her jump upon my lap brought me back to the moment. A quick look at my watch displayed that the ferry would be leaving in twenty minutes. With barely enough time to make it before its departure, I placed Lilly back on the floor. Half running down the hall to the family room, I came across June sleeping peacefully with her knitting resting in her lap.

"June!" I whispered just loud enough for her to hear but not startle.

"Brian." She adjusted herself in the recliner. "I must have dozed off."

"I have to leave now. I will be late for the ferry if I do not go immediately."

"Oh!" she replied, slowly getting to her feet. "I'll see you to the door.

Proceeding back up the hall, I took a quick glance into the study as we passed the open doorway. June noticed my slowing at the threshold.

"Did you finish all that you needed to do?" she asked.

"Well no." I replied. "I will have to think over what Vincent is proposing."

"Are you sure? You are welcome to stay the night and finish in the morning."

I hesitated for a moment, which June picked up on

and gently rested her hand on my sleeve.

"June, I am thrilled for Vincent's offer to stay and use the resources of his study and trust to continue on, but I am not all that sure I am the right man for the job. At present, my interest would be to find that certain individual that lifted me up then left me stranded to almost die in the seclusion of the mountains." June smiled at the recognizable sarcasm in my voice and inference to Shawna. "The whole experience has been quite a shock to me and I do not think I can handle any more adventure for a while. Besides, we have no idea where the pursuit of the bowl will end, the time it will take, and what is involved.

"Do not underestimate your abilities, Mr. Alexander. Your pursuit of the girl could in fact be that of the bowl. The two seem to be intertwined. And I believe if you find the one you will find the other close by. "

"Thanks for your confidence, but it would be unethical of me to use the resources of the trust to pursue my own personal desires."

"How noble of you, Mr. Alexander, but a little misguided. Do you not think that the majority of men and women working in this field, and others, do it for some form of self-gratification, personal satisfaction, notoriety or financial gain? Human nature is the same no matter where you are when it comes to individual ego. We all like the sun to shine when our name is mentioned and experience the reward. There are individuals though, that just don't mind if it stays a little less obvious for a time."

June gave a smile and took a breath; I knew she was thinking of Vincent.

"The majority of scientists in this field have

something to gain with the enigmatic disclosure of these artifacts. In this particular case, the study of early North American civilizations, and the keys that we turn to unlock the mysteries that they hold, can be a lifetime study and in most cases with very little to show in the end. Most of the greatest finds and achievements in this area over the last century have gone for the most part unnoticed. With little notoriety, there have not been the financial gains that most administrations cherish. They all like the substantial finances to wear on their sleeves at the dinner parties. So you see Brian," she said with a noticeable smirk, "Everyone has something they need fulfilled. Our society, at present, with its desire for instant gratification, would have us fill in the blanks without the assurance of an exact fit. It also does not wish to recognize that it has failed in giving humanity what it so desperately needs, to be recognized, appreciated, and loved." June picked up her gloves and spade by the door, "The pieces to your puzzle, Mr. Alexander, may not exactly fit, and you will struggle with the picture, I am sure, but what else can you do?"

She stopped momentarily to collect her thoughts and place the tools in the bucket by the door. "Vincent liked you. He saw something in your work and in your personality. You cannot deny the strange circumstances and happenings that caused you to cross the threshold of this house."

She was right; what were the chances of this being coincidental? With that she smiled, "I'll see you out."

I followed June slowly and wondered about this spectacular lady with unfinished knitting tossed over her shoulder.

"I would like to go and visit Vincent some time. Can you give me directions?"

"Yes," she replied and gave me a gentle hug. "Don't be a stranger."

She waited till I was out of sight before she went back inside the house. I knew I had made the right decision to leave, but a feeling of incompleteness tarnished it.

For the next several days, I sat and read in the loneliness of my Kitsilano apartment. I turned to reference books and made several trips to the Museum at the University, but it was useless. Visits with my sister and forays to the mountains to take pictures did little to ease the uneasiness I had carried away from Ossette. The dream-time and the memories of Shawna would not leave my thoughts. I had to go back.

As I drove the winding road back into Oak Bay to visit Vincent's internment site, the haunting memory of Shawna, as I remembered her sitting beside me in the car, laughing and making fun made the drive difficult. Perhaps she had left a forwarding address or notice at work that would help direct me to find her. Frustrated, I pulled into the cemetery and slowed the car to a crawl as I followed the directions that June had given me. Within several minutes I had found the site with its freshly turned earth and bouquets of wilted flowers lying across. There was no stone monument yet to mark the grave, but a small, clay pot in the likeness of a traditional, Haida oil jar that housed freshly-cut, garden flowers, resting at its head. I was alone except for one man, who stood in the distance reading the lettered engraving of one of the stones. I felt for a moment that he was watching me but brushed it off as over-emotion. The wind had picked up while I stood and reflected on the many possibilities our relationship; my eyes watered and my nose began to run; I had no tissue paper.

Vincent's voice reciting the story of the bowl and the evening we had spent together talking, echoed in my mind while the others had slept. There was an excitement in his voice that helped to kindle the interest that I held in my own heart for the West Coast Nations; his words of caution about the Jaguar Men of Central America, and his hesitation to tell me of their rituals and beliefs. I remembered my own dream of the young woman painted blue, sacrificed by the man in the feathered headdress. Both these warned me of the possible fate Shawna could face in the not-so-distant future should she come in contact with these men.

Feeling anxious at the notion of Shawna being in danger, I bowed my head in silent prayer and returned to the car. Leaving the cemetery and heading back down town to the museum, it was only minutes before I had parked the car.

Ascending the escalator, something in me hoped to see her sitting behind the counter; but the chances of that were next to nil. As I rounded the corner at the top of the escalator, my heart took a leap as I saw the top of her shiny, black hair. She was face down working behind the counter. Half running to greet her, I was stopped short. It was not Shawna, but a native girl of similar color and build. My shocked and startled look must have given her a conflicting impression. Lifting her head to my startled face, the young woman's countenance dropped.

"Hi!" I half sighed in disappointment." I thought you were someone else." Feeling apologetic at my negative response, I continued sheepishly, "I was looking for the girl who worked here before you."

"You mean last shift?"

"No, no!" I returned, "last week. She was here last week."

"Oh, Shawna. She hasn't shown up to work for days. I'm not sure but she may have been reassigned or something."

"What do you mean, reassigned?"

"Well, we work for the same agency. She may be working at another job."

"Oh! Can I find out where she is working?"

"You will have to phone the office."

"What office?"

"Drake Personnel, it's on Cook."

"Thanks for your help," and I left.

The office was relatively small but neat. There were several young women working in reception area and lifted their heads as the door chime alerted them to my entrance.

"Hi! " I gestured approaching the counter.

"May I help you," came the voice of the girl closest from behind a desk?

"Yes. I would like to enquire as to one of your employees. Her name is Shawna."

After a brief moment they both looked at each other and then back to me. The first responded, "Yes. In what regard would you like know?"

"Uh, I am not sure! We were supposed to meet today and she did not show. I was just wondering if you knew where she might be?"

"Yeah, she's the new girl with the placement at the museum. She hasn't shown up for a week."

"Oh. I don't suppose she left a forwarding address?"

"Sorry. We can't give you that information."

"No." I said, disappointed. "I suppose not."

With that I nodded, left the office and headed back to my car. I must have sat there for an hour, watching the play of life that surrounded me, trying to decide what to do. One option was to go back to her parents near Neah Bay, but the braves that protected the way were to be considered. I don't suppose the chief would have allowed it anyway, besides he did say she was gone.'

Intervals of bright sun were giving way to an overcast sky. I was in no particular hurry to get back to Vancouver and the next building project, I reasoned, was Steve's responsibility. He could take care of the business for a while. Rose had a good head for numbers and could keep him focused while I took some much needed R&R. One chore that I needed to complete was to develop the film in my old camera; I'd hoped it had not been ruined during my escapades; an unpleasant thought especially when my digital worked as well, and much less hassle at printing. I would need my darkroom in Vancouver, for that.

Just as I was ready to leave, a group of young schoolgirls strolled by in their uniforms, giggling and carefree as only young teens can be. One of them was a native girl, as pretty and vibrant as her youth could reflect. She impressed me, and I found my thoughts drifting once again to Shawna and the predicament that had caused our meeting and intimacy. It was at that point that I knew there would be no way to go on with my life, in peace, without the knowledge of where she was and whether she would be safe. There was only one way in which that was going to happen, 'I had to find her'! The possibilities may have been slim and hopefully, the clues were somewhere in Vincent's papers. I needed to go back.

As I re-entered the drive and approached the picturesque oak door at June's front stoop, Lilly growled and yapped from behind. In a friendly way, as if she already knew who was approaching the door from the other side, she whined and waited patiently. I had hardly dropped my hand from the knocker when June eased the door open slightly, to peek from the space.

"Brian, what a pleasant surprise! Come in. Come in."

I gently closed the door behind me and gave her a grin.

"I decided to reconsider your offer, and would again like to spend some time looking over Vincent's papers."

She smiled back at me, and grabbed me by the arm, "Would you like a tea Brian?"

"Actually, June, if you don't mind, I'd like to start right away.

"That would be fine," she replied, leaving me at the door of the study and continuing down to the family room.

I entered the room and took a deep breath. "Shawna, you are in here somewhere."

Sitting behind the desk again, I started to review the reams of material that Vincent had compiled. As I looked around the room I began to realize the extent of the research involved. There were materials here from everywhere. The American North West; the American South West; from Northern Canada stretching all the way down to Central America and Peru, some were even labeled Europe. One, of course was labeled Belmopan. It would take weeks to glean all the material, and it was wishful-thinking to assume I would find information that would point me in the direction of Shawna.

Tapping my nails on the desk, I began to hear a strange clicking noise that echoed the pattern I tapped. I tried to take no notice, but, as I continued to peruse the literary material, the clicking persisted and became noticeably louder and louder. In a small way it reminded me of the tremendous buzzing in my ears whenever I was to experience one of the vision episodes of the last weeks. I did not feel that was the case now, but it did start me thinking of the circumstances surrounding the bowl; my last memory of it, somewhere in the desert as the man with the jaguar ring interrogating me, was rolling it in his fingers. At a loss as to know how to process the thought, I began to leaf through the files before me. A footnote in one of the papers in the Belmopan file referred to the jade bowl being of the same crystalline formation and color as the infamous Jade Skull that had been found in one of the temple ruins at Altun Ha, near Belize City. Could this be a clue to where Shawna and the elders of her tribe were taking the bowl?

The more intent I became on trying to resolve the riddle, the more unbearable the clicking noise became. Getting up from the desk, I scoured the study in search of its origin; lifting boxes filled with papers, behind pictures, under chairs but found nothing. It would start again, and then stop with no warning, then start once again. It was if the clicking's intent was just to aggravate.

Giving up on finding it, considering it to be a mouse in the wall, I returned to the desk and to my studies trying to ignore the intrusion. A short and almost inaudible snicker teased the air as I prepared to continue. To my surprise, in the reflection of one of the glass-encased pictures adorning the huge desk was the image of a small, shaggy, half-naked doll in a loincloth. Atop the shelving unit that covered the wall behind the desk, the nine-inch, masked figurine peered down like an overseer. Swiveling the chair around to the rear, I gazed up at the little doll, wondering at its prominence. The more I stared at the little guy, the more the notion that his conspicuous, bandit mask covering his eyes was the same as I remembered of the mythical Kuwatsi, the orphan Makah boy.

As I sat and pondered the possibility, ghostly scenes, which I had forgotten of the strange little boy running through the woods as he followed us near Ossette; the theft of the bowl and bag, at the fire in the dream circle; the strange dream I'd had as I slept at Shawna's family's cabin, of a little boys' smiling face before me as I lay at the bottom of the inlet near Cape Flattery, they all haunted me. My vision of the old man and the pillars of light ascending up into the sky before the totems in Stanley Park, all pointed to a story yet to unfold. It was becoming more and more evident that all that happened, since that fateful day at the Museum of Archaeology in Vancouver was for a reason. The great mystery was yet to be revealed, but where was it to end?

And now, several months later, sitting in the parking lot, overlooking English Bay, I was anticipating my travels down to Belize. It would be hot and steamy; but now was the time to go, before the rains set in. I had found that Shawna had worked at the Museum of Natural Sciences, in Albuquerque, New Mexico, and had an ongoing relationship with a group of archaeologists working throughout the Yucatan Peninsula. Finding her would be a chore, but with the leads I had acquired, I was more than confident that she would be found. The bowl, with its mystery, would be less obliging.

From the papers Vincent had left me, I was able to ascertain, that bowls of this nature, with similar hieroglyphs, were used in sacred ceremonies and were greatly sought-after by less than desirable members of the occult. Bent on re-establishing the greatness of the ancient Mesoamerica of thousands of years ago, these groups have searched far and wide, to recover the lost artifacts of these civilizations, hoping to rebuild their glorious past. Whether this old ideology has a place in our modern society is yet to be determined. With its cast system of social structure, and the unrelenting desire for bloodletting, I highly think not.

NEXT...

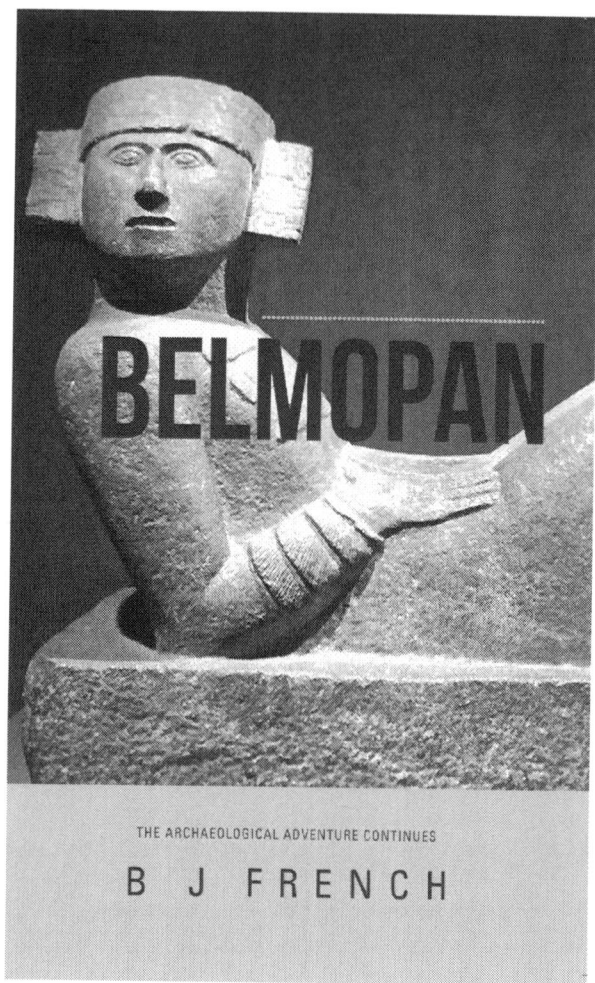

THE ARCHAEOLOGICAL ADVENTURE CONTINUES

B J FRENCH

Proof

Made in the USA
Charleston, SC
07 March 2013